After One Time

After One Time

A Novel

Cedric Dey

iUniverse, Inc.
New York Lincoln Shanghai

After One Time

Copyright © 2007 by Cedric Dey

All rights reserved. No part of this book may be used or reproduced by any means, graphic, electronic, or mechanical, including photocopying, recording, taping or by any information storage retrieval system without the written permission of the publisher except in the case of brief quotations embodied in critical articles and reviews.

iUniverse books may be ordered through booksellers or by contacting:

iUniverse
2021 Pine Lake Road, Suite 100
Lincoln, NE 68512
www.iuniverse.com
1-800-Authors (1-800-288-4677)

Because of the dynamic nature of the Internet, any Web addresses or links contained in this book may have changed since publication and may no longer be valid.

This is a work of fiction. All of the characters, names, incidents, organizations, and dialogue in this novel are either the products of the author's imagination or are used fictitiously.

Author Photo by Phoebe Dey

ISBN: 978-0-595-44864-7 (pbk)
ISBN: 978-0-595-89188-7 (ebk)

Printed in the United States of America

My daughter and I were returning to Surrey from Vancouver, British Columbia, having just visited a friend from bygone days, the irrecoverable past. I was in Surrey spending a few days with my youngest daughter Alisa, who resides and works there. She was gracious enough to accompany me on the visit to my friend Warren and his wife. I was disheartened to see Warren so different from the way he looked when I saw him only a few years previously: a bit gaunt and not as animated, but the genuine smile that emanated from him and the twinkle in his eyes dispelled the gloom I felt at first seeing him. I was comforted when I remembered his wife telling me on the telephone that he refused to see local friends but was very anxious to see me. He seemed relaxed and at peace when we knew he was very ill. I could not help but wonder what was the secret to his calm and contented demeanor and if such peace that passeth all understanding would manifest itself when the bell tolled for me. Warren seemed willing to talk about death and dying and I would certainly have encouraged him, had not his wife and daughter been present. Instead, I steered the conversation to more mundane matters like golf. I was to play the Seymour Golf course in Vancouver the next day with a member who used to be a golfing partner of my late father-in-law, so I asked him if he had ever played there.

"No, never. My game was always too limited for such a course. I promised myself to get serious and take lessons after our last outing in the prairies. Of course, I never did. Maybe it's not too late."

We all laughed.

Ruminating on the visit, on other friends of the era and on the years that slipped away so quickly, I must have looked lost in thought to my daughter. Perhaps we were thinking the same thing. Going through my head were the words my father had said to me in one of his rare philosophical moods: "When a man get older, he na mek new friends like when he growing up."

Although he was referring to himself after just burying one of his friends from boyhood, his statement is as valid now as when he uttered it.

My great-great Uncle Poo phrased his opinion differently: "Boo-Boo," he said referring to me, "the older you get, the less friends you have that you grow up with." And since he was just a year short of his ninetieth birthday at the time, he certainly made sense. Now I am at the age where I can admit that many of my mates from college are no longer with us, some not even crossing the threshold of three score years.

Both he and my grandmother Baba addressed me as Boo-Boo. Uncle Poo's friends should have taken some pages out of his book of living. While they were out drinking bush rum, made illegally on one of the other islands of the Essequibo River, he was drinking bush tea. He used to visit us at our home in Fredericksburg from his home in Arthursville, about one half a mile away. Often he would arrive early in the morning when the cocks were still crowing and he would pick and chew the young leaves from certain fruit trees scattered all over the property, then would drink the juices of the plentiful young coconuts and fill his bags with the fruits in season. When the waves and tide were propitious for swimming, he swam just about every day in the part of the Atlantic Ocean that became a branch of the Essequibo River, lapping on our shores. I have a correction to make: Uncle Poo rarely swam; instead he would submerge himself in the water and stay under for the longest time. Physically, he seemed to be in good health; his posture was straight as an arrow, he was lean, and possessed all his teeth. He encouraged us to watch our health but those sweet sugar cakes were already wreaking havoc on our teeth. His tall erect figure should have been an inspiration to all of us who used to swim with him.

One day when we were all swimming naked—the young, the very young, and the very old Uncle Poo with his pubic hair not yet white—one of the older boys Vincent, about 12, asked this question: "Uncle Poo, to what do you owe your longevity?"

"Yu wha?"

"How come you live so old?"

"Well, Vincent, dat's an easy one. The main reason is because ah neva marry."

"How come you neva marry Uncle Poo?"

"Cause women deceitful like starapple. Got one colour a top, another one a bottom."

All of us boys swallowed too much water that day as we just could not control our laughter. Vincent was always a hero to us younger ones. He excelled in every task—track and field, captain of the cricket team, and of course, in academics. He won a government scholarship to the prestigious Queen's College in Georgetown, worked for awhile in the civil service and later studied law in the United Kingdom. We were colonials then and for higher education the U.K. was the place to be for most of us at that time.

When Uncle Poo died in his sleep four years after this conversation all the boys gathered at the Sea Wall as part of the celebration of his life and Vincent presented the eulogy at the funeral. Uncle Poo attended church for the last time.

Alisa was blessed with what my mother referred to as woman's intuition and sensed my sadness at seeing my friend. She allowed me to be introspective and became quiet as I closed my eyes. The memories began to cascade like a miniature Kaieteur Falls.

Of my closest friends in the past fifty years or so—and I have made many along the way—there are three who have remained steadfast through thick and thin. Mike, Alwyn, and Boogie are irreplaceable.

Mike and I were boyhood friends in our ancestral home, British Guiana. British Guiana was ruled by the British since 1831 (the Dutch occupied it before that time) and it was not until 1966 independence was granted to the colony. It became Guyana that year. Mike and I met at a Boys' Scout Camp when we were seven years old in New Amsterdam, Berbice. Berbice is one of three counties comprising the country, each named after the three main rivers that flow into the Atlantic. The other two are

Demerara, where the capital of Georgetown is located, and Essequibo, where Wakenaam, the largest inhabited island in the country is situated. Co-incidentally, both Mike and I lived on the island of Wakenaam and had never met before the camp in New Amsterdam. I lived on the eastern part and he on the western side. We were separated by a distance of only four miles, which was quite a stretch for boys traveling on bicycles or on foot when the roads were not always in a good state of repair, especially during the rainy season. There was no public transportation. Once we became acquainted, we visited each other when we returned.

When we were nine years old, Mike and I both moved to Georgetown to attend high school. High schools were privately owned, which meant there was a monthly fee for tuition. High school in British Guiana was a generic term—a general term for private schools—and had nothing to do with the age of the student. Students were prepared for external examinations sent from London, England, and returned there for grading. Even the examination site was neutral as students from other schools would assemble to take tests with everyone else. For children who did not enroll in high school at an early age, the public school system run by the Department of Education was available with a different curriculum.

I enrolled at Central High School, one of the leading schools at that time in both erudition and sports (I was interested in making the cricket team) and many graduates would occupy prominent positions in government and professional ranks. My dad had wanted me to join him in the ferry business between Leguan Island and Wakenaam. My mother had other ideas. She wanted me to obtain a high school education before joining the business. I believe my dad was convinced they were doing the right thing when he read an invitation I was sending out to relatives and friends for my eleventh birthday. It was written in the third person and since he had never seen anything like it before—and neither had many of the recipients—he realized my high school education was worth the expenditure and time.

I started out boarding with relatives and when I complained to my mother about the treatment I was receiving, tears came to her eyes. "Mom, they are starving me to death."

"What do you mean?"

"They only give me bush tea and bread with salt butter for breakfast and dinner."

She spoke to my dad, who decided to buy a small two-bedroom house on D'Urban Street and my mother moved to Georgetown to make sure I was properly fed and supervised. My dad would visit on weekends and I would accompany him to the cinema. His love affair with the cinema was of a short duration. One evening while I was enjoying an Abbot and Costello movie, he whispered to me, "Dis is stupidness." I was surprised at those words coming from the village jokester. He never went back to the cinema. Some of my high school friends regretted his decision, as he always allowed me to invite one or two to join us.

My friend Mike wanted to enroll at Central High but he had no choice because his cousin was married to the principal of Enterprise High School. It was at Central that I met the other two boys who would become my lifelong friends. I wish I could pinpoint the time and place where I first met Alwyn and Boogie, but the memory is not there.

After high school Mike and Alwyn joined the teaching profession, both carrying on a family tradition. Alwyn's father, headmaster of a public school, was renowned for turning out scholarship winners, and both of Mike's sisters taught in the public school system. Boogie and I opted for the civil service, a prestigious position at that time, even if the salary was minuscule. For us it was spending money and we still had to be subsidized by our parents. I suppose Alwyn and Mike had to be helped by their parents as well; Alwyn lived at home and Mike was boarding with relatives. When my mother returned to Wakenaam, Mike and Boogie moved into the little house with me. We were trailblazers in a way, because we knew of no other 16-year-old boys—and definitely no girls—leaving the comforts of home and home-cooked meals, to live by themselves. We employed a housekeeper old enough to be our mother and she acted like one six days a week.

Even with good grades, it was not easy to secure a position in the civil service those many years ago. Fortunately, my family and I knew Reverend Biles, a Scotsman who was head of one of the church denominations in the country and his recommendation stood me in good stead. In his younger days he was the minister of our church in Fredericksburg. He lived in the manse, the home provided for the clergy on an acreage on the southern part of the road leading to the launch stelling—our word for dock, wharf or pier. It was a large two-storey house with balconies on each floor, a large drawing room that could have served as a ballroom, a kitchen that was spacious—as most kitchens in the village were not—and four bedrooms upstairs. I used to visit quite often with my grandmother. When he was transferred, we would visit him at his new location. I remember vividly the first trip to Mahaica to see him at his manse. I was six years old. We boarded the train at its terminal on Lamaha Street in Georgetown. I was dressed in new black short pants, black boots, and a white shirt with a tie that matched my grandmother's blue dress that reached almost to her ankles. She also wore a white panama hat that matched the white collar of her dress. We were the first ones into the first class carriage. Later on other passengers joined us: two men dressed in almost identical brown suits (my grandmother thought they were lawyers attending court at one of the villages) and an expatriate who looked like an overseer at one of the sugar estates, dressed in a khaki shirt open at the neck, shorts made of the same material and greenish-coloured socks that ended just below the knees. He was also wearing a khaki-coloured helmet and smoked a pipe—or tried to—throughout the trip. My grandmother introduced me to a gentleman dressed in a white gabardine suit; he carried in one hand a small briefcase for papers and in the other, a white panama hat he had just removed from his head to greet my grandmother. He used to teach at the school at Fredericksburg but was now headmaster at the public school at Betverwagting. The name of the village indicates the presence of the Dutch in Guiana. Wakenaam means 'waiting for a name' in Dutch.

The Dutch were the first Europeans to establish a permanent settlement on the coast of Guyana and many place names remain today. Europeans had heard of the golden city of Manoa and the legends of El Dorado from independent adventurers seeking their fortune in South America. Guyana specifically lured men with tales of its city and lakes of gold. The first Europeans who visited Guyana also found Amerindians smoking tobacco.

Another product they discovered was a red dye called annato, used by the Amerindians to colour their bodies. Traders saw the commercial value of the dye and took it back to Europe at the same time as they introduced smoking.

But I didn't know all that history yet in that railway car with my grandmother. The itinerary of the train was from Georgetown to Rossignol, where there is a large sugar estate. Our destination was Mahaica, the fourteenth stop on the route. Meeting us at the station was our father's nephew Gene, who was head of the other workers at the manse. He had joined the staff at Fredericksburg as a youth and was the only one to continue on to Mahaica. Rev. Biles was the consummate host and included me in his conversation with my grandmother during lunch. Later he occupied me with some jigsaw puzzles which he remembered intrigued me. I have always cherished the memories of those visits. His parting gifts of Peak Frean biscuits, Cadbury chocolates and the box of soft McIntosh toffees stand out—they seemed more delicious than the same ones my father brought home whenever he visited Georgetown.

I have always coupled the memory of our trip to Mahaica with what happened on our return to Wakenaam. Two of my father's nephews were involved. I have mentioned Gene, who was the *major domo* at Mahaica and am about to speak of the other nephew Arturo.

Due to our late arrival from Georgetown, I was allowed to sleep in longer than usual. When I awoke neither my mother nor my grandmother was to be found. I could not locate the cook and no one was in the house. The larger homes were built on concrete blocks about ten feet above ground as a preventive measure against flooding during the rainy season; Daddy was able to house his car, some tools and even a bateau under ours as well as all the bicycles. I decided to look under the house and there I found Doreen, the woman who washed the clothes and sheets. Boy! Was that a relief!

"You know where Mom is?"

"Me na know nuttin. Some boy come heh early an seh somebody fall overboard and drown and she and yu grandmother gone to the stelling."

I ran all the way in that direction and changed my route when I saw about eight men and women heading to my Aunt Jane's yard which was not too far from the stelling. Aunt Jane is my father's sister and the mother of Gene and Arturo. When I reached her premises, many of the villagers, men and women and even some school children were huddled under the house talking softly. Since my mother was nowhere in sight, I climbed the tall stairs at the back of the house and entered the kitchen. My mother and grandmother were seated with Aunt Jane on a long brown couch. Other women were sitting nearby on chairs and benches and a few men were standing with their backs against the wall. The conversation was very quiet.

My mother immediately took me to the front of the house, where we could speak quietly. "Wha' happened, Mom? Doreen say somebody drowned at the stelling."

"Trust Doreen. The drowning part is true. Your cousin Arturo drowned in the Mazaruni River."

"Oh no. How you know, Mom?"

"A friend in Bartica sent the telegram to Aunt Jane. Let me get it and read it." She took the telegram and read. "'Arturo Willems drowned at falls today. Boat capsized. Tell Sula.'"

My mother explained that Sula was a girl who lived at Zeelandia, a village about four miles north of us. Sula had visited Fredericksburg for a wedding followed by a reception and a dance a few months earlier, and Arturo was smitten by her beauty. The men in the village had said after the dance that they felt sorry for Arturo, because they believed he had not aroused a reciprocal feeling in Sula. Sula was twenty-two years old. Arturo was twenty-five.

Bartica is situated in an area of land called the Bartica Triangle at the confluence of three rivers, the Mazaruni, the Cuyuni, and the Essequibo. It is a mining town. The Mazaruni is a branch of the Essequibo and is the gateway to the gold and diamond fields. Gold diggers, known as pork knockers, would paddle up that river to the gold fields. It is rumoured that Sir Walter Raleigh's son met his death in the Mazaruni district. The pork knockers with their caches of gold would return to Bartica to celebrate before traveling to Georgetown to cash in the balance of their treasure. The prudent ones would arrive there just in time to catch the steamer but many others would never make it to the city, squandering their earnings in booze and the flesh. Temptations were always there: gambling, beautiful ladies of the night, demon drink and new friends who were always ready and willing to celebrate. The saying 'A fool and his money are soon parted' could have been coined in Bartica.

Many of the older men in our village were surprised to learn that Arturo had become a pork knocker as he had earned the reputation of being easy going. Perhaps love had something to do with his bold move to Bartica. All this was surmised before the arrival of the telegram, and now everyone was reading from the same page, thinking kind thoughts. Some of the men could be seen wiping tears from their eyes. A young man volunteered to ride the four miles to Zeelandia to convey the sad news to Sula.

Sula arrived at about four o'clock that afternoon dressed for mourning—black dress almost to her ankles, black shoes with heels about an inch high, and a black scarf tied around her head. She looked so beautiful even the women were saying they wished Arturo was there to see her. The wake lasted until daybreak. Four days after the wake there was still mourning and crying. Since there was no body to be buried, there was no closure to the death. On the fifth day a boy came running to our house, out of breath, with a message from my father to meet him at Aunt Jane's home. When my mother wanted to know the reason for going to Aunt Jane, the young man replied, "Me na know, mam. Nobody na tell me nuttin.'"

When we arrived at Aunt Jane's yard, everyone was saying the same thing. "Arturo na drown. He save. He upstairs with the Captain and Aunt Jane."

We proceeded upstairs to the living room where my father, Aunt Jane, and some relatives and close friends were gathered. Tears were still being shed, but everyone was smiling and appeared jubilant, quite a different demeanour from a few days earlier. Arturo and Sula had ensconced themselves in an easy chair, like two peas in a pod. Arturo was holding forth, repeating how he had not become a victim of the falls, like so many men before him.

"When we capsize, I jus float with the tide. De others try to swim against the tide to reach some trees they see close to shore. When I look back fu dem, dey disappear. Soon I see a big log and I scramble on top but when the timber want to go he own way downstream, I tek off me clothes and start to swim to shore. When I tink I gettin' closer, it look like ah still far away. Ah start to feel wary and start to pray and ready to give up when a boat almost run over me. Dey trow me an old tire tie to a rope and pulled me in and took me to a island full a buck people—ah mean, Amerindians. Ah never gwine call dem 'buck' no mo. Dem Amerindians tek me in, give me some ah dey medicine and food and clothes and put me on a boat to Bartica."

Arturo had become a hero. Sula thought Arturo needed some rest and took him to her parents' home. There was a beautiful beach nearby where they could relax and get to know each other. If Arturo's rescue and his reconciliation with Sula were a part of a movie, it would have probably ended with them on the beach drinking rum and coconut water. But that was not to be. Ten days after the hero's homecoming, some pork knockers from a nearby village returned home. They had been making a living from gold digging for many years. They had traveled the same route from Bartica as Arturo, arriving at Fredericksburg on the two o'clock launch from Leguan. When they heard of Arturo's adventure, they laughed until the tears came. When told the date of the accident, mention was made of seeing Arturo in his favourite rum shop in Bartica that day.

In the end Arturo's creative scheme paid off, as Sula interpreted his chicanery as proof of his love for her. Many of the men in the village were surprised to see the change in Arturo after his marriage. He joined Sula's father and brother in the fishing business, extending their markets to new clients in Georgetown.

After graduation I went to work in the civil service for an embarrassingly meagre salary. In our day just about every one of us found work right out of high school. There were no centres of higher education in the country. I had plans to work for a few years, then return to Wakenaam and continue the long tradition of boat captains in our family. I would have been the fourth of the lineage to operate the ferry service between Wakenaam and Leguan. Wakenaam and Leguan are the largest and second largest inhabited islands respectively in the county of Essequibo. Both are situated at the mouth of the Essiquibo River as it enters the Atlantic Ocean. Wakenaam is on the western shore and Leguan on the eastern. Three nautical miles is the distance the ferry travels from the stelling at Wakenaam to its counterpart at Leguan. My great-grandfather began the service "with an ordinary fishing boat." My grandfather continued and improved the system with outboard motors and my father updated it even more by installing inboard motors.

My mother gave me a lecture on what was expected of me, before returning to Wakenaam and leaving me to my own resources. She knew that Boogie and Mike would be joining me, and when they did, our home became a clubhouse for all our friends. Every Sunday we had a routine. Around three o'clock in the afternoon when the breezes from the Atlantic prevailed—and this was not a conscious thought of avoiding the heat, since we never discussed the weather—we would put on our Sunday best and ride to Alwyn's residence. Shirt and tie, no jacket, polished shoes, shiny bicycles, the four of us would ride from there to the Sea Wall. We would start at the eastern section, which bordered the Kitty subdivision and make our way to the Georgetown section.

It bears repeating that during the sixteenth century Europeans of all stripes—Spanish, Portuguese, English, and Dutch visited South America after the circulation of rumours of the existence of gold in the legendary city of El Dorado, which was supposed to be in Guiana. They were all individual marauders rather than government agents. It was left to the Dutch to establish the first permanent settlement early in the seventeenth century on the coast of Guiana. The native people were Amerindians and the name Guiana means 'land of many waters' in their language. The northern boundary of Georgetown is the Atlantic Ocean. Georgetown and most of the northern part of the country are below sea level. To prevent the waters from flooding the coast during high tides, the Dutch in their wisdom as long ago as the eighteenth century built a concrete wall, or levee, along the shore. It runs from Georgetown, at the mouth of the Demerara River, which flows into the Atlantic Ocean, to Rosignol, at the mouth of the Berbice River. The Georgetown section, including the part adjoining the suburb of Kitty is known as the Sea Wall.

The Sea Wall has remained a very popular area for all ages. Anyone can look out over the horizon, see the ocean-going vessels and conjure up dreams or pleasant images. In one area stood a hut with wooden planks for seats for the populace to relax, meditate, just sit. On special occasions, certain holidays, and always on Sundays, the Militia band, resplendent in their uniforms would play from their repertoire of classical music as well as local favourites. At Easter there would be an exhibition of the fine art of flying a kite in a crowded sky.

The Georgetown section was always crowded when we arrived there on a Sunday afternoon. On our way we would encounter groups of friends and we would stop to greet each other with "Wha' happenin'?"

It was a ritual in a sense, young men—boys really—admiring girls in their fancy frocks, our name for dresses then. Most of them were home-made or made to order by their favourite seamstress. We would stop briefly and chat with some of the boys and girls standing in groups and we would remain on our bicycles with our feet on the ground before moving on. The fun, however, was to ride in style and act like monarchs even though we did not have any girls of our own. We followed this ritual just about every Sunday as juniors and seniors in high school and even after we graduated. We were still teenagers, after all. I cannot pinpoint the turn of events that brought Alwyn and Boogie and me together. I have tried but the memory is not there. I was the only student from Wakenaam and I had to make new friends. Mike was at another school, so I was the link that brought us all together.

Boogie was friendly with a girl working with him in the same government ministry. I refer to her as a girl, since she was still in her teens. Her name was Olive. We never knew how deep the friendship was between the two of them. Were they at the hand holding stage? We knew he was very fond of her because he spoke of her constantly and they went to the movies a few times. Then she left to pursue studies in the United States, and we never saw a more devastated human being. They stayed in touch through letters while she was a student at Howard University, planning a career in medicine. She told him that the United States was a country replete with opportunities for anyone willing to work hard and sacrifice. All this sounded great on paper but we knew it would not be that easy.

The letters from Olive kept coming and one day he showed us a letter he had received from Howard University in Washington, D.C. He was grinning from molar to molar. He had applied to the university without telling us and had just received his acceptance. Now he wanted us to join him in sending in our applications. Imagine our surprise and disappointment that he had not told us before. There was no doubt in his mind that we would travel together, live together, study together. We had no idea what attending college in the United States meant—the cost, the timetable, anything. We had heard tales but had no way of separating fact from fiction. We were young and confident and thought we could be masters of our fate. We pondered our decision for a full five minutes and agreed to send in our application. Before receiving Olive's letter, traveling to the United States was at the low rung of our priorities. I always believed I would return to Wakenaam and work on the boats.

In the meantime, I was more interested in solidifying my position as opening batsman and medium pace bowler in the "A" team of my cricket club. Boogie was working on his table tennis ranking; the same could be said for Mike with his chess manoeuvres and Alwyn was building his muscles in somebody's back yard.

On my next trip to Wakenaam I discussed this new development with my parents. After all, it had come out of the blue and none of us had set such lofty goals. My father was still expecting me to join him, especially when he found out what my salary was. My mother was pleased but cautious: "Go ahead and apply, and we will see when and if you get a reply." My grandmother was so happy that she started to call me Doctor until my mother stopped her. "Don't put any bad luck on him."

We knew of two cousins who studied in North America. One studied in Alabama and became a veterinary surgeon and the other obtained a medical degree from McGill University in Montreal, Canada, and neither of them was better off financially than my father. He had been in the ferry business with his father since the age of twelve and became the sole operator three years later when his father succumbed to a heart attack at the age of forty-six. My father was well known and respected in the county of Essequibo and was the only person from Wakenaam to be included in the inaugural issue of *Who's Who in British Guiana.*

Time has not suppressed my reverence for what my father accomplished as I was growing up on the island those many moons ago. I will bet my bottom dollar that our home was the only one at that time with indoor plumbing that allowed us to have a shower, toilet, and running water in the kitchen. He installed tanks on the flat roof of the addition he had built and water collected from the rainfall could be pumped to the tanks on the roof. Many middle class homes in Georgetown still had their toilets outdoors. He constructed a separate building to house his generator, which was big enough to supply electricity to all his neighbours if they had been set up for it. For us it meant electricity in our home to operate such luxuries as a turntable, which he made himself, amplified through the radio. Once a year he would tear down, as he termed it, the Ailsa Craig engines for his launches, taking out all the moveable parts to clean, lubricate, and replace them. All this from a man who never left British Guiana, probably never used a telephone and who left school at the age of twelve.

Where did his insights originate? When Uncle Poo came to our home to view the electric lights he could not believe his eyes. He answered my question by saying, "He born with it. He been heh before."

During freshman orientation at Howard University we were given a questionnaire to answer. The only question I remember after all these years is: Who had the greatest influence on your life? I debated whether I should try to score points by naming a philosopher or religious icon and decided on neither. I wrote down the names of my parents instead.

My mother's expression 'Empty vessels make the most noise' became my eleventh commandment. She also had me learn: *The heights by great men reached and kept Were not attained by sudden flight, But they, while their companions slept, Were toiling upward in the night.* My father used to say 'The nail that sticks out gets hammered down.' I wish now to my regret that I had followed more of their precepts. One in particular—'neither a borrower nor a lender be'—not quite those words because my mother was not a Shakespearean scholar. What she implied was that if I borrowed a book and lost it, I would have to buy two—one to replace the lost one and another for myself, because I would not want to borrow again. It was the same with lending. Most people never repay the loan and I will lose a friend in the process because he will want to avoid me. And of course her advice 'If you can't afford it, do without' reigned supreme.

When I received my letter of admission from Howard University my father joined my mother in my corner. When I questioned Alwyn and Mike about news from Howard, their response was always the same, as if rehearsed and recorded—"No man, don't know why they teking so long to answer."

My 90-year-old Uncle Poo used to say to me, "Boo-Boo, the older I get, the smarter and braver I used to be." Now I know what he meant. In my younger days I had no fear. Once the decision to attend Howard University had been made, there was no slacking off. So much had to be done; medical examination, visa from the United States Embassy, U.S. funds from the bank, airline reservations were just some of the items on my list.

But getting all those essential tasks done was the easy part of my preparation to leave.

The highest hurdle I had to clear was the decision to travel to the United States in the first place. It looked as if I would be going alone. Even Boogie did not have a plan. He wanted to accumulate more funds so that he would be able to relax when he got there, and of course, Alwyn and Mike had not heard from the school. Thank heaven for my parents. Once they were satisfied that I was serious about my intention to travel and study, they made sure I had enough funds to last more than the school year with a promise of more to follow. I must mention that at that time the British Guiana dollar was at par with the U.S. dollar. Hard to believe, but it was. I should also state that I did not know anyone to call when I arrived in the United States. True, I knew Boogie's friend Olive casually, but she was a struggling student and I had no desire to add pressure to her busy schedule. These days the Guyanese diaspora can be found in every continent. Just the other day a cousin who resides in London called with a request for me to find lodgings for her granddaughter who was attending a course in Los Angeles, California. It took me two phone calls to accomplish my goal. One call to a friend, who called me back in about thirty minutes with a telephone number and a name. My second call was to this stranger, who agreed to take in my young cousin after we traced our roots.

Whoever said parting is such sweet sorrow knew what she was talking about. I had said farewell to everyone in the village during the few days I spent at home before my departure. Many were blood relatives and all were loved ones, young and old. It was quite a distressing parting for all of us, but especially for the older members of the community. They realized that time was not on their side and that we might never meet again.

Then came the moment to leave for the launch stelling. My mother and Baba—that's right, my grandmother—wanted to say good-bye at home. They were too sorrowful and apprehensive to walk with me to the stelling. I agreed with them because I, too, was disconsolate. We had shed tears and I did not wish to repeat this emotional display before the other passengers. Baba had a parting aphorism for me: "Boo-boo, remember what I always tell you—show me yu company, ah tell yu who yu are." My mother used to phrase this advice as 'Birds of a feather flock together.'

I walked alone to the stelling where my father's launch would transport me and the other passengers to Leguan, our first stop on the journey to Georgetown. My cousin Jasper's bus would take us to the eastern part of the island where we would sail on a government steamer to Parika, less than an hour away. From Parika we would take a train to Vreeden Hoop, then board a steamer that would take us across the mouth of the Demerara River to Georgetown. One of my friends from the village was a fellow traveler that very morning. His name was Randy. Standing on the stelling before boarding the launch, I looked up in the sky across that branch of the Essequibo River toward the Atlantic Ocean. I perceived the skies to be very bright, brighter than I had ever seen them before and I had been on that spot many times, early mornings, late at night. It seemed as if Georgetown had turned on all its lights and moved them over the ocean. At that moment I felt calm, and my skin began to crawl, an eerie feeling which my children would refer to as goose bumps. Then I heard a voice whisper: "Don't be afraid, I am with you." As I pondered the meaning of all this, I thought I heard the voice of Uncle Poo saying "Is yu grandfather John talkin' to you. I see him every day." Of course both my grandfather John and Uncle Poo had passed on. I wished Uncle Poo was still around. I would have asked him the significance of hearing voices from the dead. My grandfather I never did have the pleasure and privilege of knowing.

In his later life Uncle Poo became a skeptic, a dramatic change from his early upbringing. Once George, one of the boys from our swimming group, asked him on a Sunday, after we had all attended church and were allowed to go swimming: "Uncle Poo, how come you na go to church no mo?"

"Wah ah dey givin' way deh, boy?"

Uncle Poo had been a regular attendant all his life, teaching Sunday School and singing in the choir, working on church repairs, refinishing the pews. One day an eminent clergyman from Georgetown visited the parish at Fredericksburg and read from the Bible. It is a well-known passage, the one where God led Moses and the Israelites to freedom by opening the Sea of Reeds and made the sea dry land as the waters were divided. When the Egyptians pursued Moses, God had the waters return and drown Pharaoh and his army. Uncle Poo jumped up from his seat in the choir and shouted during the reading of the Bible: "Wha kinda God ah dat? Dat got to be a damn lie."

The minister said, "It is not a lie. I believe every word of the Bible because it was written by God."

Uncle Poo got up from his seat, retrieved his hat and left the church, never to return except to the cemetery on the grounds of the church.

When thoughts of Uncle Poo subsided, the only way I could articulate my experience under the stars was to turn to Randy from the village and say, "Life is a dream, isn't it?" To me at that moment it felt like a dream, a hallucination.

He thought I meant everyday life and replied accordingly, "It may be a dream to you, but it's real to me."

Randy was not as fortunate as I was to have a father who provided all the comforts that I took for granted. He was on his way to Georgetown for a job interview at one of the daily newspapers. He would become one of the renowned journalists in the country until he wrote one too many scathing editorials about the Prime Minister and had to seek employment in one of the islands of the West Indies.

Randy is one year older than I am. I remember visiting him when I went home to Wakenaam on a weekend visit to see my parents and Baba. I had been working at the Audit Department for a month. Randy lived about five minutes on foot from my home. I knocked on his door and when he opened it with a book in his hand, he looked surprised to see me. His house was built like a trailer—long, narrow, low, and compartmentalized into three sections, each with steps to the ground, almost like three condos.

We chatted for awhile about past and future and mundane matters, when he said with a sheepish grin: "John, I would gie you a glass a wine (I could see two bottles on the table) that my aunt made, but I ent open the bottle yet."

"Say dat again?"

"I ent open the wine bottle yet, so I can't gie you no wine."

"Ah don't want none anyhow, Randy. Ah going to the stelling to see my Dad and ah don't want to smell like a rum shop."

Years later in my extracurricular readings I learned that I might have had a mystical experience that morning. The writer described such incidents as an awareness of God's presence. Leaving my mother, father and grandmother, I was receiving a message of faith, but of course, I did not think of what I now call the sign in those terms then.

I reached Georgetown with mixed feelings and was greeted by the boys, Alwyn, Boogie, and Mike. They had arranged for my Cousin Boyo to drive us to the airport where we said our goodbyes and made promises for the future. Now I was alone for the first time in my life. I was a few months over eighteen years, but more a boy than a man. We still did boyish things. I was beginning to wonder whether I was doing the right thing, heading into an unknown country with no one to greet me on arrival. The boys had given me a card to be opened on board and, as is my nature, I never opened it until we were midway through the flight. It said: 'Fare thee well for we must leave thee, do not let this parting grieve thee, and remember that the best of friends must part.'

I remember thinking that they had it backward. I should have given them that card, since it was I who was leaving. I suppose it could have been interpreted either way. I am convinced that Mike and Alwyn did not send their applications to Howard until days after my departure. Boogie had the same excuse about finances, and it was ironic that he, who was the catalyst for our exodus, never did get to the United States. We did not learn of his reason for not traveling to the United States until years later. It seems he must have read too much into the friendship with Olive. Boogie had received a letter telling him she was about to be married. Because of either a broken heart or embarrassment or both, he did not want to confide the truth to his friends about what he viewed as a rejection, when in fact he must have interpreted their relationship in a different way than she had. It may have been some relief to him that the marriage did not last very long and he regretted he was not nearby to give her comfort.

Sitting next to me on the plane to New York was a young man from New Amsterdam, Berbice, and he remembered me from one of our Boy Scout camps there. His name was Oscar and he was immigrating to the United States, sponsored by relatives. We chatted for awhile until we were both overcome by the tiredness from our pre-flight experiences. When he found out that no one was meeting and greeting me in New York, he volunteered his cousin's assistance in finding me a hotel for the night. They took me to the Theresa Hotel in Harlem, the same hotel that Fidel Castro later made famous by staying there on his visit to the United Nations.

Every experience was new. Registering at the hotel was a first. Riding up the elevator was a maiden voyage and fortunately my friend's cousin knew enough to tip the bellhop. The next day my new Berbician friends returned and took me to a restaurant, Horn and Hardart, where the food was in automated dispensers against the wall. All a patron had to do was insert the correct number of coins and presto, you open the glass door and your selection is on a tray.

You know I was impressed.

Later that day they drove me to Grand Central Station and made sure I boarded the train for Washington, D.C. Sorry to say, after keeping in touch for awhile, my new friends and I became too busy with the everyday hustle and lost contact with one another.

When I arrived in Washington by train from New York I took a taxi and asked to be taken to a hotel near Howard University. Those were the days of segregation, of course, and that meant my choices were limited. The taxi driver took me to what seemed like a fairly new hotel, clean and respectable-looking, and which turned out to be not very far from the campus. He helped me to the registration desk and left his card, saying, "Call me if you need to go anywhere."

The next day I was up early to get to the university to do what first year students do: register for classes, a formidable task I discovered soon enough. Those early hours made me very reflective, realizing that I was going it alone since my arrival in New York. Leaving the hotel and not knowing that I could have walked the distance, I stepped out of the hotel and opened the door of the first cab I saw. To my surprise, the driver was the same one who had brought me from the train station the day before. His name was Franklin Delano Roosevelt Smith and he turned out to be one of the kindest persons I had the pleasure of knowing in the United States. He drove me to the campus and I spent many hours in what was called freshman orientation. Although I thought the orientation was a waste of precious time, I was able to hook up with some West Indian students and through them I found a place to stay. I took the first room I saw in a house where two first-year Barbadian students and a student from my home were already living.

Mr. Smith, the taxi driver never gave up on me, returning to the hotel that evening to see how my day had progressed. When he learned that I had found a place to stay, he insisted on driving me there free of charge. I spent many holidays, especially Thanksgiving and Christmas at his beautiful home in northeast Washington with him and his wife and many of his relatives. He and his wife drove me around Washington, pointing out places of interest. Foremost among my disappointments and regrets is that

I allowed the relationship to lapse after awhile, when I no longer lived in the United States.

Moving into that rooming house made me feel a bit more relaxed, especially when I found out the student from British Guiana was a member of the staff at the Freeburg Public School, the very school where Alwyn was a teacher. He was older than Alwyn and he was a no-nonsense type; all he did was work and study. He never drank, did not smoke or fornicate. He was an excellent student but did not live long enough to compensate for the sacrifices he made to become a renowned surgeon.

Upon reflection, I gave myself a good grade for those first weeks in Washington. No relatives to rely upon, no buddies with whom to share the fear. Just about everything was a first for the boy from Wakenaam.

I had been living in that rooming house for about two weeks when I happened to visit a snack bar just off campus. After I had placed my order with the waitress behind the counter, there was a student behind me in the line who said to me "Where you from, boy?" almost in a condescending manner. I wondered why he asked the question and who was he calling boy? Instead I replied politely, "British Guiana."

"Is that so? And what school did you attend?"

"I went to Central High."

"Well, I'll be damned. What a co-incidence. Welcome to Howard." He explained that he too had attended Central and his brothers could have been there when I was. It turned out I knew both of his brothers and was very friendly with the younger one Ivor, who played on my cricket team and did tell me he had an older brother in the States studying medicine. This gentleman was indeed Roy, who was in his final year of medicine.

The upshot of that encounter was that he invited me to join him and his roommate, also from British Guiana, in their apartment. It was a small place but we were hardly ever going to be there at the same time. So after one month at Girard Street I moved to Riggs Place.

1339 Riggs Place North West housed a fourplex building with two units on the ground floor and two on the upper level. It was the only apartment building on the street. The stairs to the upper level were slightly to the left upon entering the building through the front (there was no back door) from the street, leaving a passageway on the right for the two ground floor apartments. Ours was the first on the right, and as you proceeded to the rear, you reached the second apartment whose entrance was left of our wall—a kind of inverted L-shape.

When you opened our apartment door, you stepped into the living room/dining room/kitchen. Straight ahead against the eastern wall was a fairly large sofa with a coffee table in front and a floor lamp to the right of it. To the right, facing Riggs Place, were two upholstered high-backed chairs on each side of the room. Behind each chair were two windows that had to be pushed upward to be opened. Most of the wall facing Riggs was enclosed in glass. As you stood at the entrance, you would see a dining table with a glass top and four chairs around it. To the left against the wall that separated this large space from the bedroom stood a refrigerator and to its right was the stove, sink, and kitchen cupboards. The passage to the bedroom was to the left, past the fridge toward the back of the building. It contained two single beds, a tall clothes closet against the wall separating the bedroom from the kitchen, and a tall metal clothes locker was located close to the toilet and shower.

All in all, it was not a bad set-up. Much better than being cooped up in one room without conversation.

Roy suggested I should prepare myself for the work force, unless my father owned a bank. As such, he arranged with one of his friends to teach me the use of a switchboard and how to operate an elevator. Many Caribbean students were operating switchboards and elevators in apartment buildings and hotels all over Washington, D.C. At that time there were no private lines to rooms and apartments so all calls came through the switchboard. After two weeks of training he pronounced me ready and I made my way downtown to an employment agency. I also took the elevator operator's licence and fortunately passed it. My guardian angel continued to keep watch over me because very soon after a vacancy occurred at the Cairo Hotel, and thanks to Roy and the Caribbean network, I became employed. Roy graduated from medical school at the end of the term and headed to New York for his internship.

Roy's apartment mate was not only a student from British Guiana but was a graduate of Central High as well. He too had relatives attending Central during my sojourn—two boys and a girl whom I knew fairly well. They lived in a huge two-storey house on Durban Street, about an eight-minute walk from Central.

He was known to his friends as O.J. and was well-liked by everyone. Since he pre-dated the infamous one, he will remain for me the only O.J. He made quite an impression on me. He was in his last year of Pharmacy and had been accepted into Medical School for the new term. He was tall—six feet plus—and was considered handsome, well-built without going to the gym, and suave in every way. He had adapted the American style without the affectation. In other words, women just loved him. His proclivities demanded more than most men would dare tackle. He had two girlfriends in our fourplex without either knowing. One young beauty, married without children, lived on our floor, and the other—older than he was—lived above us with her brother. I do not know if I knew the occupant of the fourth suite or I do not remember. She could not have been attractive or O.J. would have been visiting her too. Besides the women in the building, he had others. Sometimes his timing would be off. If I arrived at Riggs Place to find a nervous lady marching up and down at the entrance, I knew he was trapped inside. That meant she was early for her appointment; very early, because he was always a stickler about time. To save face, her face, I would tell her he was delayed for another hour, giving her time to leave and return, and allowing him time to get his act together. You might say I was growing up.

One time I stayed put, continuing to sit at the kitchen table with my back to them, pretending I was reading while he and his guest were ensconced on the couch. It did not take long for him to grab me on the shoulder—gently I must add—pull me into the bedroom and stuff a five-dollar bill into my hand before whispering his famous three words: "Get lost, kid."

Any time I returned home and found the safety latch on, I took my cue and disappeared, then called home after an appropriate interval to see if the coast was clear. To tell the truth, I did not protest and never complained, inwardly or otherwise. Not only was this a real liberal arts education but I knew I should not consider biting the hand that fed me. After all, most of these women came bearing gifts: food baskets that were very much appreciated. The larder was always full and belonged to all of us, share and share alike.

O.J.'s brother, who was a professor of Medicine at a New England college, owned the building where we lived. It was the only apartment building on our street, and many streets around us. He was very compassionate about keeping our rent at a reasonable level.

My first term at Howard had come to a successful end. I was surprised how well I had done because I had been out of high school for awhile and had given up any idea of post secondary education. I gave all the credit to the teachers at Central. I was floored one day when our English professor read an essay to the class, commenting how well it was written and I soon realized it was my work. I expected an 'A' for the paper and was disappointed on receiving only a 'B plus.' One of my classmates told me I should be grateful since the professor was reputed for not giving a grade higher than a B.

Although I was working at the Cairo, I would have to find a day job. I didn't have to look very far. O.J. had worked at one of the prominent hotels—the Wardman Park—for a number of years as an attendant in the swimming pool locker room. Since he was now a graduate pharmacist, he no longer needed that job. He took me to the hotel and actually told the manager he would like me to be his replacement, saying I was his roommate and a countryman. That was all there was to it. Life was so simple then. Mr. Sutton, the manager, was always well dressed in a dark blue suit and shiny shoes. I found out later he was also a gentleman when he checked with me to inquire how I was and how I was being treated—me so low in the hierarchy of the work force.

I started working at the swimming pool the first of June and O.J. accompanied me to show me the ropes. He introduced me to the head lifeguard in charge of the pool, and we met the other attendant, also new, who became my assistant. We meshed quite well. He was also attending

Howard and was recommended by his friend who had just graduated after working at the pool for three years.

O.J. was leaving for New York where he was to work in a pharmacy, so I was left to man the ship. Two weeks before his departure Mike and Alwyn wrote separately, advising me of their arrival dates. They were to land in New York a week apart. At the time I thought it strange that they were not traveling together but rationalized that their reservations probably depended on the availability of seats or they might not have bothered to co-ordinate their schedules. Whatever the reason, they were indeed coming and I was elated at the prospect of them joining me in Washington, D.C. I decided I needed to get a part-time job to enable me to buy some new threads to impress them. I did not want to dip into my savings for college, because from experience I knew I would never replace the money borrowed from the nest egg. I planned on getting a new sports jacket, a couple of slacks and a new pair of summer shoes. I wanted to look sharp, to let them still believe that they had come to the land of milk and honey. In short, I did not want them to be depressed upon seeing me. And I wanted to ease them into the real world. They loved clothes.

It was not hard to find a part-time job in downtown Washington and I found one washing dishes. It was labour-intensive work and after six weeks, just before their arrival, I quit. I received my cheque and did not bother showing up the following day. That was my revenge to the owners for working me like a slave. As I have said, I still had two other jobs: my night job at the Cairo Hotel, which I kept throughout the year, and the one at the swimming pool at the Wardman Park Hotel, later changed to the Sheraton. I started my shift at the swimming pool at eight in the morning, worked right through to four thirty and caught a cab to the restaurant, finishing at nine. I would then catch a cab to Riggs Place and hang around until it was time to go to the Cairo. During my extra duty at the restaurant I hardly spent any time at home. Catching a cab was a common thing to do as all three jobs had the bonus of tips being part of the job and cabs were relatively cheap then. I was also able to have my supper at the restaurant.

Alwyn arrived a week before Mike. He must have landed in New York when I was at work at the swimming pool, and I had no way of knowing he had caught the train to Washington. I was at work at the Cairo when he arrived. Although I had sent him information on reaching me at both places, I found out later, to my chagrin, that he had not received the letter. The post office in British Guiana had a reputation for mishandling overseas mail, a euphemistic way of stating the obvious. He took a cab from the train station and arrived at Riggs Place to be greeted by silence and darkness. Undaunted, he walked east and knocked on the first house that was illuminated.

This was a Saturday evening in the summer and the neighbours were up and engaged in conversation and card playing. Those were also the early days of television, at least in our area. He must have explained his dilemma in his British Guianese accent to some bewildered people who had never met anyone who looked like them speaking a language they could barely understand. He had to repeat himself several times and, for him, it must have been equally fascinating to hear an American accent different from the Steppin Fetchits of the movies. These newfound friends were transplanted from the South and had brought their southern hospitality with them. Upon hearing his predicament, they invited him to spend the night and would not allow him to leave in the morning without a proper breakfast. They then helped him with his luggage and escorted him to 1339 to be sure someone was home. They were very kind, caring people—a man, his wife and young son who went out of their way to help a total stranger. Alwyn remained friends with them even after he left Washington. It is a reflection of the changing times that an incident such as Alwyn's might turn out very differently today.

Alwyn came to the pool with me and it happened to be the day a photo shoot of Miss Washington contestants was taking place. He had a chance to see some bathing beauties in the flesh and discovered that those Esther Williams movies were a pale imitation of the real. Later he joined me at the Cairo Hotel where a dance competition was in full swing in the ballroom. It was strictly Latin American music and contestants came from as far away as New Jersey and New York. Alwyn was intrigued not only by the technique of the contestants but by their attire as well. Although we had considered him a virtuoso in both the rhumba and the tango, he confessed his performance was different to theirs as night to day. After this little bit of excitement the hotel became quiet and I found a room for him to get some sleep until my shift was over.

Mike arrived the following week and Alwyn was there to greet him with a fake American accent. Perhaps because of the long journey, a first for all of us, Mike was a bit tired and was not amused by Alwyn's joke. "You ras bin heh one week and you gone crazy. Ah gwine go back home tomorrow." Mike must have really been on edge, to have fallen back to speech patterns he used in Wakenaam. Sometimes when we were all together, we would relax and speak the way we did in Georgetown, not always the King's English. We took comfort in the fact that Thurgood Marshall gave us permission to do so. He had said there was nothing wrong with speaking the language of your culture when you are within that culture. And we often spoke of Boogie. After all, he was responsible for the three of us going to Howard and he was the only one not present.

Washington D.C. is a relatively easy city to navigate, having been laid out in quadrants. Numbered streets run north and south. The streets that run east and west are arranged alphabetically. So if the address was 1424 U Street NW, the simple way was to find Fourteenth and U NW and plot a course from there. That was how I taught the boys to find their way in the city. We were living very close to the busiest intersection in our part of town—Fourteenth and U. This was a major intersection that served the inner city. 1339 Riggs was only a few blocks away. On my days off I introduced them to the section of Washington I knew best. Just about everything I needed was within walking distance. Okay, so I walked a lot in those days. We went on foot to the campus, quite a stretch for boys not used to walking. We knew we were going to a segregated country and our imagination conjured fearful thoughts that never materialized. When they wanted to buy winter coats, I took them to a store where the owners were regulars at the swimming pool. Sometimes we went sightseeing but most of our activities were confined to the area between U Street and Seventh and Fourteenth Streets.

That section was always busy, teeming with bodies like a Boxing Day sale, and before the boys arrived I had a secret I shared with no one. I told myself I was rounding out my North American education by visiting one particular dance hall on U Street a few times that summer. No thought of personal safety ever crossed my mind. For all those years I spent at 1339, I never encountered any threats or heard of any muggings or shootings, morning, noon or night. Now they tell me Washington D.C. is the murder capital of the world. What happened?

It took me about thirty minutes to walk to the Howard campus if I did not stop and gawk at people on the street, trying to hear what they were saying to each other. Usually I would leave 1339 and turn left and when I reached Thirteenth Street, make another left, then I crossed U Street and continued until I came to Fairmont Street where I turned right. Fairmont Street would take me to Georgia Avenue and Howard University. To vary the scenery, I sometimes followed U Street up to Eighth and turned left. Upon reaching Barry Place I turned right and continued on Georgia Avenue. That was when I saw a Salesman Wanted sign on a storefront. It was like a signal from heaven and so I went in. It was one of those narrow stores—a generous guess would be seven hundred square feet of space with a counter and showcase displaying household products as well as beauty supplies for women and shaving supplies and cologne for men. The position was not selective; anyone with time and a few dollars to invest could start working immediately. Thus I became a salesman.

I bought a few items at my reduced price, obtained some brochures and hit the road that day on my way home. My route could not be random as before; I had to be more organized in spreading my wings to include a larger area with more potential customers. On my way home from Howard I would knock on doors, show my brochures and the few samples, take a deposit for the orders and arrange a delivery date. My clients were for the most part women, though I did have my share of men customers when they were home. The whole enterprise was very rewarding; it was as easy as pulling teeth. Of course, whenever I reminisced about my salesmanship, I concluded that many of my customers were really trying to help me. One particular family—husband and wife—always bought something and there was no doubt in my mind that they were poor. I still have the greatest respect and gratitude for those extraordinary people who knew I was in school and was a foreigner.

That is how I met Marge. She was my favourite customer who later became a friend. She introduced me to an aspect of American lifestyle I had never encountered in my parochial student existence. Like most of the women on my client list, Marge was a stay-at-home wife, not because the husband commanded a large salary but because it was the norm then. The husband went to work, the wife stayed home.

Marge invited me to my first rent party at her home. Food and liquor were sold, ostensibly to pay the rent or in her case the mortgage. There was music and dancing and in one of the rooms at the back, away from the dancing, men and women would be busily engaged in some form of gambling—dice and/or cards. Booze would be served to those participants also. I never did ask Marge how much money she recovered from her night of open house and I still do not think it mattered. I believe the main purpose was camaraderie, friends getting together and having a good time.

Marge also took me to an after hours club or joint. That was the place where the participants gathered after the bars closed and the musicians moved to a private establishment, usually in a basement where the noise would be subdominant. Most of them worked the night shift, like bartenders, waitresses, musicians and even some professional people. Musicians would move from one job and start another. Food and liquor were sold, illegally of course, and the party lasted until daybreak. Those gatherings were limited to friends and acquaintances and guests who could be vouched for, since total strangers could not be relied upon to keep this unlawful activity a secret. Marge always knew somebody who sold alcohol after the stores were closed. In retrospect, I can only conclude that not too many people kept bottles of liquor at home, as is the custom now. Perhaps it was the economics of the time. Not too many people could afford the luxury of extra bottles, and the bootlegger extended credit when payday had come and gone.

One of Marge's favourite expressions was 'my old man'—"I have to check with my old man" or "I don't know if my old man can afford this."

Marge was twenty-four years old with a pleasant face that embraced you with an attractive smile. Her constant concern for her old man added to my already positive estimation of her. The reverence I had for my parents had already passed the high water mark of the launch stelling at Wakenaam, and Marge was passing this test by showing her father the same respect. At least that was my belief.

One day when I was making a delivery to Marge's home, a tall refined-looking, solidly-built man answered the door. He must have known my mission because he invited me in without hesitation. He was older than Marge, but not old enough to be her father—to my thinking, anyway. After we were introduced, I realized that this man, Edward, was her husband. Welcome to America.

And Marge became my favourite customer and a friend. Early in the summer, before the boys arrived, she surprised me by inviting me to a dance on U Street. Her husband gave us his blessing. He did not enjoy public dances and he disliked crowds. I knew it never occurred to him to be jealous of our relationship, and of course, he was right. More boyish-looking than I should have been and underweight at five foot ten, I posed no challenge.

It was an inexpensive evening on my part. Thinking it was the noble thing to do, I offered to buy a round of drinks for Marge and her two girl friends, Ginette and Minnie. They smiled and snickered. I checked my crotch and was assured that the giggling was not due to the exposure of body parts. Then Minnie said, "Oh, you are so sweet wanting to buy us a drink. Put your money away, boyfriend, we will treat you tonight. You ready for a drink? Good, we gonna have one too."

They poured some coke in a paper cup, slipped me a mickey and directed me to the men's room to pour my drink into my cup. At the same time they headed to the ladies room, since each of them had a mickey. Throughout the evening, whenever anyone said, "Care for a drink?" we repeated the pattern. I continued to use that trick until the end of my student days.

The next Saturday when I was off from the Cairo, I returned to the dance hall. I had discovered on my other visit that the patrons were only interested in their own group, and did not pay much attention to anyone else. I could blend in with the crowd and my foreign label would not advertise itself. I kept a low profile, nonetheless, observing the interplay between the sexes, trying to decide whom I would ask to dance. I did not want to make the mistake of asking someone's old lady—the opposite of old man. I was overwhelmed to see a young lady heading in my direction and was more surprised when she addressed me by name.

"Imagine seeing you again," she hissed, grabbing my hand. "I bet you don't remember me, John."

"But of course," I replied, because I had met her through Marge the first time I went there dancing. "Your name is Mattie."

My children would be very surprised I remembered Mattie as I sometimes falter in remembering the names of some of their friends. But I was better at it then. I had to survive.

She held on to my hand and pulled me toward her girlfriend. Mattie was about my age, about my height in her heels, not skinny, not fat, with a lovely backside. She had a face I had seen a few times before—plain but attractive; so perhaps her beauty radiated from within. A beautiful smile with perfect teeth. She was from North Carolina and although she had a high school diploma with secretarial emphasis, she could not find office work anywhere and was employed as a domestic, as was her girlfriend, Doris. She worked for a professional family, both doctors, in nearby Chevy Chase, Maryland. Mattie and I stayed friends during my entire sojourn in Washington, even after I left and came back in the summer. I started to reminisce about U Street when the old memories began to cascade like the Mazaruni River.

Every day brought the return of my roommate O.J. closer and closer. That meant it was time to find Mike and Alwyn a place of their own. This was a new life for Alwyn, free from curfews or having to pass his father's inspection. An incident from our boyhood days comes to mind: we once accompanied him home with a drink or two more than his custom of Guinness stout and tried to sneak him into the house. It was about 11 o'clock. As we quietly opened the door, there was his irate father greeting us: "What do you rumsuckers think you're doing?" We were all out of high school and working, but of course, we were still in our teens.

Back to the problem I was facing. I knew of no apartments other than Riggs Place. Some students rented large old houses and shared the space. Some had landladies to monitor their comings and goings. In my case I was fortunate to have been rescued by one of my countrymen, who took me under his wing.

Sometimes I attended a church within walking distance. I didn't have a regular timetable; I went when the spirit moved me and when my schedule permitted. There was a lady member who made it her duty to speak to me every time after the service before I left the church. This particular Sunday was no different and when I broached the subject of finding a place for my boys, she whispered: "God be praised." She knew someone who could help. This friend, who was a Christian lady, had a nice room and she was sure the boys from Ghana would be pleased with their choice. When she gave me the lady's number and said she would give her a call as well, I did not have the heart to correct her.

With a reference from a church lady I felt comfortable taking the boys to see the place. They were impressed. It was a big, old two-storey house with clean, spacious rooms. Each room was furnished with desks, reading lamps, two separate clothes closets and beds. They shared one large room with two single beds and the use of a bathroom for all the tenants on their floor. An African student—and I mean bona fide African from Nigeria—named Sunday occupied one of the rooms on their floor and the other was rented by a woman named Amarit. Amarit was what the male students at Meharry called high yellow, which meant fair, or what Guyanese refer to as light-skin. The landlady Maria, a voluptuous woman in the positive sense, had her own self-contained manor on the first floor with dining room, living room, bedroom, and ensuite bath. Everybody was to use the very large kitchen in her place, having individual cupboards assigned to each. All in all, it was not a bad set-up.

Mike, Alwyn, and Sunday quickly became friends and Sunday introduced them to another part of U Street at Seventh Street, a couple of street car stops from their residence. It was within walking distance, if they felt so inclined. Sunday seemed to have an unlimited supply of money and was not reluctant to treat his new friends, who were watching every penny they spent. He was in his second year of college and that was another advantage he had over them. When the school year started, their forays onto Seventh Street came to a dribble, if not an end. For boys who had never cooked for themselves, they sought the easy way out by eating at some inexpensive neighbourhood restaurants or out of a can.

On weekends they were frequent visitors at Riggs Place. The boys were adapting to life in America except for the seasonal change. Autumn had taken the place of summer, and wearing heavy coats did not sit well with their tropical upbringing. Thanksgiving was and still is a very big holiday in the United States. Sunday was leaving for Philadelphia for the whole weekend and I was invited to spend the day with some people named Smith, who had befriended me soon after my arrival in Washington. Just as I was feeling perturbed about the boys being alone for Thanksgiving, they called to say that their landlady had invited them, if they had no other plans. Of course, they had none.

I don't want to imply that all Guyanese men are gentlemen, simply that those whom I have been fortunate to know well, were. Mike and Alwyn were a part of that tradition. Dressed in their best suits, made to order in Georgetown from expensive English tweed imported from Great Britain, they arrived at Maria's living room with flowers and a bottle of wine. They had observed this protocol in the movies, but were not prepared for the relaxed nature of the afternoon. They promised themselves to be on their best behaviour, for although they had been tenants for a few months, there was not much communication with their landlady. They paid their rent on time and exchanged light conversation in the kitchen and hallway. Maria was dolled up and they were surprised to see that dinner was for four. Then Amarit appeared, displaying her fine figure in a dress that made them wonder how the stitches did not pop.

The sumptuous meal of roast turkey, cranberry sauce, country ham, asparagus with pimentos, and sweet potatoes with marshmallows had them breaking their promise of not overeating. The meal was followed with Napoleon brandy and when they thought nothing could top what they had experienced, Maria brought out a bottle of Johnny Walker Blue, which they had never seen or heard of. Those drinks were an aphrodisiac to these young men whose experience with the opposite sex had amounted to no more than a surprise kiss on the cheek, or surreptitiously brushing a girl's bubby, as we used to refer to the breast in high school. These ladies were a little older and much more experienced in every aspect of life than the girls they knew back home. Amarit was twenty-four, and Maria claimed to be twenty-eight. What made it so exciting was the fact that these ladies had made it known that they liked their lifestyle. They were not looking for husbands.

The boys must have impressed the ladies as well, because, fearing they might overstay their welcome, they excused themselves at a reasonable hour that Thursday evening, only to be invited for another party the next day. They were learning that Thanksgiving meant the whole weekend. We had planned to get together on Saturday, but they called to tell me they were too tired to travel to Riggs Place. It was their way of bragging about their wonderful weekend and change of manhood.

It seemed that Maria liked Mike all along, and Alwyn could not believe his luck ending up with Amarit. I suppose they had to tease me. They had arrived a year after me and had beaten me to the punch. I am waiting for quality, I said, spelling the word out. Truth be told, I was not looking for any conquests. I realized soon enough that the journey ahead was unpredictable and arduous and many times when the urge surfaced to slacken off in my studies, the image of my mother appeared to strengthen me. I was very busy working, attending class, and studying, and too tired in between. Although I could catch a few winks at the Cairo, I think those short naps created more stress than relaxation.

My shift started at eleven in the evening and this meant I had to be in the building at least thirty minutes before to change into my bellhop uniform and be briefed. I had to be informed of guests who were arriving late, special requests of guests, that sort of thing. In other words, stay awake, but if it's a slow night, try to relax.

The bellhop is a rare bird these days. There was a night manager who did the bookkeeping—this was long before the days of computers. He retreated to the office behind the registration desk, ostensibly to do his book work but the intention was to get some sleep inbetween. During his sojourn at the back, I would be left to steer the ship, answer the switchboard through which came all calls, in or out. I would register late guests and still tend to the requests of guests who were not smart enough to be sleeping. Get me some cigarettes, drinks, or even liquor. Whatever they requested, they received—within limits, of course,

And there was my fan club. Just about every week and sometimes more than once, a girl would call the switchboard after midnight. I realized from her voice that she was not from my neighbourhood. I would answer, putting forth my most pleasant voice always.

"Good morning, Cairo Hotel, may I help?"

"Yes please, we are just down the street and we seem to be lost. Can you tell me please how far we have to go to Pee?"

There had to be more than one person involved in this charade since the voice differed from time to time. I allowed them their fun. It was a joke, of course, and before I could answer, the line would go dead. I have to explain there was P Street, along with Q, R, U etc. I never did find out the source of the call but I know it was not from the inner city where I was living.

The boys could not believe their good fortune. They were within a short walk to the campus, so they were able to save time and money for transportation. Now they were also saving on meals, since they were no longer customers of the greasy spoon diners they used to frequent. They were eating nutritious meals in their own kitchen, thanks to their new status. Their youthful impetuosity continued until the end of the school year. I often wondered how they combined study with romance, but then they did not have to spend eight or nine hours at work. They still had enough money from home to get them through that first year.

They both found summer jobs. Alwyn worked in one of those drive-in restaurants where the waiter came out to the car, took the order and brought it back on a tray, which was attached to the open window of the car. The drive-in restaurant seems to have been replaced by the drive-through. Mike quickly learned his mantra from former newcomers to the American work ethic. Indoor work only, no heavy lifting. He opted for part-time relief work, mostly at apartment buildings, taking care of switchboards. Like hotels, every apartment building had a switchboard through which calls were forwarded to the apartments instead of direct lines. Whenever I tell this to young people, I see a look of disbelief, but I guess I have participated in the passage of time. Many of the switchboards were manned by Caribbean students, so it was easy for him to find work, when the operators wanted time off, or left the city in the summer for better-paying jobs. I think the Caribbean students started this networking trend more than half a century ago.

So the boys were enjoying their freedom. Maybe I should refer to them as young men, because they were in years, but I could never think of them that way. I know they were not contributing much, if at all, to the weekend celebrations taking place on Fairmont. The girls knew of their financial situation and did not hesitate to provide the food and drinks that go with a party. They loved to party, too. Amarit had a well-paying job with the federal government and although Maria did not work outside the home, she had inherited the property with no mortgage attached, as well as the benefit of an insurance policy from her late husband. He had been a prominent boxer, ranked second in the world in his division. He had just signed a contract to fight for the boxing title when the unexpected happened. He was sitting on the verandah one hot summer evening, when he was shot accidentally, as two passing cars exchanged fire. He had done well in real estate, and had left his widow financially secure. So both women had funds. In addition to all this, both ladies had male friends who contributed, although they had families of their own.

As I always remind myself, everything is impermanent, nothing good lasts forever, and there are not too many things that are free in this world. It took Mike and Alwyn quite awhile to discover those precepts, but discover them they did.

Late one Saturday evening when Mike, Alwyn, Maria, and Amarit were relaxing with music and dim lights, two men appeared. Well-dressed, they looked like accountants, but their demeanour bespoke another line of work. One of them displayed his gun attached to its holster, as he unbuttoned his coat. Just like in the movies, the boys told me later. Maria would have none of their intrusion, though her perfidious behaviour was now clear for everyone to see. Mike and Alwyn had never seen their rivals before, although they knew of their existence. They knew their visits were usually during the day when they were on the campus, or early evenings, but never on Saturdays until now. The boys knew the men were not gainfully employed but had their own lucrative hustle on the streets.

They were older men. Mid-fifties, was the boys' guess. They lived in the Northeastern section of Washington in a so-called middle class neighbourhood and were well thought of by their neighbours. They belonged to a church congregation that worshiped on Saturday evenings and Sundays, and their offering to the collection plate was above average. On Sundays they gathered together with their wives and families. Because they dressed well and always drove new cars, many in their community thought they worked for the government in a high-paying, secret job. Maria would not be embarrassed by a disruption to her party and led the visitors into the kitchen to give them what she later described as a tongue lashing. Amarit accompanied her for support. These were two ladies, who, even if they were playing a dangerous game, were not going to show fear. In other words, they could be really tough, when the occasion warranted it. The boys, suddenly aging into young men during the confrontation, pondered their situation. Sunday, the African, who was also there with his girlfriend, one of Maria's friends, eased his way back to his room. The others followed his example and waited in their room until the ladies sought them out.

The incident dampened their ardour. After all, they did not want to be caught in a crossfire, or worse yet, be the recipient of a jealous lover's bullet. They had heard Maria tell the men that if they ever brought their guns to the house again, she would not hesitate to shoot. This tough talk worried Mike and Alwyn. They had grown up without ever having seen a gun, and their imagination was getting ahead of their thinking. Now they were calling me every day to find them another place to stay. One day when Mike called, I was preparing to visit Mattie who had invited me for lunch. He sounded so desperate that I invited them to tag along with me. I think that exposure to the guns had a more chilling effect than I had assumed. I called Mattie to notify her of her extra guests, and she was more than considerate. "I hope your friends are hungry, because I have beaucoup of everything."

Mattie lived quite a long distance from our neighbourhood of Fourteenth and U Street and it took us almost an hour by streetcar and bus to arrive at her yard, as my Jamaican friend would have said. The inconvenience of the time-consuming trip was expiated by the cordial reception and sumptuous meal that greeted us. The chicken, shrimp, and vegetable casserole was washed down with Southern Comfort, a liqueur we had not drunk before, and the boys showed their appreciation by imbibing more than their custom. It was the same with the meal. It looked like this was their first for the day and Mattie took their enthusiasm as a compliment. After a decent interval, we were ready to go. I had to work at the Cairo that night, so we thanked Mattie effusively and took our leave. On our short walk to the bus stop they started to snicker.

"Share your joke," I exhorted.

"Whe you find her?" asked one in a derogatory tone, while the other proclaimed, "Wasted yella!"

The 'wasted yella' term is an expression they picked up in Washington, D.C. to describe a certain type of Afro-American girl. As much as I dislike describing a particular people by colour, this is the only way I can explain the term. I remember when I had to pacify my infuriated daughter one day when she came home from school. She was still very young and wanted to know why a girl who used to be one of her best friends joined with another girl to call her 'black' and even used the derogatory 'N' word. Previously many in her class had told her how beautiful she was. I told her to fetch the dictionary and find the meaning of the word black. "Does that describe you?"

"No, Daddy."

"Why don't you look up the meaning of the word 'white?' Does that describe your so-called friend?"

"No, Daddy."

"Then there is nothing to worry about. Remember, ignorance is bliss."

The rationalization for the term 'wasted yella' is that the closer the skin colour is to the dominant race, the more beautiful the girl should be. If the girl has the required complexion and is still not considered attractive, then that facet is wasted, of no benefit to her. Strange, I have never heard that expression applied to men. This must have had its roots during the days of slavery when yella meant related to the master in more ways than one. The expression 'fair-skinned' to describe someone of African descent says it all.

Taking all this into consideration and smiling inwardly at their quickness at adopting the new culture, I told them how ungrateful they were. Their attitude was not all that surprising, since they had a full belly and had drunk too much of the free liquour; in other words, I understood that the oxygen needed for thinking was being used for digestion at that moment. I told them that their behaviour since arriving in the United States of America reminded me of a classic behaviour change in Fredericksburg when I was very young.

I then related the true story of a boy named Dudley who lived in Georgetown but would spend his July/August holidays with his Fredericksburg grandparents. City boys always thought they were smarter than their country cousins and his behaviour was, therefore, more uncontrollable than the other boys, including me, in the village. We knew our limits. His grandparents tried to discipline him by words and entreaties and when no change was forthcoming in his attitude, they tried the remedy that worked for most of us: licks. Corporal punishment followed the threat, when the threat had no effect. As you can imagine, they had to resort to the punishment when there was no change in the boy's conduct; whenever the grandmother tried to administer the punishment, Dudley would run and hide, behind bushes, a wall, a tree. He would pick his hiding place in such a manner that his head would be hidden but his shoulders or feet were visible. His reasoning was that if he could not see his pursuers, they could not see him. His grandmother would take her time and quietly grab him by the scruff of his neck and the licks would fly. Dudley came to the conclusion that country folks were not that stupid after all. He thought his grandparents could read his mind and therefore, knew what he was thinking. He changed completely. His behaviour became so exemplary that our parents would say to us: "Why can't you boys be more like Dudley?"

Both Mike and Alwyn giggled. Mike said, "You should change your course and become a preacher man."

The timing was unbelievable. I had just finished relating the history of Dudley when we arrived at our stop at Seventh and U Street, the same area Sunday had taken them to a club where he was acquainted with some ladies of the night. They had never mentioned this to me, so I casually let it be known that I knew of their peccadillo and outlined it for them.

"Whe you get dat from?"

"Oh, ah heard it through the grapevine."

"Well, dat's a damn lie." When both of them protested simultaneously, I knew I had made my point. By the time we reached Fourteenth and U on our way to Riggs Place, the teasing of Mattie had long been forgotten. After all, they did not intend to be mean. It was their way of having fun. You must remember that we were still young in the grand scheme of life, and boys will be boys. Whoever said boys will be men had a lot of waiting to do, when it came to us.

Not forgotten was their predicament at the rooming house, once we reached Riggs Place. Of course, O.J. had been told of the situation. After all, if he could not broker it, who could? He agreed they should move, pointing out the effect the proximity of Amarit and Marie could have on their studies. To show them how negative the relationship was, he concluded with: "Even a dog does not defecate on its own doorstep." Or words to that effect.

It was definite that they would move; the only stumbling block was finding another place. Riggs Place was too small for four, three maybe, but not more. Finally, the telephone rang at home one day: "Ah hear you lookin fu a place fu yu boys."

The accent was unmistakable. Two medical students from British Guiana were living on Belmont Street, not far from Riggs and very close to Howard. It was a fairly large, self-contained suite with two single beds, ample closet space, two chests of drawers, a table and chairs, and a pull-out couch against the wall in what was known as a co-op building, which was the forerunner of the condominium. It was an apartment without a kitchen but with its own small bathroom. The absence of a kitchen was no problem, since the lady who owed the apartment would allow the use of her kitchen. She hardly used it anyway, since she worked all day at a government job and hardly cooked even on weekends. The boys did not plan to do much cooking either, so the offer seemed tempting. The bush drums had rolled: the network was active.

We decided to visit Belmont and inspect the premises. The medical students were vociferous in their praises for the set-up. On entering the apartment, the suite was to the left. A hallway to the right led to the domain of the landlady. Inside, almost immediately to the left was a washroom and a few paces to the right was the kitchen. Further along was a wall that separated the drawing and dining room from the rest of the house and from there a hall led to two bedrooms, which occupied almost the width of the house. The dining and drawing room, enclosed by an ornate door, was straight across from the rental suite.

The boys were impressed with the layout and eager to secure the place. The rent was the only drawback, I gathered, and I anticipated their request to join them, even before they asked. After discussing this with O.J., he agreed that I should help them. He had found out from a friend who worked in the registrar's office that their marks needed improvement and he believed I could be a stabilizing force in their lives. The suite was large enough with two single beds and a pull-out couch, especially since we would almost never be there at the same time.

I moved to Belmont with the knowledge that I could return to Riggs Place, if the experiment proved to be a failure. The boys settled down to their studies, as far as I was able to discern. They did not give up their gratuitous behaviour entirely, however. They continued to visit Fairmont Street, when they deemed it prudent—after all, Howard was very close—but for the most part, the girls would come to Belmont Street, either individually or together.

On a few occasions we took in some shows on Fourteenth Street within walking distance of Belmont. Among the artists we saw there were Ray Charles, Ruth Brown, and Sarah Vaughn. They performed in what must have been a converted warehouse. It looked like a gymnasium with a stage for the performers and the band entertaining a multitude of worshipers on a floor without any seats; maybe there were some against the wall, but we always stood in front of the bandstand. Needless to say, we never did try to pick up any chicks. I have a feeling this type of entertainment has disappeared with time and integration. Saturday night was always a busy, rollicking time in the inner city when segregation ruled the land.

Coraye, our landlady, was a very attractive woman in her early thirties. She was friendly and accommodating, meaning that if we were not prompt in paying the rent on the due date, she would not leave reminders for us. She would accept our apology for the delay every time we were late. On at least a couple of occasions we would pay our rent, only to borrow a portion later to attend one of those concerts on Fourteenth Street. Of course, we always repaid her. She even invited us for what she called brunch a few times. She introduced us to chitlins, a traditional soul food considered a delicacy by many. Mike used to say, "If you can stand the smell, you got it licked." For my part, I thought an appreciation of such a treat had to be ingrained at an early age.

For all this kindness and friendliness, she was never intrusive. When the boys sneaked their female companions into the crib, they never did find out if Coraye knew of their artifice. It seemed as if the decision to settle in at Coraye's was a wise one. The boys were paying more attention to their studies and I went to work every night at the Cairo.

Once all the planets were aligned properly, which meant that I was off on a Saturday night from the Cairo, it was payday, and examinations were behind us for awhile. We were planning to take the bus to New York to attend a British Guianese dance that had become a tradition there, and return the next day. Coraye overheard us talking in the kitchen and offered us her car. We left on a Saturday just before noon and returned the next day at about the same time. At that dance we saw so many of our countrymen and women whom we thought we had left back home, only to learn they had been in New York even before we arrived in theUnited States. How come? It was this way. We knew many of them but only as acquaintances, meaning we did not fraternize on a weekly basis, but would meet occasionally at school functions, cricket matches, dances, so when they left the country, only their very close friends and relatives knew. There at the Empire Ballroom we joked that most of Georgetown was at the dance. Talk about brain drain. It was a beguiling evening, because we were able to turn the wheel back to the carefree days in British Guiana.

On our return trip to Washington, Alwyn insisted on driving, and went way above the speed limit. Ignoring our admonitions to slow down, he continued to test his mettle, to the point that Mike and I were getting very apprehensive. Mike shouted: "Look like you gwine get another ticket." Alwyn looked in his rearview mirror and did see a motorcyclist behind him. Thinking it was the highway patrol, he started to reduce his speed and even wanted to exchange places with me, while the car was in motion, an act that required nothing less than an acrobatic feat. I was on the passenger side and Mike was alone at the back. Mike knew all along that the cyclist behind was not the highway patrol, and let me in on this fact with a wink. Alwyn was driving below the speed limit when the motorcyclist passed us at high speed and Mike could not contain his gloating. Alwyn gave him a few minutes to restrain himself, then said, "Okay, you've had your fun. Maybe I should let you drive the rest of the way." Ray Charles would have been a better driver than Mike.

Alwyn had reason to be afraid. On a previous trip to New York he was driving with some Jamaican students—above the speed limit, of course—and was given a ticket by a patrolman. He was hauled before a judge and had to pay the fine forthwith. All this at night. Now he knew we had only enough cash for gas, so he must have had sudden fears about spending time behind bars. Why did he do it?

Tempus kept doing what it was famous for; tempus fugit: time flies. Everyday we grew older but not necessarily wiser. I kept thinking of a fish that came in with the tide to the beach where my father's boats were moored and where we went swimming as boys. Nobody in our village bothered to catch them with their cast nets for the simple reason that they were too elusive. And too ugly. They were small to start with, about six to eight inches, and their appearance did not conjure up a piquant meal. In a word, they did not look appetizing. We called them four eyes. Maybe there was a scientific name for them, but that was the only name we knew. Two large bulging eyes on the sides of their heads and two eyes under those two to see underwater. They were able to avoid their predators from above and below. I believe it would have boded us well, Mike, Alwyn, and me, to have had four eyes each during our early days in Washington, D.C. If one or two became blurred with the overwhelming pace of life and the temptations that confronted us, there would still be one or two left to see the errors of our behaviour. But then again, why take all the fun out of living? How were we to garner our life experiences? The boys and I continued to enjoy each other's company, as friends are supposed to do, especially friends who were essentially alone on a wide, wide sea. If we had a rudder, we certainly did not have the compass we needed. Or was it a compass we had and not the other? Looking back, I think our move from a simple, safe, regulated society—that shame-based society with relatives and elders monitoring our behaviour—to a complex society without restrictions may have had a more psychological effect on us than we cared to acknowledge at the time.

Time stood still for none of us. Seconds ticked into hours and days became months with hardly a change. *Plus ça change, plus c'est la même chose.* A favourite expression of my mother: the more things change, the more they remain the same.

Summer was once again upon us and that meant double duty; during the day my time was spent at the swimming pool at the Wardman Park Hotel. I could not call it work since work entailed expending energy and I was not guilty of that. At night I went to work at the Cairo Hotel. The Cairo Hotel was 'once the jewel of high society and a magnet for visiting celebrities.' It was and still is the tallest building in Washington, but its decline was in effect during my years working there.

Every Saturday I started my shift earlier than usual. I had a private arrangement with another bellhop who wanted to leave early because he had to do what he had to do. I never did ask him his reason and he did not volunteer to enlighten me. I always remembered what happened to the curious cat.

There was one young lady who used to visit the hotel on Saturdays, having reserved Room 615 earlier in the week. She would check in around 9 PM. She was an attractive redhead named Mildred, about five feet, seven inches—taller if she decided to wear high heels—who looked more like a college student than a call girl. Over her long red hair she always wore a beret in a selection of colours but her favourites were black or purple. She definitely stood out. Other girls frequented the hotel as well but there was no doubt they belonged to a lower tier than Mildred. I knew all the regular girls because I had to transport them up and down the elevator and cater to their wants—taxis, liquor, cigarettes, ice, and inconsequential requests. I knew them all, the night crawlers and early risers. One young lady, when she buzzed me to pick her up from one of her trysts with one of the officers from Andrews Air Force Base in nearby Maryland, would always say to me: "Damn, that was lousy. Think you're man enough to finish what he started?"

My reply was always the same: "You bet! But who's gonna run the switchboard and elevator."

The night manager started his bookkeeping about the same time I started my shift, but not long after—around midnight—he would retire to the inner office, ostensibly to continue the balancing act, but more likely to get a few winks. He was an older man, stooped in his posture, almost as if there was some discomfort in his back. Although he was the overseer, I cannot remember any time when I had to disturb him to solve a problem.

On this particular evening, which I have not relived for a long time, everything seemed to be a copy of previous Saturdays, but with more intensity. It must have been payday at Andrews Air Force Base, as there were an inordinate number of officers milling around the lobby and in the dining area cum bar next to the lobby. I had also noticed the full moon earlier and it looked as if all the regular ladies of the night had decided to visit us. There would be no rest for the tired tonight.

As if on cue, I knocked on Room 615 at 10:45 and escorted Mildred to the Oriental Room, which was just off the lobby. Mildred was always treated like a debutante and a table was reserved for her. The waiter would immediately serve her a tall glass of Dr. Pepper topped with crushed ice.

He knew the ritual. As he handed Mildred an unopened pack of playing cards, she would be joined by three officers. She would give the cards to one of the men and ask him to shuffle the pack. She would then deal three cards to each of the men. The person with the highest score won the privilege of taking her to his room. Shortly before the last call for drinks, Mildred appeared at the front desk, indicating she wanted to be taken up. Her companion, an older-looking officer, seemed impatient, champing at the bit, as I was taking my time leaving my post at the switchboard.

I took them to the sixth floor where both of them had rooms. I then returned to the lobby, and took other guests to various floors. For awhile I was very busy. When there was a lull, I checked the bar for stragglers. In the lobby there were four young ones, two pairs who were trying to decide whether to stay the night. In the end the ladies must have won out, because they came to the desk and asked me to call a cab. Then there was a call from Room 615. I heard a voice saying, "Ah wonda wha she want dis time ah night" and had to smile when I realized I was talking to myself.

"Hope you weren't sleeping?"

"Sleeping? No ma'am. I never sleep on the job."

"In that case, could you bring me a Dr. Pepper with some ice? The door is unlocked, so don't bother to knock. Just come right in."

I had delivered items to her on many previous occasions but not in my wildest daydreaming was I prepared for what confronted me. There was Mildred on her back as naked as a newborn babe. There was just enough light to showcase her slim shapely figure. I fell into a trance, hypnotized, spellbound, with my brain between my legs. "Would you pour some of the drink with ice and bring it over?"

I complied as requested.

"What's the matter with you? Cat got your tongue?"

If by chance we were alone in the elevator we chatted as if we were old acquaintances. She would interrogate me as if I was a witness, and so she knew a little about my plans while I knew hardly anything about her. I must confess that this was my first exposure to a naked woman and in such an alluring position. "No, ma'am," I stuttered in reply to her question.

That Ma'am business I picked up from my co-workers. In my case it was little ass kissing to swell the kitty, to augment the tips.

"Will you stop calling me Ma'am and come over here," she said, pointing to her bed.

I went over to the bed and sat very close to her, sneaking a peep at my watch.

"Are you waiting for a formal invitation? Don't you find me attractive?"

"Are you kidding? You have the most beautiful body I have ever seen in my entire natural life, but if I remain up here much longer, the old man is going to have a stroke."

"Fu—fu—forget the old man."

"Wish I could. In any case we can't hurry love. Let's not and say we did." I leaned over and gave her a warm kiss on the lips, fondled her bubbies—I mean breasts—and hurried out of the room. After that encounter, I never did see Mildred again. When I checked with the other bellhops, they were none the wiser. Maybe she had decided to move to another location.

When I recounted my night of adventure to my friends, Alwyn said: "John, don't you know women can smell a virgin? She wanted to initiate you and boast to her friends."

"So you are an expert now after fooping one woman?" I replied.

One Saturday morning on leaving the Cairo I decided to stop at Fourteenth and U and have breakfast at one of the restaurants that I infrequently visited. I had planned my menu the night before: scrambled eggs with pork chops, hashbrowns, orange juice. It was my twenty-first birthday, I was off from the Cairo and had the whole day to do what I wanted. I could not help but recall all the birthday celebrations my mother, and of course, my father had held for me in Fredericksburg with music, cake and homemade ice cream. This was one of the occasions when Dad would start the generator and the lights would shine and the turntable would get no relief. And as soon as I was old enough, dancing was added to the festivities, even though I was related to almost all the girls who came to the party. Today I would treat myself to a birthday meal instead of the prescriptive cereal in Coraye's kitchen. I would get a few hours of shut-eye, then get the boys and visit O.J. where a party could be enjoined at the drop of a hat.

When I arrived home, the boys had already left, presumably for the library to study so they would be free for the rest of the day to do their laundry, shop and help me celebrate. Sleep came quickly, as it always did in those days, and I would have slept longer than I intended, had I not heard a knock. Almost immediately, someone, who turned out to be Coraye, was shaking me, and when she thought she had my attention, said: "What's the matter, are you going to sleep your life away? Come on over and have a birthday drink." Then she told me Mike and Alwyn had gone to the university but would be back in a while. So I did get up, quickly showered and shaved, put on my birthday present to myself—grey slacks, black long-sleeved shirt, and black loafers, which were fashionable then—and knocked on the door to her living room. It was an ornate door, or rather two sliding doors that came together and which she sometimes kept closed. This time it was partly open. At the summons of "Come in" I entered, and there they were: Mike, Amarit, Maria, Alwyn, and of course, Coraye. Already in the sauce. The girls shouted "Surprise!" I heard Mike say "Weh the pawty at?" and Alwyn chimed in: "The pawty's gwine on rat now." Real British Guianese-Americans. That 'Weh the pawty at?' became our mantra for the rest of our lives.

My twenty-first birthday was a real party. Impressive buffet lunch, brands of liquor I had never seen before, champagne to toast the birthday boy, and of course, a birthday cake with appropriate candles. Since Mike and Alwyn could not afford this spread, I knew the benefactor to be Coraye. Everybody made a toast with Alwyn outtalking them all. After the customary Happy Birthday singing, I thanked them, Coraye in particular, holding back genuine tears. I was thinking about my parents and the birthday parties they always had for me. Of course, everyone present thought the occasion had moved me to tears. And it certainly did.

After a few hours of merriment, dancing, snacking, and imbibing from choice liquors, the boys were satiated with food and 'luscious liquor' and were ready to leave, probably to consummate the occasion elsewhere. Coraye called them a cab and I was conveying my gratitude once more when she held my hands. Like the boys, I was feeling no pain, and was about to call O.J. when she said in her soft ladylike voice: "Will you stay a bit longer?"

This late in the day my other plan was in disrepair; why take a chance on Riggs Place, when, as they say, a bird in the hand is worth two in the bush. So I willingly remained after asking to use the phone to call O.J., because I was sure he was expecting me. We continued to celebrate with soft, slow romantic music—Jackie Gleason's *For Lovers Only*.

"Want to dance?" she asked.

"I am not a very good dancer," I replied.

"Can you walk?"

"Of course, I can."

"Then you can dance. Come here."

I complied. You can hardly call what we were doing dancing. The term is slow drag, because drag was first used to describe a musician who lagged behind the beat for dancers who dragged their feet. I found this out from a member of my fraternity in his serious scholarly manner. Whatever the origin, the dancers hardly moved, just dragged their feet. I had become very proficient at this dance. Before Mike and Alwyn joined me in D.C— we referred to Washington that way, not to confuse it with the state maybe—I had a secret life I shared with no one. Every Saturday night there was a dance at the student nurses residence; the dance floor was dimly-lit and the music was the slow romantic variety. You'd get a partner in that dark hall—a partner that seemed to be a silhouette—and you would embrace, pretending you were lovers, and dance away. More like grinding away. Although I had to leave early for the Cairo, I hardly missed a week. The admission could have been twenty-five cents, probably to pay for the music system, but I am sure it wasn't the price of admission that made that place so popular. Although O.J. had told me about it, I never did tell him I was a participant. He never brought it up, but perhaps he knew. He had contacts everywhere. The many male students at the dance never referred to it as slow drag; they had a ruder, cruder expression—a dry foop, which was a very descriptive term. Everybody must have enjoyed this Saturday night, as there never was a shortage of partners.

But back to the birthday celebration. We danced and held each other so closely that I started to get what the Guyanese call eyeturn—that giddy, yes, dizzy feeling. This was different from the rendezvous with the nurses. There were only two people at this dance and nobody was thinking of catching the Trans P to the Cairo Hotel. We would have a sip of our drinks at the end of a number and continue our embrace in dance. Then the kisses started on my neck and moved gradually to my forehead and eyes, face, and finally to my lips. This was for real. And this was enough to drive a neophyte in this business up the wall. I felt her hands move to my groin, and in my embarrassment, she giggled. With a euphoric expression on her face she blurted out in the most unladylike manner: "My mama always told me that boys are like potatoes. If they are big enough, they are ripe enough, and you know what, you are not only ripe, you're ..." She giggled and seemed so exultant that tears came to her eyes. Tears of joy? Maybe.

Next thing you know we are on her couch and she is all over me, a very excited woman indeed. She massaged me with her hands and with kisses, deep kisses. I don't want to give the impression that this was all one-sided. I was doing the best I could letting instinct be my guide. More kisses from her, all the while asking questions: "Do you love me? Tell me you love me." When she eased off a bit, I managed to blurt out: "How can I tell you I love you when I can hardly breathe?" Her sense of humour showed naturally as she burst out laughing.

Nevertheless, she wanted to know if I loved her, and when I told her what she wanted to hear, she became—well, let's just say I did not sleep in my own bed that night. The next morning as I was trying to sneak away, I was given a lecture and breakfast in bed. And so started, as Alwyn referred to it later, my sexual down slide. I was now not content to wait for another twenty-one years. Knowing Coraye was attracted to me did something to my ego. Oh sure, girls at our parties at Riggs Place would say things to me like "Where have you been all my life?" but I never left those remarks go to my head. I always suspected they were saying the same thing to all the other chaps. On the other hand, when a beautiful woman who could have her pick, chose you, that gesture became a flattering unction to my soul, if I remember my Shakespeare.

Sharing my first experience with Coraye may be considered a late start in the North American tradition, but it was the norm for most of my friends in British Guiana at the time. Was it self-restraint or fear, or a combination of the two? I know the girls we wanted to be around did not even think of putting out. British Guiana was then a class society, as well as being purity-conscious, and status determined behaviour. Mothers inculcated in their daughters certain standards to follow to maintain this purity status. Believe me, status was a big thing then, and the thought of it lingers forever. I was amused, therefore, when we moved from Guyana to that small prairie town and saw the man who owned a cesspool cleaning business dancing gallantly with the daughter of the town physician. That is what an egalitarian society must mean, I thought. It would never have happened in British Guiana. The boys at Central High would have referred to the young woman's situation as infradig.

Contrary to what was expected, I did not drop everything to see Coraye as often as I wished. School and the Cairo kept me busy, and of course, I was not off every weekend. I also knew my manners. If I saw that sliding door closed, I never ventured there. If I happened to be in the kitchen and she came in, I left the invitation to her. That way she was free to frolic elsewhere and I was always ready when she was. Knowing she was seeing other men did not threaten me. Coraye was a great lady, full of passion. I was only her student. I remembered my Byron from Central days:

> *In her first passion woman sees her lover*
> *In all her others, all she sees is love.*

Much later, when we were having breakfast in bed one morning, relaxed and satisfied, she said: "You know, I am glad you didn't think after your birthday party that you owned me."

"Don't be silly!"

What I really was thinking was how close you came to what I thought. In actual fact, I had wondered at the time—Does this mean we're engaged? And when I thought she was avoiding me, I, too, was staying away until the smoke had cleared. You see, I know of a few fellows in British Guiana who got themselves engaged the first time they really kissed their girlfriends.

She went on: "I have seen how understanding you are, so I will tell you something about myself, if you haven't figured it out yet."

"Please do."

"I am a little like Mae West. In her philosophy anyway."

"Mae Who?"

"Mae West. You have heard of Mae West, haven't you?"

"You betcha!"

Here is what Mae West said: "We are never too old to get younger," followed with, "Whenever I have to choose between two men, I always take the one I haven't had before." God bless her soul. She was honest in her own right. I didn't tell her her philosophy suited me. Every time I was with her—or should I say, after I was with her—I could hear my mother's voice saying the devil always finds mischief for idle hands to do.

The celebration staged by Coraye with Mike and Alwyn and their ladies became the mother of all previous birthday parties. Later on Coraye said the occasion ignited a spark she thought had been expunged, and she was afraid of becoming an old fool falling in love with someone who was struggling against all odds to achieve a goal. Remember that Mae West reference? That was an invention. She wanted to keep our relationship strictly physical since she believed that I had more than a passing fancy for her. Bless her soul. She was very perceptive indeed.

Summer was once again upon us and that meant a return to my day job at the swimming pool. Although it was a public pool, many prominent guests graced our waters. Scientists from the National Institute of Health, Congressional aides, staff from foreign embassies, including the Canadian and Argentinean. The son of the Ambassador from Argentina was always in our locker room and why not? We were both from South America. A famous cartoonist did a sketch of me and signed it. Visiting one day was a quiet, well-dressed, good-looking man in his forties. A companion, who seemed to be his chauffeur did the talking, and asked for two tall lockers. I instantly found them two at the back of the room and locked them when they were ready to go poolside. I watched them go out and watched them swim. After completing a specific number of laps, they relaxed next to the pool and later returned to the locker room. The buzz in the locker room was that he was a prominent lawyer. He handed me his wet swimming trunks and gave me instructions to mail them to a hotel in Chicago. He could have discarded the trunks and bought a new pair at his next destination with the fat tip he slipped into the breast pocket of my shirt—the largest tip I ever received anywhere.

The next day I saw his picture in the Washington Post. He was an attorney representing some Mafia types. Years later at a Dental Convention in Chicago I thought of that attorney when my good friend and classmate Ulric, and another classmate Sammy, and I stayed at the Palmer House, the same hotel where I had sent the trunks. We rented a suite on one of the upper floors and invited a select number of our confreres for the cocktail party we staged. I guess we thought we had arrived.

And of course there was Dr. Cary Middlecoff, who came frequently to the pool when he was in Washington, D.C. He was a dental surgeon by training but gave up dentistry to become one of the icons of golf. He won the Masters in 1955 and defeated the legendary Ben Hogan in the 1956 U.S. Open, one of two wins for him in that tournament. At that time my knowledge of golf was abysmal and my interest was non-existent. Dr. Cary, as I used to call him, was so unpretentious that I was not aware of his stature when we first met at the swimming pool. He told me he used to be in dentistry only after learning that I was aiming at the same career. The summer of the year I left for Nashville and dental school he brought me a set of golf clubs and bag in very good condition, and after wishing me success in my chosen field, almost a bit embarrassed, said to me: "I think it's about time you get started with the game. You'll enjoy it for a lifetime."

What an understatement.

So if Coraye was responsible for igniting one spark, Dr. Cary was responsible for the other.

If I said that the citizens of Guyana consume large quantities of rice, would someone consider that statement disparaging or boastful? I hope not. I was fortunate to have chosen parents who provided our home with luxury those many moons ago. And servants galore. We had a housekeeper in charge of the household duties which included cooking and cleaning. Sometimes she would have a young person to help her. My mother would post a schedule so she knew what meals were to be prepared daily for that week. It was not written in stone, however, as the menu could change according to circumstances. For instance, if my father was bringing home some guests for lunch, different dishes could be prepared at a moment's notice. Mother was very organized.

Besides the main housekeeper and her helper, there was a woman who just did the washing and ironing and another woman whose sole duty was to keep the yard neat and tidy. There was no lawn as such; the yard was a mixture of dirt and sand, shrubs and flowers, fruit trees and rocks. We also had a maid whose duty was to take care of me from the time I was born until I left for Central. She was a relative of my father and stayed on after I left for Central. Instead of just giving the family cash, everybody pretended she had to work for it. Even to this day I remember how excited she was when my dad brought my first bicycle—a boy's bike—which she had never seen before. Mine could have been the only one on the island as most boys had to learn to ride on their fathers' bikes. He had made a special trip to Georgetown to present me with it on my fourth birthday.

My father owned a car, which he kept under one part of the house. At the stelling were his boats, two motor launches—one about thirty feet and a smaller one about twenty feet—and at least two bateaux, which could be propelled by Evinrude outboard motors. One of the launches was used exclusively for taking government and quasi-government ministers and engineers and officers to various areas of the Essequibo River and for the Cable and Wireless Company for placing cables along the rivers. Which came first—the idea or the pursuit? I know we had indoor plumbing and electricity before many homes in Georgetown and will wager my prized golf club that we were the only family in Wakenaam to possess such luxuries. This is not intended as a pompous reflection but only to illustrate how blessed I was to have had such a father.

In looking for work I was not about to prove anything to anyone. I adhered to the same philosophy Mike espoused. Inside work, no heavy lifting. The job at the pool sparked the entrepreneurial spirit. The job description was what the name implied: locker room attendant. My assistant and I were to collect the tickets, purchased from the cashier at the entrance to the locker room, distribute the towels to each patron, see that everyone took a shower before entering the swimming pool, and of course, keep the room clean and dry after swimmers came in and out of the showers and pool. The patrons would enter our section, change out of their street clothes and put them into an available locker, then ask us to lock it for them and head for the pool. We always told them to take their valuables with them, and during the many years I worked there no one ever complained of losing an item from the locker room. The ladies had their own locker room.

There were at least sixty lockers on our side: tall ones where suits could be hung and small ones where clothes had to be folded. If it was a very hot day, the swimming pool would be busy and all the lockers would be occupied. Clothes were then folded and left on the benches, the owners taking their valuables with them. O.J. had told me that most patrons usually tipped after their visit to the pool, but after our first week, the tips were nothing to cheer about. The second week we came up with a scheme. We kept all the lockers locked, regardless of the time of day. Each tip was not much—on average a quarter—but we thought we were providing a service, after all. On a busy day, if most men tipped, our effort could be worth while. There was a saying in British Guiana when I was a little boy: 'Wan (one) wan (one) dutty build dam.' Dutty means dirt. In the small prairie town where I now reside there are beavers' lodges. A little twig or a limb from a tree missing here and there and soon the beaver has a palace.

Back to the lockers. When our early customers enter they find them all locked and when they sneak a peak poolside there are not that many swimmers to be seen. He checks the lockers again to reinforce his first impression and finding them still locked, he approaches me standing at the entrance of the locker room collecting tickets, or more likely pretending to appear busy doing nothing.

"Say, are there no lockers available?"

"Did you check, sir?"

"Yes, I did. They are all locked."

"Then I suppose they are all taken, sir."

Pause. We stare at each other. I sit on the table and wait for his next move. I see from his vacuous expression that he is not seeing the picture.

"Can I leave my clothes with you?"

"Sir, you can leave your clothes on one of the benches over there. Please fold them and take your valuables with you. When a locker becomes available, we will put your clothes in the locker."

If he is hip and tips before he goes to the pool, we put his clothes in a locker as soon as he leaves. If he does not tip, he finds his clothes where he left them on his return from the pool. The regulars soon figured out the scheme and reach for the tip as soon as they entered. "Have a locker for me today?" he says, surreptitiously giving me the tip. By this time we are on a first name basis—on his part, that is, because he addresses me by name. We are co-conspirators.

"Wait here. I'll see." And I run to the back of the room and open a locker for him. Our scheme began to pay dividends. I could live off my tips and deposit my salary at the bank. A dollar could go a long way then. Our immediate boss was the head lifeguard and if he was wise to our hustle, he never did let us know, as he never said a word. He considered the locker room our domain. If he had a friend visiting, he would bring him in and of course, we would find him a locker. And his friends always tipped. But there was one customer who tried to hoodwink us. He was about six feet two, two hundred and twenty pounds, and looked to be in his fifties. He was always dressed in suit and tie and wore glasses and we both thought he was a Congressman. The first time he appeared he was as smooth as silk, and as slick as Jello. I was returning to the front after taking care of another swimmer.

"Hello John," he said, calling me by my first name. "O.J. always kept a locker at the back for me," he continued, all the while marching to the back and taking off his coat, showing me his red suspenders. I opened a locker for him and he slipped me fifty cents.

"Your ticket, sir?"

"Oh, I gave it to your assistant."

He performed this routine a couple of times until one day he went to the well for the last time. When he told me he had given his ticket to my co-worker I said he must be mistaken because my assistant was away for the day at a dental appointment. He laughed and said it was his mistake. The next time he appeared and had a ticket, which he made sure he gave to me. And he continued to tip fifty cents.

O.J. said he remembered him. He used to walk right in and give him fifty cents. By the time he found out he was not purchasing any ticket it was too late to do anything about it. He thought he was a chauffeur for someone in the government.

I had discovered that some Americans have a schizophrenic personality when it comes to race. If you were a foreigner, you could be as dark as midnight in Essequibo where there is no electricity or moonlight, and they would treat you with respect, providing you carried out your part of the bargain. That was my experience anyway. For all the years I spent there going to school and working, my memory is one of kindness and generosity extended to me.

Here is an example. Once I had car trouble outside Baltimore. A white gentleman stopped to help. He pushed me a good distance to a gas station and advised me to stay there until morning. Just as I was settling into the back seat, two tall policemen pulled in and began to question me. Suddenly there was a call on their radio and after a brief conversation they left abruptly without a word. When the attendant arrived in the morning I related my experience to him.

"We've had some break-ins," he said.

It was then I suspected my benefactor might have been someone important in the area and instructed the gendarmes to leave me alone. Had my accent saved me?

Coraye had what was considered then a top-level job in the U.S. government. It could have been the State Department but do not quote me. Her job required her going out of town several times during the year, sometimes for short periods, sometimes longer. I knew she had attended Harvard and obtained her PhD. in Political Science but I had also learned from a Trinidadian friend not to ask too many personal questions, that it was not good manners. Often the appearance of someone with expensive garmenture can belie his occupation. This warning proved prophetic, as I was later to discover at the Cairo Hotel.

Coraye was away on one of her extended trips—to Paris, this time—and left her sister Selma in charge of her domain. Selma lived in the building two floors up and would drop in to check on Coraye's place, to water the plants and to see that her tenants did not burn the place down with wild parties. None of us smoked. I had met Selma a few times when I was with Coraye in her living room when she dropped in. I always found an excuse to leave after a few minutes of her arrival. She seemed opinionated, always spoke in a low dulcet tone, almost like a musical instrument. And she spoke constantly, never stopping to catch her breath. She was younger and taller than Coraye, and I am sure was considered beautiful. She had the same complexion as her sister, that olive look that many people die slowly in the sun every summer to attain. Her hair, curly or straight, was always pulled back in pigtails when she was not working. This particular Saturday it started raining early and continued throughout the day. It was not a day for sitting by any pool. Not good for our private hustle either. I sneaked away early, leaving my assistant to close up. I thought I would go home, get something to eat, rest a while, perhaps visit Riggs Place. Saturday afternoon, something had to be stirring. I am in the kitchen, trying to decide what gourmet cuisine I should open from a can, and who should appear but Selma.

"How would you like to have a home-cooked meal instead of that?" she whispered condescendingly.

"Thanks, but you don't have to go to all that trouble. I never have time for a three-course meal any more."

"No trouble at all."

"In that case, thanks for the invite. I have to clean up."

"Take your time. A couple of hours? I live upstairs, you know. The number is 315 and I'll leave the door unlocked."

"Muchas gracias." I always liked to add a little Spanish flavour. After all, I was from South America.

O.J. and my other mentor Roy, the doctor, my two connections to Riggs Place, always insisted that an invitation for a meal was not to be sneezed at. "You never refuse, banna." I was just following their maxim, I rationalized. I often think how long it takes me to get ready now, even when I am rushing. In those days I could change in half the time. Youthful exuberance, no doubt about it. I knocked on the door and not eliciting a response, I pushed the door open. I quietly stepped into the hallway. This aspect of my life has not changed. I still move as quietly as a mouse. My wife has often said that I walk more softly than Tassel, our cat. I could see no one. I ventured in more. The layout seemed similar to Coraye's. I could see the dining table formally set but no one was in sight. I retreated to the stairs and returned to my room to change and present a more dashing and debonair appearance by donning a summer jacket. Then I hightailed it across the street to the flower shop for a bouquet to take back to No. 315.

This time Selma was ready and waiting for me. I was glad I did not look like the janitor. She welcomed me in a low-cut floor-length aquamarine dress that achieved its desire effect. I could not take my eyes away from her. She was truly beautiful. Why had I not noticed this before? Perhaps for some underlying reason I prejudged her and ended up with a negative impression.

The apartment was tastefully decorated. Even with my limited knowledge, the place looked as if a decorator's insight was used. The ceiling was painted red and the walls, a leafy green, like green mangoes, and hung with original paintings done by a family member. Family photos were also on display, some of women and men on horseback. One wall housed a bookcase filled with bound books, and another with hardcover best sellers. Selma offered an apéritif, as she called it, and I took what she was having. What did I know about apéritifs?

The meal was sumptuous and reached all my taste buds. It was the first time I had eaten lobster Newberg, which I enjoyed immensely. Along with the lobster were baby carrots and asparagus. After a full belly, as they still say in Guyana, we retreated to the drawing room. Soft brown rustic leather sofas that I wished I could move to the Cairo for use between the hours of two and four, really impressed me. She left to fix us both a drink, asking me what 'my poison was.' I had seen a few bottles on her sideboard and requested Cutty Sark, a Scotch blend that Mike learned to drink with Maria. I could never afford the brand, but if someone else was buying, why not?

I sat on the sofa and she sat on a matching chair opposite, watching me as if she was seeing me for the first time. Relaxing music could be heard everywhere but the source was elusive. Just as I began to feel relaxed, the fantasies inhabiting my head or mind or whatever, she brought me back to the present with a slew of questions. I was a disappointment even then with small talk. I have become better at it, by force, I imagine. I have noticed all my daughters are very good at it and can converse with anyone. I am my father's son.

It was like a cross examination—Selma was full of questions—about my background, what were the courses I had taken and was taking and why Howard University? I told how it all started with Boogie receiving that first letter from Olive and how he was the one left at home. Would I be returning home after my studies were completed, did I have a girlfriend at Howard and was there one waiting for me at home? She spoke as usual barely taking a breath and paused only when I answered, or when she stopped to freshen our drinks.

"Whoa! Not so fast. I hardly know you. Aren't these personal questions?" I asked when she took a sip of her cognac.

"Of course not. How else am I going to know anything about you? You are the first person I have met from South America."

"Only the shadow knows." One of O.J.'s saying in sotto voce.

"Beg pardon?"

"Oh, nothing really. There's not too much to know. I have to earn a couple of degrees. When I achieve my goal, I hope to return home, much as I like and admire your country. In answer to the girlfriend question, the answer is no twice. Didn't leave a girlfriend back home and I don't have one here either."

A sultry smile flickered across her face. "Why not? What's the matter with you? You are not—" and she laughed "—no, I don't think so. A good-looking young man like you should have one for every day of the week. No, no, every working day of the week. Perhaps you can leave one day for church."

(Long after that conversation I did meet a young lady in church who invited me to her apartment for tea. It must have been the accent.)

I told her I was not a bit interested. For one thing I did not have the time or the means. When Selma returned with another refill, she sat on the couch very close to me. "All these questions. Is this a job interview? I already have two jobs."

"Who knows?" she said.

"You sound like an attorney questioning a witness."

"What gave me away?"

"Are you really an attorney?"

"Why the scepticism?"

"None intended. Where did you get your degree?"

I thought she said Howard and I said something like "at least we have something in common" when she said, "No, sweetie, Harvard," and she spelled it this time.

"No shit," I said in my best imitation of the American accent.

So we sat there while the questions and answers continued. After awhile I said something about how much I enjoyed the afternoon, the food, her company, and the music. She liked Spanish guitars and the Latin beat, all the Titos. So did I.

"As pleasant as this has been, I think I should leave. Ta Ta."

"What's the rush? I know you don't have to work tonight. How do I know? Have you forgotten I'm an attorney? Learn to relax, boy. Take your coat off and pour us each another drink while I slip into something more comfortable."

I may have been a neophyte in relationships; my mother may have brought me up to be as chaste as the morning dew, but I was no fool, at least I didn't think I was very foolish. I had heard those words too many times in the movies. But when she returned a few minutes later, I was not really prepared for the look. Boobs partially hidden under a halter top looked more tempting after the booze, and legs that could only have been carved by a sculptor. God is love. She changed the music to some slow-moving blues and pulled me off the couch to dance. We danced and danced. The music stopped and we stood there unable, or having no desire, to move, to break the spell. What would O.J. do in a situation like this?

"If I said you had a beautiful body, would you hold it against me?" (Thank you, O.J.)

Maybe it was the Cutty Sark, maybe the natural born tropical instincts were kicking into gear again, maybe it was the scent of a beautiful woman. Whatever it was, she braced her body against me and whispered, "I was beginning to think there was something wrong with me. You didn't seem interested."

"You got to be kidding. I was always interested. All I needed was a little prodding."

For some time after that night of real rapture, her loving affirmation of ecstasy "Oh Lordy Lordy, Oh damn, Oh Jeez" could always bring a tear to my eye. In my naïveté I used to tell myself she earned my respect for being so pious—you know, thinking of the Lord at a time like that. In my learning process it took quite awhile to realize that not all women were as demonstrative or emotive as Coraye and Selma. They wore the crown and were never dethroned.

I came away from that experience thinking many beautiful women do not ever believe what their mirror reveals to them. We have all seen a woman of outstanding beauty being escorted around town with a companion who could only be described as ordinary. In British Guiana most observers would acclaim "Ah wah she see in him?" In North America the comments might be more generous, as the spectators might wonder about the mystery of the relationship.

One of my daughters would later ask me: "Daddy, do you think I am pretty?" Many of her friends of both sexes from Junior High School were always telling her how beautiful she was.

"Of course, dear, I would consider you beautiful."

"Would I be considered beautiful in Regina?"

"Yes, dear."

"In Toronto?"

"Yes, dear. You would be considered beautiful anywhere. In Georgetown, Guyana, in New York, New York, in London, England, in Paris, France."

"You think so?"

"Yes, I flatter you not." I took her to Europe—to Paris where she turned the heads of the French—but of course, she never believed me.

After that night with Selma I returned to my pad and slept like a lamb. I awoke with the sound of her voice in my ears.

A few days later I ran into Chumel at one of my eating holes at Fourteenth and U. Chumel was one of the previous occupants of our apartment or better yet, our room. After the usual 'wha' happening, banna' and the usual gossip about our compatriots, we started to go our separate ways when he shouted: "Wait a minute." The tone of his voice prepared me for ominous news. I stopped and turned to face him. "Any more shootings at Coraye's?" he asked.

"Shootings, what shootings? What you talkin' about?"

Seems Coraye had a problem with one of her fellows. Shot him dead in her bathroom. It was ruled a justifiable homicide. He used her as a punching bag. Her so-called friend when he drank too much used to say, "Coraye, your ass belongs to me and you can't do shit about it." Famous last words.

Working two jobs kept me as busy as I wanted to be. If the tips were adequate, I would indulge, splurge a little and eat at one of my favourite emporiums around Fourteenth and U. I hardly saw the boys any more. Alwyn was working two jobs and spending every cent. Mike was still relieving on a part-time basis. The next time I saw Mike, he informed me that he was leaving the ship, since he had the good fortune to live rent free. Seems he had a new girlfriend and was spending most of his spare time at her place anyway. She was an instructor at the School of Nursing and lived in a large comfortable home that belonged to her parents. They were both physicians and were sowing good seeds somewhere in Africa.

Accordingly, Mike moved out and still there was no sign of Alwyn. I went looking for him. I had an idea and an address and I was right on both counts. I found him with the original party animals. These were the real 'the party's gwine on rat now' people. Non-stop twenty-four hours going on thirty-six. After cashing his paychecks on Friday he was broke by Sunday. He was the big spender. Fortunately, it was only spent on booze and food; what I mean is, there were no drugs in the mix. Through patience and tender care I was able to get him away peacefully. Nobody likes a party pooper, especially if it is a free party for most.

Registration for the new school term was just around the corner, and many of the Caribbean students were already gathering on campus. Occasionally I ran into Mike but there was no trace of Alwyn. Alwyn was supposed to be still living with me at Belmont but we were like ships that pass in the night. When classes did start, I was gone most of the day and went home a little before six in order to get some sleep before heading to the Cairo. I had assumed he was in when I was out. Perhaps he was trying to avoid me, although he had not been seen on campus by anyone else I knew. I checked with Mike every time I could but he was none the wiser. I did not have to wait much longer to clarify the mystery.

That Saturday I decided to wait around the apartment and my hunch paid off. Alwyn arrived later in the day and, just as I was about to let him have it with my prepared speech, he floored me with a rabbit punch.

The reason I had not seen him was that he was spending a lot of time with a fairly new girlfriend who was also a nurse. Actually, this was the first time I was hearing of someone new in his life. She suggested that since he was there all the time, why not move in rent free? That way he could save quite a bit, since even his meals would be free. She had a nice apartment and he didn't have to worry his handsome head about small matters.

"Where are you guys finding these kind nurses? First Mike and now you. Do they have friends or sisters?" Maybe I should quit my job; I too could find someone to watch over me. I was thinking about that switchboard ringing every time I thought I could get ten winks. The Cairo switchboard had a lasting imprint on my psyche. For years, no matter where I was, visiting or at home, if a telephone rang while I was sleeping, I used to think I was still at the Cairo and would jump straight up at the first ring to answer.

Moving in with the nurse who, by the way, was related to Mike's nurse, was not as big a bombshell as what he told me next. He was not only moving out of our apartment, but he was moving out of the country at the end of the year. He would continue his studies in Toronto, Canada, and had no intention of registering at Howard. He would keep working and save toward that end. What's going on, was my silent reflection. Seems my compassionate spirit has dug another hole for me. Sometimes I blame my mother's influence, sometimes I have regrets, even for a moment. This was one of those times. Remember the only reason I had moved from Riggs Place was to help reduce their share of the rent and, at the same time, put a dampening effect on their free spirits. Now I was left in an embarrassing position, holding the bag, as the saying goes. I called O.J. and did not have to go into details.

"Come whenever you are ready," he said. "Hope you still have your key."

Coraye understood. I always knew she was very perceptive and full of compassion. She would have no problem finding new tenants for the room. She had felt the winds of change blowing long before I had a whiff of what was going down.

So I returned to Riggs Place. Sometime after my return, Mike and Alwyn dropped in. O.J. happened to be home. We were all in a relaxed mood that Saturday afternoon when there was a telephone call for me. The crisp male voice, which I did not recognize, said he had a package to be delivered to me and wanted to be sure I was home. "Sure, I'll be here," I replied. "I don't plan to leave for quite awhile." When I relayed the conversation to my companions, the others laughed at Mike's suggestion that it could be a bomb.

Half an hour later there was a knock on the door and I opened it nervously with Mike's remarks still reverberating in my ears. It was the most pleasant of surprises: a smiling Mildred of the Cairo Hotel stood there. I invited her in, shocked at her blonde hair and the way she walked in like an actress surveying her audience without the least bit of hesitation. She introduced herself to each of my friends as Mignon and told them we were very old friends. In her hand was a copy of her book *How To Make Money*

The Old-Fashioned Way. It was a best seller after only a few weeks in the book stores. After taking the chair I offered her, she slipped off her shoes and continued in conversation with us all. As soon as O.J. realized Mignon was the author of the best seller, he excused himself, went out the door, and returned shortly with a bucket full of ice. While we were wondering what he was up to he retrieved from the bedroom a bottle of champagne, Mumms no less, and said he hoped we could wait until it was chilled. After an appropriate time he filled our glasses with the bubbly drink and made a brief speech to Mignon and her success, concluding with "not every day we have the distinct pleasure of meeting a bona fide author."

Shortly after that all three friends realized they were late for appointments and I was able to discover two important details about Mildred. Mignon was her real name and she was a natural born blonde. To my great surprise I found in the copy of her autographed book a cheque for six hundred and fifteen dollars. Although I was never to see her again, every Christmas during my stay in Nashville, I received a cheque for six hundred and fifteen dollars. The last cheque for that amount arrived shortly before my graduation from Dental School with a note: "Take good care, life is a peach."

When the time came for Alwyn's departure from Washington, he said he had postponed his departure time from January because his latest research indicated that Toronto was the coldest place on earth that time of year. Of course, he was exaggerating, but I realized I didn't know anything about Canada either. The only connection I had to Canada was through a cousin, who was a medical graduate from McGill. I have mentioned him before. He is the one who, upon taking the medical history of his male patients would ask: "How is the boy?" referring to the patient's sexual function or dysfunction. He also believed in nutrients, which his father before him, not trained in traditional medicine, had concocted from various bushes that grew in Guyana. Although the son did not get rich from his services, he was satisfied with the many followers who filled his waiting room six days a week and who often traveled days to be seen by him. Many couples who were having troubles conceiving were able to have the children they wanted, and they were truly grateful to him.

The only other Canadian connection was a Miss McDougall who worked at the Canadian Embassy and who lived at the Cairo. She had a small apartment on the twelfth floor. She was from Calgary, Alberta, and informed me that she didn't know too much about Toronto and didn't seem too interested. Seems there was a regional bias and years later, I found that bias to be still thriving. Once during the playoffs for the Stanley Cup, the emblem of superiority for professional hockey in North America, I asked one of my neighbours the name of his favourite team. Any team other than the ones from Ontario or Quebec, was his answer.

Alwyn did finally move to Canada, catching the bus to Buffalo and then on to Toronto. Before his departure we gave him a good send-off with two formal parties, one where Marie and Amarit were present and the other where the nurses were the ladies-in-waiting. Of course, there were other parties held at Riggs Place, spread out in time because they had to be held on weekends.

For the rest of us it was another summer of work. Maybe I should add that I graduated from Howard during this time. I was not as excited as I thought I would have been, probably because I still had a darn long row to hoe. Coraye had a party for me to which Mike and some of my classmates were invited. O.J. brought one of his favourite ladies and Selma was there looking very provocative. It was a wonderful party. Selma had another one for me with only Mike and his nurse as our guests. I also said farewell to Mattie and enjoyed one more of her delicious meals.

It was almost time to head south to Nashville and Meharry Dental School. Seems I was a better planner then than I have become in later years. I am sure I became complacent because of a little success. Before I quit my job at the Cairo, I took a friend, a student from Grenada, and introduced him to the head bellhop. He would take my job during my sojourn in Nashville and since he always went to New York for the summer to work, I knew the job at the Cairo would be secure for me the next summer.

That first visit to Nashville was truly a journey into the unknown. Mike, Alwyn and I had visited New York City a few times by car and bus. The Big Apple, as I first heard it from O.J. We had also taken one-day excursions to Baltimore and Virginia, driven by the nurses, but Nashville conjured up other images. This was the South. I had read that 1952 was the first year in 21 years of tabulation that there was no report of lynchings. The homes of some Afros did not escape the violence of bombs, however; I hoped my impressions of the South and of Nashville, in particular, would turn out to be as innocuous as the ones I brought with me when I arrived in Washington from British Guiana. Now that I knew my way around, Washington had become a sort of second home. I liked my world. Segregation never entered my mind, even at the Cairo or the swimming pool. I knew both were low level jobs but they paid the bills and I believe I was not disliked at either place. I don't recall an incident where race or colour was the issue. I rationalized that the work at both places prepared me for the real world, a sociological experience, seeing how the privileged lived and behaved. That experience at the swimming pool has always stood me in good stead.

I have mentioned how I came up with the idea of locking the lockers to get some of those tightfisted swimmers to be more generous. And how that one gentleman in particular (and there were many others who tried) would bypass the cashier and try to bribe me or my assistant by giving us fifty cents for a free entry. We did not succumb to that temptation not because we were so honest but because we believed someone could be testing our honesty by sending in spies pretending to be slick swimmers. We never did find out because we refused to take the bait. Everyone had to have a ticket unless our immediate boss brought him in.

Here's an example of what I carried with me from that swimming pool. My foursome won a golf tournament and the first prize was a trip to Las Vegas. Manet, my wife, very much wanted to see the Pointer Sisters who were appearing at Caesar's Palace, and since we could not get through from our hotel phone to make reservations, we caught a cab only to find the line at the box office a mile long. I have always had an aversion for long lines. I could see the disappointment in Manet's face when I said I was not about to join that line. "Wait here," I said and walked to the entrance of the auditorium where an armed guard was standing.

"Any way I can avoid that line?" I asked him, placing my right hand in the pocket of my trousers and keeping it busy, so he would know money was about to talk.

"You betcha, sir," he said with a polite smile.

I signaled Manet to join me about the same time he must have signaled his cohort, the usher, who was ready to show us our seats. I thanked him, shaking his hand with a bill I had palmed. The usher escorted us to two of the best seats in the house and when he returned later with our tickets at a price less than we expected, I slipped him another crumpled bill. That look of respect and surprise from Manet said it all. Then a couple at our table—a man and wife from Nashville—wouldn't let us pay for our drinks, much as we tried to reciprocate. The man told us he had prospered financially, that he owned corner stores at home and that he seldom got the chance to meet such nice people. Working at both the Cairo Hotel and the swimming pool was indeed a 'learning experience' as Uncle Poo would have said.

But I am digressing too much. As I said, I knew my way around Washington and my safety was never in question. I had made many new friends. I have already mentioned the Smiths, Marge and Mattie, Coraye and Selma, and of course, O.J., and there were others. So at the risk of becoming repetitious, I must say again that leaving Washington was like leaving home. I had arrived as a boy and after four years I had become a man, wiser in a few things yet still naive about many others. With a couple of trunks, a suitcase, and the golf clubs given to me by Dr. Cary, as I always called him, I was the first to board the Greyhound bus. I headed for the seats at the back where I planned to stretch out, if no one joined me. I was embarking on a new phase of my life, feeling excited about the direction it was taking me and forgetting everything I feared about the southern destination. Mike and his nurse, whose name was Ann, had come to see me off. They had left at my behest since I was anxious to get that long seat at the back of the bus and that meant boarding early.

As soon as we pulled out of the bus terminal, I fell sound asleep. All the activities of the recent weeks and most likely months, contributed to a tired body and soul. The first stop I missed completely and perhaps that happened for the best. At the next stop still sleep-eyed, I went into the coffee shop and placed my order to go. In the meantime, I used the men's room before collecting my snack to eat in my own private dining room at the back of the bus. I continued this routine every time the bus driver pulled into a stop. Along the way I did notice that I was the only hyphenated person ordering anything at the snack bar or in the men's room. I concluded the Afro-American travelers were carrying their own lunches in paper bags as I had been told and did not need to order as I did. It was a couple of stops before Nashville that I realized the truth. At every bus stop there was a Whites Only section and Coloreds Only section. The washrooms were the same—Coloreds Only, Whites Only. Without thinking, subconsciously probably, I was following the white passengers, going in to their restrooms and buying sandwiches at their counters, albeit to take back to the bus.

Nobody said anything to me. The waitresses took my order and did not bat an eye. Perhaps it was my British Guianese accent, very noticeable still, even after my stint in Washington. That's not so extraordinary since I am reminded now and then by my daughters when I get really comfortable and readily fall into the Guyanese rhythm. Maybe it was none of the above. Maybe I looked like a somebody. Ha Ha Ha.

Back to the bus, however, and it was at the back that I had set up my private quarters.

After a few stops a young man about my age came and pointed out the grave error I was making. "Ah notice you going into dey washrooms and lunch counter ordering dey women around. You tired o'living or you just plumb crazy?" I did not venture out again, even to the Coloreds Only section. I never could understand how such a great nation like the United States of America could have allowed such mistreatment of its citizens. I know some people would be surprised to learn that discrimination in some form still exists today, many years after my initial visit to the south. I have always maintained Africans on the whole love everybody—look at the presence of whites in African societies. One of these days I'll have to have an in-depth discussion with my psychiatrist friend and fraternity brother Hi in California. Until then I am inclined to go along with Eldridge

Cleaver and blame it on penis envy. After all, only the strongest of the strong survived the Middle Passage when Africans were shipped under inhuman conditions to the West Indies and North America.

My sleepy entry into those coffee shops was nothing; forgetting where I was a different matter. The movie version of Heat of the Night with Sidney Poitier is a glamourized version of the truth, as most moviegoers would agree. The real story would have been over at the train station where Sidney would have been shot right there. End of story.

Not long after I arrived in Nashville, a 14-year-old boy from Chicago visiting relatives in Mississippi was brutally killed for allegedly whistling at a white woman. His name was Emmet Till. For all the years I spent in Nashville, whenever I heard the word Mississippi, the mere mention of the name would conjure fear. I cannot take credit for starting this, but the same year of Emmett Till's murder, segregation on buses, waiting rooms, and railway coaches in interstate travel was banned. This happened in the late fifties; that's not so long ago. Years ago, one of my daughters, very young at the time, had seen something on the U.S. television news that made her turn to me and ask: "Daddy, why do people hate Afro-Americans so much?" My reply was: "Not all people do, dear," and I hoped she was satisfied with my answer. Years later as we were taking her to Edmonton to enroll at the university, we ran out of gas on the highway. The closest help was a farm we passed about six hundred yards back and my youngest daughter volunteered to accompany me. She was worried the farmer would not help. I remember not encouraging her fear, pointing out that she should not think of every experience along racial terms. The farmer not only had some gas, but took us back to our car and got us started. He probably took one look at me and arrived at the correct conclusion that I didn't know enough about cars to start one that was out of gas.

Of course, once I realized the mistake I had made on that first bus trip, I never ventured out at any stop again. An older gentleman, who had spoken to me earlier in the trip, brought back for me sandwiches and milk after he had not seen me with the group in the Colored Only Coffee Shop.

He thought it was time for me to eat something. I was able to survive until we reached Nashville. After all, I was used to long periods between meals.

From the bus depot I rode a cab to the campus at Meharry—not much of a campus at all. It was a small university numerically, composed of the schools of Dentistry, Nursing, and Medicine. Registration was a breeze compared to Howard and in no time I was enrolled in first year Dentistry and had found a room in what looked like a fairly new dormitory for men. I was able to secure a single room for myself with a little help from the manager of the dormitory. There was a new cafeteria adjacent to the dormitory, bright, airy, modern—wide open with glass all around—and for a few days I had my meals there. Then I was re-united with a Jamaican medical student whom I had known at Howard, and he recommended an eating place not far from the school.

The small diner was housed in a converted older home and that's where I had most of my meals—breakfast, lunch, and dinner—during my stay in Nashville. Not only was the food tasty and cost effective but even in my most impecunious state, meaning I did not possess a nickel to my name, the two sisters who owned the business, would carry me on their books and not one of my eating companions would be the wiser. I could have been mistaken, but I believed my portions were always larger than the others. On more than one occasion I left Nashville in debt to the sisters, sending them their due after my first paycheck along with a present. Add the Berry sisters to the list of kind people who pulled me along the early part of my professional journey.

Of course, it is not a pleasant experience to know poverty, even in the hope that it would only be temporary. I was able to talk myself into a job as part-time overseer at the dormitory. Its lobby was like the hotels then—a front desk, cubicles for letters and messages, and a telephone. There was also a payphone at one end of the hall on the first floor of the two-storey building. No personal calls were allowed at the front desk but messages were written down and placed in the cubicles. My job was to deliver the letters as the students arrived at the front desk but everyone would just walk behind the desk and get his mail. Easy work for little pay. Oh yes, I would give out the number of the payphone for callers, mostly girls calling guys.

Another hustle I organized was a dry cleaning and laundry business. I arranged with a business downtown to collect and deliver the returned product to our customers in the dormitory. Through the manager of the dormitory I was able to use a closet on the second floor as my depot, where the students could pick up their clothes. I received a thirty per cent commission for my trouble and I always slipped the manager a bottle of demon drink from time to time for allowing me to conduct my business.

After the first year in Nashville, upon my return from the summer in Washington, D.C. I purchased a very used car with a reasonably low down payment. I was then able to deliver and pick up the dry cleaning and laundry, increasing my commission to fifty percent. Weekends and holidays and especially at Thanksgiving and Christmas, I used the car as a taxi, taking students around town, to and from the bus stations and trains. For this additional enterprise I enlisted the aid of my friend Norm. Norm was especially suited to the job with his good looks and southern charm. We visited the campuses of the three Afro-American colleges in close proximity: Meharry and Fisk were separated by a street and Tennessee State was only a short ride from these two. I do not recall knowing anyone who used the airlines then.

One of my daughters was always consumed with curiosity about my experience in the south and particularly my stay in Nashville. I have assured her I was not affected physically, though perhaps psychologically during those days of segregation and discrimination. She wanted to know how it was for us socially and I told her in that respect, we could not have asked for anything more. Nashville was and still is a university town as far as I know. During my sojourn there, segregation of the races was still in vogue, was still the law of the land. There were three predominantly Afro-American colleges and if you loved to party on weekends, that was the place to be.

Once the famous poet Langston Hughes was in Nashville on one of his book tours and our fraternity wanted to honour him with a cocktail party. They asked me to be in charge and I looked upon the assignment as a privilege and took it seriously. Since my knowledge of staging cocktail parties was limited, I relied exclusively on a couple whose daughter was a friend. I had been invited to their home on several occasions for formal and informal gatherings and they steered me in the right direction, and even made suggestions for the toast which I had to deliver. Needless to say, the occasion was deemed a huge success and the news of our social event soon spread all over the campus. For many years the autographed copy of a collection of short stories *The Ways of White Folks* by Mr. Hughes was a fixture on our coffee table when our children were growing up.

Many years after that cocktail party I learned much to my regret, that Langston Hughes had worked as a busboy at the Wardman Park Hotel in Washington, D.C. about a quarter of a century prior to my stint there at the swimming pool. He had one of the first public readings of his poetry there. Another co-incidence is that he attended Central High School, albeit in Cleveland, Ohio, and one of his early short stories was, get this, 'Cora Unashamed.' I am not making this up.

Another noteworthy event occurred when a young anesthesiologist at the Hubbard Hospital invited me to a Christmas soirée at a physician's home in a section of Nashville called the Gold Coast. It was appropriately named because only the well-to-do, mostly professional Afro-Americans, lived in that neighbourhood. The beautiful properties spoke for the group, as this was still the era of segregation when the option for upwardly mobile minorities was very limited.

That Christmas party was a lesson in living. I was the only student among the professionals and I thought I carried off my role playing very well. Hardly drank at all; even though I would have liked to sample some of that expensive booze I saw on display, my glass was always full. Many at the party seeing me for the first time thought I was one of them, and the ones that knew me kept my secret. Of course, I had this beautiful lady who would not let me out of her sight and her prestige must have helped to make my presence bona fide. In addition to that, I was nattily attired, my suit purchased at less than half price from one of the frequent visitors to the swimming pool. Made me realize what was in store for me if I continued to work hard and play by the rules. The parties at Riggs, enjoyable as they were, were a learning experience too, but that is where the comparison ended. It was like learning to swim in the trench and then battling the waves in the Essequibo River at high tide against the flow of the current.

Having lived in Washington, D.C. and Nashville and interacted with the residents with different economic, academic, and social backgrounds was an education in itself. Uncle Poo would have said "Better than book larnin." More credit should be afforded Afro-Americans for surviving slavery, for being disconnected and separated from their heritage, uprooted in other words, for their hard work without recompense, for the humiliation and suffering they endured and still remained sane, for the most part.

Even the highest law of the land, the Supreme (meaning the greatest, most excellent) Court took forever to help them, and continued to endorse the law of segregation. Early in their history the Supreme Court had ruled that a black man, a slave, cannot sue for his freedom in a free state, even though his ancestors had lived in the United States for over two hundred years, because he is property, had never been, was not then and could never be a citizen of the United States. A 'black man' has no rights that a white man has to respect. Many of these racists' decisions were usually pronounced in the name of the Lord. Some voiced what many were thinking, that the 'racial order' was ordained by God. One defender of that notion summed it up this way: 'Black is not God's colour, white is God's colour.'

I have always wondered what those who make specious statements about race say when they are told that we are all descendants of Africans, that their family tree dates back to Central Africa and that a time machine would connect them to their ancestors fifty thousand years ago. Science has the proof in DNA markers.

And the churches? Segregated in every way. They worshiped the God of their own creation. Where was their 'generosity to the poor, their protection of the weak, and their defiance toward the strong?'

During my years in Washington, D.C. and in Nashville, my very best intentions were to return to British Guiana, the name of my native land at that time, to practise my profession. Some of my classmates were heading into private practice, some to graduate school and a few to the armed services. My friend Norm was one of the few. They were all native born Americans, of course, since I was the only foreigner in the class—only one was accepted into the Dentistry program each year. An instructor, who had always shown kindness toward me, showed me an advertisement in a dental journal relating to an internship at the Toronto General Hospital and advised me to apply. A positive response was quickly received. Seems like the journey of my life had already been plotted. Every little piece of the puzzle was falling into place without too much hassle or long planning. And that's how I came to Canada. The insouciant confidence of youth must have taken a leave of absence as the years rolled forward. I am not that fearless young man anymore.

I notified Mike of my plans to visit Washington, D.C. en route to Toronto and he was genuinely pleased. I was able to arrange a ride with one of my classmates who was returning home to set up shop. When I called on Mike, I could see he had traveled as well. He was living in an elegant neighbourhood of well-kept homes on Georgia Avenue North, quite a contrast to the days on Fairmont and Belmont Streets. He was living the life that befits a professional architect. Of course, he was glad to see me and I had a few days to relax in Washington without thinking of any kind of hustle, work or studies. For the first time in eight years my only decision to make was what to wear and where to dine. My first real holiday. I did the tourist bit—visited the Smithsonian Institute again, the National Art Gallery, paid Coraye and Selma separate visits and enjoyed Mattie's home cooking one more time. I even squeezed in a visit with my generous friends, the Smiths, the kind taxi driver.

Time goes quickly when events are propitious and once more I was about to set out on a journey of uncharted waters. As I said good-bye to Mike, he blurted out: "Be seeing you sooner than you think—keep a spare room for me. Regards to Shortman. Have Dick, will travel," he ended with one of his favourite refrains. It was an adaptation from a 50s TV western series *Have Gun Will Travel;* the men at Meharry had changed it to Mike's version.

Mike didn't just shut things down in D.C. and hightail it to Toronto. He took his leisurely time, as was his nature.

During my internship housing was provided on University Avenue across the street from the Toronto General Hospital. It is located downtown, not too far from the business section, the University of Toronto, and close to the waterfront and Greyhound bus depot. I had spent the night in Detroit with Ulric, a classmate, and he drove me through the tunnel to the bus depot in Windsor, Ontario, and I arrived in Toronto around noon. In no time I had found my room in an old elegant house, met some of my house mates—all medical residents—and discovered that I had arrived on a holiday weekend. It was in honour of Queen Victoria. My first day on the job would not be until Tuesday, so I decided to relax a bit, then took a shower before venturing out on a sightseeing expedition. I walked north to College Street, then east to Yonge, which I soon learned was the main drag and longest street in Canada. From there I headed south to the waterfront, then retraced my steps, and I felt thirsty from so much walking, or at least convinced myself that I did. At the sound of jazz music I followed the sound, entered the lounge, and ordered a beer. When I finished my first Canadian beer ever, I headed for a restaurant I had noticed earlier and had something to eat. During this whole jaunt I had not seen anyone who looked like me and I was truly surprised.

Tuesday I began my professional journey, getting measured for uniforms and meeting the staff at the dental clinic, including assistants and the doctor in charge of the program. During my lunch break in the cafeteria a few days later I was more than surprised to see two nurses giving me the eye as I walked in their direction. I took their smile as an invitation to join them. I was the only doctor not Caucasian and I was not sure if they knew my status or took me for an orderly.

"May I join you beautiful ladies?"

"Of course. Have a chair."

They were pleased when I introduced myself. From their accents I gathered they were Canadians; one was from Toronto of Jamaican parentage and the other, who looked mixed, was from Nova Scotia. We became friends. They were both married at the time. One lost her husband at an early age and the husband of the other became a popular writer.

I used to slip out of one of the side doors of the hospital and visit Eaton's and the Bay and other stores nearby for items and supplies I needed, since I had arrived with just the bare necessities. On one of those visits to Eaton's I took a different route just to vary the scenery; as I was passing a picture framing art gallery I looked in at the window display and happened to see a tall, good-looking brown-skin man working on a picture frame. I went in, introduced myself, and started a conversation that led to a lifelong friendship. His name was Victor. His parents were originally from Antigua but he was born in New York and spent most of his adult life in the United States including a stint in the armed forces. He had moved to Canada about fifteen years prior to our meeting.

As far as I know Victor is the only man who would sit on the toilet to take a pee. He had a hilarious reason for this habit but time has erased it from my memory. I can hazard a guess as I get older, but it would only be a guess.

After a short year my stint at Toronto General was at an end and I had to join the working class if I wanted to eat. Thanks to Victor I was able to start immediately without going into debt. He had a friend who was a dental surgeon and who was thinking of taking on an assistant. Here again the timing was right. His surgery was located on Bloor Street between Avenue Road and Bay in a large office complex in the Yorkville area.

Once more British Guiana had to wait for my services. As I was about to leave my free room provided by the Toronto General, Alwyn was soon to finish his articling at a Toronto law firm. He would soon take his bar exam which would enable him to practise law. This co-incided with my passing the Ontario dental exams that would allow me to practise dentistry. It could not have turned out better, if we had planned it.

Now we both had to find a place to hang our hats. Alwyn had been living in one room in a private home but it was time to move on. A nurse came to our rescue. Three of her co-workers were giving up an apartment on Isabella Street not far from Bloor and Yonge area, and we could have first choice. There was no hesitation in agreeing to move into the three-bedroom apartment; a few of Victor's pieces of African art and some of his water colours completely rehabilitated the atmosphere of the living room.

As if on cue Mike arrived when we had settled into the apartment, furnished in a casual, tentative manner until our finances improved. But while Alwyn and I were excited to be starting a new phase in our upward struggle, Mike was of a different attitude. He wanted to relax and recharge. He wanted time to think, to which Alwyn replied: "He who thinks too much is guaranteed to be full of sorrow."

Mike was insistent about watching and waiting. Money was not a problem because he had accumulated some savings. "After all," he said, "this is not D.C. The city is different. Even the people are different."

"What did you expect?" I asked.

"I have to tiptoe first, to feel my way around."

Since he would be sharing equally in the expenses of the apartment, we decided to let him be. Perhaps his time for introspection would do us all some good. You have to remember that throughout his life Mike was the recipient of motherly care by the women around him. His two sisters, who seemed old enough to be his mother, really brought him up as a prince. He lacked nothing that money could buy and they loved him like a son to boot. When his sisters were no longer around, the women in Washington, D.C., carried on the practice. I realize he was a real charmer, but I would like to think it was something else. Maria was the first, and then came the others; with every move, her status improved.

"Nah mind how pumpkin vine run, he must dry up one day." He quoted a British Guianese proverb, and then added: "Why settle for fried rice when you have the smorgasbord? Variety is the soul of pleasure."

"Is this some new philosophy garnered from a dream?" I asked.

"Oh, you referring to D.C.? Buddy, this may surprise you, but I have no regrets."

For days he was content to remain at home and enjoy his music. He never seemed to get supersaturated with the sounds of John Coltrane and Miles Davis emanating from his expensive reel to reel player. When I took him down Yonge Street to A & A Records he was like the proverbial kid in a candy store browsing through the old and new releases of his favourite musicians.

But man cannot live on music alone and so Alwyn and I decided to have a house christening. We had quite a mixture. My guests included people I knew from the hospital—nurses, receptionists, and two doctors who were in specialty training. One, born in Ireland, used to lend me his automobile whenever I needed it and the other used to greet me every Saturday with 'Fockey Night in Canada.' He was from Spain. Alwyn had his own invitées and Victor graced our presence with two extraordinary-looking ladies.

Our strategy was partly successful, since Mike showed some interest in a buxom redhead, a nurse from Sudbury, Ontario, and invited her for cozy lunches downtown and even for drinks at one of the establishments along Yonge Street, but he never invited her back to 'the crib.' Maybe his attitude was changing. Although he would accompany me to the golf course, he never did show any interest in the game. He would complain that golf was one way of interrupting a good walk. He had an ally in Alwyn. I did tell them that since I had played so much cricket as a youngster, it was for me an easy transition into golf. I had started playing cricket at school in Fredericksburg after my father supplied the school with the necessary equipment; then played on the teams at Central and after Central captained a team to play weekend matches with other teams. We were a touring team without a clubhouse or a field.

The dentist with whom I worked turned out to be more helpful than I expected. From him I not only learned the practice but also the business of dentistry. I was a willing student. He, Peter, was a kind gentleman. His wife Joan was a certified dental hygienist who no longer worked in the office. They lived in a luxurious apartment nearby.

Just about every Friday when we closed shop Peter and Joan would stroll over to the neighbourhood pub where they joined their friends in the ritual of the times, in songs and music. This was the period of coffeehouses and sing-a-longs. Peter played a mean piano and Joan often sang and accompanied him on guitar. It was a rollicking time, in spite of the fact that Joan did not drink and Peter stopped at one glass of wine. I only remember declining their standing invitation a few times, and when Mike arrived, he became part of the group. Alwyn? His office was quite a distance away and in the early days of his practice he tended to work late.

It was at one of these gatherings that I met Mrs. K who not only overwhelmed me with referrals from her circle of friends but was instrumental in getting us started in a little business venture. A friend wanted to get rid of one of his rental properties quickly and she notified us of his intent, even advising us of the offer to make. The building was in need of repair but because of its location, she believed it would be a good investment. We did not have ready cash, except for Mike who was willing to invest. The bank was prepared to take a chance on our professional potential.

That's how we acquired our first rental property. Mike, after all, was an architect, and Alwyn, a legal expert, could handle the financing. It was agreed that Mike would find a crew and take care of the improvements. The idea was to renovate the building and move in, but even before the work was finished we were flooded with inquiries for selling, and did indeed let it go for a tidy profit. It inspired us to continue improving and selling until we found a house we felt we should keep for ourselves. The business took on a life of its own, as friends and acquaintances wanted upgrading of their properties as well. Mike was doing something he enjoyed and hired a permanent crew.

Here we were living together again after all these years on a much more enjoyable level than when we were struggling in D.C. We were all busy at a practice or at a company, leaving relaxation for Saturdays and Sundays. We had a four-bedroom house including an ensuite guest bedroom on the third floor. On the outside the house looked very much like the neighbourhood, but new guests were always gasping with surprise upon entering. To show how styles never seem to change much, we had black leather furniture in our entertainment room, two walls paneled, polished wooden floor, and a fireplace that used wood.

When we moved into our first home on Walmer Road off Bloor, we decided to get ourselves a housekeeper. One who could also cook our evening meal. Alwyn had a client, Natasha, who volunteered for the position. He had extricated her from a marriage that had gone sour. Her husband, a physically attractive man, had wined and dined her through the courtship with promises of a comfortable life ahead. Once the short honeymoon was over he showed his true character by bringing a man to their apartment and wanting her to sleep with him. When Natasha refused he manhandled her. Actually, he did that only once, but when she told him she was leaving he tried to prevent her by grabbing her in a headlock. She was prepared for the intervention and jabbed him with the scissors she had concealed in a pocket. When he instinctively released her, she ran directly to the police. The police took him to the station forthwith and locked him up. When they found out he was in the country without immigration status, his troubles really began to mount.

Natasha was a very attractive redhead from Quebec. She had two immediate needs: to improve her English and her typing skills. She was a hard worker and we found no fault with Alwyn's decision. We were so impressed with her cooking and housekeeping that Alwyn procured a typewriter for her to practise. After about three months we noticed a change, not in her work but in her countenance. When she was cross-examined by Alwyn, we discovered the reason. Many of our male visitors were making passes at her and some of the romeos took it upon themselves to visit while we were away. Since we could not contain these pursuers, Alwyn found employment for her somewhere else.

For Natasha's replacement we chose a woman from British Guiana. She too was very attractive and used to be a member of the Police Force there. She did not suffer fools gladly. Whenever we wanted to entertain large groups, she enlisted the aid of her sister-in-law who could cook Chinese dishes with a different flair. Her East Indian cuisine elicited tears from our guests for their delicacy. Some people do not believe in change. They would rather cling to what they thought to be the tried and true and we allowed for their preference on the menu as well.

Mrs. K, whom I have mentioned before, was very curious and daring about the new dishes. She was an actress who had appeared on Broadway and had several substantial roles in the movies but had returned to Toronto, her native village, for a more leisurely lifestyle. She lived in an older home inherited from her parents, a home that could only be described as a mansion near the University of Toronto. She lived in the lower flat and rented the two upper storeys to professors. She used to invite me to her abode where she would serve homemade wine with various cheeses and biscuits, overworking her record player with the music of Miles Davis, and reading poetry she had written about the man. I always enjoyed those visits, sitting enraptured and hypnotized by my fantasies as I listened to the music and her poetry. I can see her even now, relaxing on the couch in that oversized muu-muu dress, braless and shoeless, as tears sometimes flowed from her eyes. It was she who invited us to a party at Forest Hills, a suburb of Toronto where the affluent lived. Alwyn could not go because of a previous commitment, so Mike and I became the flag bearers. We arrived at the exact time we were told to be there. Mrs. K greeted us at the door and escorted us to meet the owners of the impressive home complete with terrace and wet bar. After a few introductions she led us to the bar and got us started with drinks, then left us to fend for ourselves.

"This is the best spot in the house," she whispered before leaving.

At that time we were, as Cousin Boyo would have said, the only darkies in the house. He had lived in England for many years and picked up the habits of the colonials. We were among the few early arrivals. Shortly thereafter we noticed a beeline of newcomers heading to the bar. Among them was a ravishing Afro-American woman who squeezed herself into a seat next to me. No, she did not know me, although I had watched her perform with her group at a club off Yonge Street—get it? Off Broadway, off Young Street. As the night progressed, the bar did indeed seem to be the place to be, especially around Mike and me. Mike was a social creature, a natural raconteur, and with his blend of British Guianese and American accents, he was really comedic. He had strangers wiping tears from their eyes when suddenly there was a hush and two men walked into the room through the patio doors at the back dressed in identical trench coats, dark glasses, and black fedoras. They were escorted by a blonde musclebound young man who must have been their chauffeur/bodyguard. You could have heard a pin drop to the floor. Mike and I recovered first and giggled, covering our mouth with our hand simultaneously. We knew instantly what the other was thinking. Guess who the visitors were? Harry Belafonte and Sidney Poitier. We were probably the only guests who didn't know they were coming. Many people crowding the bar had expected them and, we assumed, believed we were Harry and Sidney. This is not so farfetched.

I have a Jamaican friend Les in Toronto who still, to this day, calls me Sidney. He had nothing to do with the party, of course. He and some other friends used to tease me about my resemblance to the actor. And to prove my point, a friend's grandson in L.A. quite recently remarked about our similarity as well. Out of the mouths of babes! Mike favoured Harry, as they probably still say in Guyana, meaning there was a likeness between them. Once Mike, Alwyn, and I were dining with our dates at a fairly new place on the Lakeshore Boulevard in Toronto when this well-dressed gentleman came over to our table. After making apologies for the interruption he asked me to settle a bet with a friend. Was Alwyn Hank Aaron? "Better pay up," I told him. Sometimes we looked like different celebrities to different folks.

I am reminded of a time when some friends and I were at Glen Abbey, the celebrated golf course in Toronto. After our round of golf, Ken, my partner, and I visited the pro shop to browse and buy some souvenirs. We were killing time waiting for a Barbadian friend who was a member of the club and had promised to take us to the members' lounge for beer and sandwiches, so we were in no hurry. By chance I looked at one of the cashiers behind the counter and our eyes became four. He was staring at me. Everywhere I moved he seemed to be following me with his eyes. I told Ken what I had observed and his reply was: "It's your squinty eyes, your Chinese-looking eyes that give you away. He thinks you are going to steal something. Better don't stay too close to me."

He was being ludicrous, of course, but suddenly there stood the clerk, red-faced, in front of me, about to confront me.

"Sir?"

"Yes?" I stood ready with a combative reaction on my face, as close as I could muster to the one used by my friend Leonard who left British Guiana after I did and became very rich. Whenever anyone from home asked him what he did, meaning what was his profession, he would stick out his chest, assume an imperious air, as if to say, "How dare you—don't you know who I am?" He would then tell his questioner how many taxi cabs he owned and how many impecunious foreign students were in his employ without bothering to elaborate about his other businesses. I should explain that in his time most of the students leaving British Guiana were determined to enter into the profession of medicine, engineering, dentistry, or law, a throwback to the models they saw at home. If they did not succeed, they worked hard to ensure that their children did.

"Sir, I hate to be a bother, but aren't you Charlie Sifford, the golfer?" I must confess that during those times I often used to have a cigar on the golf course and environs, not realizing that Mr. Sifford's trademark was a fat cigar clenched between his teeth. When I recounted what I thought was a humorous incident at Glen Abbey, Mike and Alwyn guffawed simultaneously. Mike was the first to recover with "Charlie Sifford, my beetie!"

Yes, beetie. A Guyanese term, mostly used by children for the gluteus maximus; the backside in other words.

Alwyn's reaction: "Stop dreaming."

Let me say a few words about Mr. Sifford. All his life he wanted to play golf, ever since he started caddying in the south. Later he wanted to join the PGA (Professional Golfers' Association of America) where he thought he was good enough to earn a living. One small clause prohibited him from joining the tour, a blatant discriminatory one that barred him from the circuit. There were not many enlightened Americans who would come to his aid for a long time. The clause:'Professional golfers of the Caucasian Race over the age of eighteen, residing in North or South America, who can qualify under the terms and conditions hereinafter specified shall be eligible for membership.' Mr. Sifford never threw in the towel; he worded hard at his game and continued to hope. After all, this was the United States of America, the greatest democracy in the world.

With the help of the California Attorney General, a Mr. Stanley Mosh and others, including the Afro-American icon Joe Louis—my mother's hero—pressure was applied to the PGA tour. In the thirties and forties when Joe Louis was defending his heavyweight title, our home would be packed with neighbours because we were the only home to enjoy the luxury of a radio. My mother and grandmother would be the only ladies in the mix, my mother the most excited of the listeners.

So after a difficult battle, with Joe Louis's help, in 1961 the Caucasian clause was expunged from the constitution of the governing body for golf in the United States. Mr. Sifford became a member three years later in 1964, the first of his race. He was forty-two years old.

What a struggle.

In 1967 Mr. Sifford won the Hartford Open, naturally the first Afro-American to win on the PGA tour, beating some players whose names are well-known—Lee Trevino, Gary Player, Chi Chi Rodriguez, Raymond Floyd. By the way, in 2006 Mr. Sifford was given an honorary degree by the University of St. Andrews in Scotland.

Brother Langston Hughes, who died in 1967, wrote:

> *What happens to a dream deferred*
> *Does it dry up like a raisin in the sun*
> *Or does it explode?*

I guess I am trying to say that I must have looked like celebrities at various times. Even with guests like Sidney and Harry present at the reception I was describing, our status was not diminished one iota. As they moved to another part of the room, Mike kept on with his chatter and if anyone followed them, I could not say. Trust Mrs. K. She made sure we were introduced to Sidney and Harry, assuring them we were prominent members of Toronto's society and were among her cherished friends. They must have been impressed by what she said about us because the next time Harry brought his show to Toronto he had his agent call me. I was to provide six Afro-Canadian women dancers to appear with him in a special number and I contacted the president of an active Afro-Canadian women's group and she was happy to oblige. For my efforts Mr. Belafonte had sent me six complimentary tickets. Since Uncle Poo often insisted charity begins at home, I offered four to Alwyn and Mike who needed no coaxing to join me. Of course I invited Mrs. K, who was responsible for the introduction; Mike took Joy and Alwyn brought one of his ex-wives.

It was an enjoyable evening and we promised our hosts we would reciprocate the next time we had a party. We had to. Mrs. K. had already regaled them with stories of our different dishes. I thought I was going to have a hard time deciding who was going home with me, a cute blonde who always asked me to repeat everything I said or the Afro-American entertainer who was sitting very close to me and playing footsie, rubbing her shapely legs against mine. As it turned out, I drove home alone after exchanging telephone numbers and the usual banalities. The coup de grâce to my manhood was there for all the world to observe. My two would-be conquests decided to leave together. Did I see them holding hands? I am still not sure, after all this time.

Mike, on the contrary, decided not to interrupt the mood of the evening by accompanying a dazzling lady in black to her place for a nightcap. She was the one who laughed at all his jokes and clung to him like white on rice. In truth, they seemed to be enraptured with each other. I was the recipient of the details the next day when he arrived with tired eyes and body and a smile as wide as Niagara Falls. Her name was Joy and she lived up to her appellation, if I am to believe what was recounted to me. She had been married for four years and divorced for almost two. Joy's ex-husband David was one of Toronto's brightest young lawyers. His parents had emigrated from England and settled in Fort St. John, British Columbia, where the father worked as a safety expert for some oil companies and was able to parlay his knowledge into riches. Their only child was sent east to one of the best private schools and eventually into Law. Joy owned her own home, a two-storeyed, older house in a part of Toronto that was considered exclusive. Her father was the founder and majority owner of an engineering company but misfortune struck when the company plane carrying him and two other executives crashed. No one survived. Her mother never recovered from the shock and spent her remaining days in a nursing home, happy as a lark but mentally incapacitated.

Joy had a routine of joining Janice, one of her closest friends, every Saturday for a matinee at the movies followed by tea and cake at a stylish restaurant or a drink at the Royal York Hotel before going home for supper.

One particular Saturday when Joy arrived at Janice's apartment as scheduled, she told Joy that she was coming down with something and would not be able to join her. The truth is, that the 'something' was hiding in one of her closets. Janice had accompanied another friend to a West Indian club for dancing the night before, her first time ever, and the spoil of the evening was the tired young man in the clothes closet. Joy didn't know this, of course, and disappointed, she returned home to find her husband in a compromising situation with their buxom young Barbadian maid. David was making sounds she had never heard from him before and never expected to hear, since he was always so conventional in every respect.

The maid was originally from British Guiana. Her name was Megan. Her father was a physician and had immigrated with his family to Barbados in the forties. Like her mother, she became a school teacher, fluent in French and Spanish. In the fifties and early sixties emigration from the West Indies to Canada was limited, and many young women could only get here as domestics—household servants contracted to work for families. After the expiration of their contract they were allowed to apply for resident status. I met many of these 'domestics' at a recreation centre on Cecil Street, established by a Mr. Moore, a West Indian immigrant who thought the girls needed a bit of relaxation and a place to meet other people from the Caribbean. This was a way of making new friends as well. By the way, Megan and David were married shortly after the divorce.

Mike had found his mate. They were both jazz enthusiasts and Mike, who considered himself a connoisseur and collector, found out to his pleasant surprise that he was a neophyte compared to Joy's knowledge and her catalogue of records. While his interest was relatively recent, her love affair with the music had been inculcated in her early years, thanks to her father.

Unlike Mike, she was into fitness and went to a member-only gym at least twice a week. I, too, had become a member of a health club, confining my activity to swimming during my lunch hour. Mike would bring Joy to our place for the occasional formal dinner, but for the most part, they preferred to visit the many top restaurants around town, inviting

Alwyn and me and our dates to make an evening of it. Most of the time I declined, as I found my taste buds were never able to appreciate to the full the expensive menus presented to us. I have a theory which states that taste buds are inured by early exposure. In British Guiana no matter what the dish was, we were bombarded with so many spices that we have grown to expect that special taste whenever we dine.

Joy was indeed beautiful, elegant, full of fun, and it was a delight to see them so happy. It seemed Mike's resolution to play the field had dissipated. When we asked him about the smorgasbord decision, his reply was brusque and came in the form of a British Guianese proverb: "Is de ansah (answer) does bring de row (fight)."

When Joy mentioned that she was thinking of taking piano lessons and would have to shop for a piano, he indicated that he would take on that project, and immediately arranged to lease one. The trouble was, to his consternation, when delivery time came, they could not get the piano through the front doors and decided to convert the basement, which had not been used for some time, into the entertainment room. So the piano was returned to the store until the room was completed, his crew doing all the work, finishing with a wet bar and polished floors for all the dancing they loved to do. Naturally there had to be party to showcase his accomplishment.

"You are both invited to a party this coming Saturday. There will be beaucoup single, elegant women, so leave your kangalangs at home."

He was trying to get even after we had castigated him for spending so much energy and time on Joy's renovation. Kangalang? Let's say it's not flattering for a woman to be described in that way.

Of course, it was a waste of time trying to embarrass Mike or to move him to anger. Our attempt had the same effect as throwing water on a duck's back.

We took his exhortation seriously, however, arriving with bottles of wine as our only escorts. It was quite the party. The guests were so fashionable and elegant that Alwyn thought Mike had rented some models for the evening. The women were tall, slim, and looked upper crust, no sluts here. The men looked as if they had spent an inordinate number of hours at a gymnasium. All flat bellies. Fortunately I was still doing those midday laps at my club.

Joy made it her duty for me to meet one of her friends. We had previously met at one of her parties and on that occasion she was with a dashing young man, and my date would not let me out of her grasp, to which I must add in her defence, that she was shy and did not know anyone else. Tonight we were both free and she seemed interested. I have never forgotten what O.J. told me those many moons ago. "Never waste your energy chasing."

Her name was April and as the saying goes, she was a knockout. Slim, long, beautiful legs, full red lips. Like Joy, she visited the beauty salon every week and was a member of the same fitness club. People often told her she ought to be in the movies. Her father was a baker who started making cookies for the children of the neighbourhood until their parents told him he should go into business. He did. The result was O'Brien's cookies, which eventually went national.

Fireworks never did explode when we were together. As a matter of fact, I would not call our encounters dates, as there was no intimacy involved, if you discount hand holding. I soon realized we were, or to be specific, I was along for the ride to complete the tableau for Mike and Joy, the two lovers. We did not join in the twosome until later in their relationship, and April's indifference did not bother me in the least. Sure, she was an enigma, as most women found me interesting and would not lead me on if our intentions did not mesh. My tutor O.J. had warned me never to fret over rejections. The odds would always be in my favour, he insisted.

Although she seemed to like my company, romance was not on the horizon and truthfully, it didn't matter. Whenever we walked into a restaurant or anywhere else, all eyes turned to her and to me, back to her and then to me. And why not? She was a beautiful lady and I was no slouch in those days either.

On a trip to a jazz concert in Buffalo, New York, the four of us found ourselves some distance from our intended destination—in short, we were lost. We pulled off the road and consulted our map. April and I in the back were the map readers and after a brief consultation, we plotted our route. I handed her the map to refold and since she was unable to do it, I had to complete the task. All of a sudden, Ulric's words were in my ear: "Watch out for any woman who cannot fold a map neatly." I can still see us, Ulric and me with a couple of binnis in a restaurant in Boston trying to fold a map. Ulric, you may remember was my classmate who lived in Detroit.

Whenever I have a problem to solve, I have a way of eliciting the help of my inner mind. The question has to be asked so that the answer is either 'no' or 'yes.' I designate one finger of one hand for the 'yes' and another finger of the other hand for the 'no.' I have done this for such a long time that within seconds the answer appears with the lifting of the finger. It is a well-known technique in psychology, known as the ideomotor response and I use it assiduously. After our return trip from Buffalo, New York, I posed the question: 'Should I continue to see April?' Whenever Mike asked or Joy called to suggest joining them I gracefully declined. I did not have to draw a picture for Mike. He understood. My finger has never let me down.

Weekends became normal again. Alwyn and I entertained at home, our cooks ever present when needed, or given a holiday when friends only dropped in for drinks or dominoes. Lazy, casual Sundays. Mike would occasionally bring Joy, but she never seemed as relaxed as in earlier times and never wanted to stay very long. They continued their exploration of the few dining emporiums that were still new to them or they revisited old favourites.

Then we noticed a gradual change. Mike was joining us more frequently on weekends and Alwyn wondered aloud if Mike was losing that loving feeling, even hummed the tune of the song.

Mike looked embarrassed. "Oh, no such thing," he replied. "Every rope got two ends. It's just that Joy is very health-conscious and is always watching her diet. I can only eat so much salad. You know me—I enjoy me cook-up, me chicken curry."

Not only was he not enjoying his meals with Joy as he used to but the bubble in their romance was beginning to dissipate. He thought that was just too soon in their relationship. He related, humourously, that whenever he broached the subject, she would laughingly ask, 'Is it your birthday again?' It had not reached that stage, but he wanted to convey what dire state he had found himself. He had a lot to think about, he said. He should have learned to use the ideomotor response.

He had confessed to me that the sizzle in the relationship had taken a downturn even before we suspected. Rather than telling us that he was not seeing her as often as he claimed, he would go down to Yonge Street and spend time at the Towne Tavern, a very popular place of entertainment. He reminded me how I had told him of someone I knew back home when we both were starting our careers. The young man Burtness from a respected family—his father was an Anglican minister—would leave home when the rest of us did, dressed in a shirt and tie, the work attire of the day. He would return home for lunch, as was the custom, and presumably, back to work for one o'clock. The only thing is, Burtness did not have a job. He had told his trusting parents that he worked at one of the ministries of the government and this was a complete falsehood. The charade continued until a friend of the family notified the parents.

One Saturday I heard Mike tell Joy on the phone that he would not be coming over at the time planned, because he was not feeling up to par. She must have asked if there was anything she could do because I heard him say, "Oh no, I'm sure it's temporary. I'll be all right. I'll call you to pick me up if my condition improves."

Alwyn, who was also nearby, remarked, "What's this about not feeling well? Your eyes look like you could use some sleep, but apart from that, you look as healthy as ever."

"I am," he replied, "I just don't feel like going over."

"In that case, let's go downtown," I chimed in. "Remember when we were very young and I thought I had that loving feeling for Doris and you guys, including Boogie, found the cure."

"No, I don't remember," they said too quickly, almost in unison. Maybe they did not want to rehash unpleasant memories.

This is the story. I had girlfriend named Doris and I really liked her. I would visit her at her home or we would just go for walks or rides on our bicycles along the famous Sea Wall. We would embrace, if the opportunity presented itself, and even kiss. Yes, kiss on the lips, but that was the extent of our romance. I was just over seventeen, and she was a year older. Talk about épaisse—she was the embodiment; long, slim, beautiful dark legs, and her future was behind her. When we met, she was on the rebound from another relationship where the boyfriend preferred someone else. He was older, was wise in his ways and left her to flounder.

Doris was a very good friend of Olive, Boogie's friend and he introduced us. We had been seeing each other for some time when I made a weekend trip to Wakenaam to visit my parents. On my return to Georgetown the following Monday I discovered to my utmost consternation that Doris and her so-called ex-boyfriend were an item once more. Imagine the pain I suffered. When I thought my friends would rush to my corner and offer words of sympathy and encouragement, they said things like, "What's this crap about not sleeping and being in pain? Your pride is broken, my boy, not your heart. We'll straighten this all out tonight."

When I heard 'tonight' my imagination took a wild flight. Although I knew my friends were not combatants, I nevertheless thought they would confront the boyfriend and intimidate him. After all, they were young and muscular and into bodybuilding. At least Boogie and Alwyn were, and I knew Mike would be good at encouraging them with the appropriate words or be engaged in fanning the fire, as my grandmother would have said. Instead of traveling to his paternal home on the East Coast as was his custom, Boogie decided to remain in Georgetown. Alwyn was over as usual that Saturday and the afternoon seemed normal, if I discounted the shh-shhing, the whispering, conspiring nature of their conversation whenever I left the room.

After calling an early end to our dominoes session, Mike and Alwyn excused themselves and left the house, indicating they would be back in a jiffy. It took more time than I expected but at seven o'clock that evening they returned. Alwyn was dressed to kill in a new white gabardine suit, blue shirt, and silk tie. They had arrived in a car. My cousin Boyo had a private car and if he was in the mood, could be persuaded to be hired. As far as we knew, we were the only ones he would accommodate this way, and I could only guess he was in the best of moods, because he was wearing his chauffeur's cap when they pulled up, joining the pretense that he worked for us, that he was our private chauffeur. Our man Boyo. In those days many of the rich and famous, and of course, all the embassies had their private chauffeurs, and at functions the drivers could be seen fraternizing where they parked their cars. We always made it our duty to take some of the goodies from the banquets we attended out to Cousin Boyo. We were the only ones serving their chauffeur that way, but we had a special relationship with ours. The other chauffeurs could never understand this treatment and our secret remained our own.

We all tried to match Alwyn with our Sunday best, and soon we showed up at the Bel Air, a posh new hotel a few miles from Georgetown on the East Coast where the Atlantic Ocean lapped against the Sea Wall. At that time of the evening sea breezes from the ocean subdued the tropical heat, and an assault of a different kind, an attack of the senses, began to take place. A large private party was in progress and we resorted to our old trick of becoming part of it. As someone was monitoring the entry, we stopped there and I waved to the bandleader who played for me on my cricket team. He waved back and beckoned us in. The sentry watched this interplay and waved us through. We were used to crashing parties and weddings, and sometimes the boys even danced with the bride, the bridesmaids, and the mother of the bride, without having seen them before. I suppose we were clean-cut, decent-looking, and confident, and no one wanted to take a chance in questioning us, in case we were important or our parents were. I've said this before, British Guiana was then a class society. My mother always said, 'Clothes maketh the man' and so we adhered to that maxim.

In an instant we became part of the celebration at the Bel Air. The party was in honour of a Dr. Broomes, a native son who was a noted neurosurgeon in California. As well-clad as we thought we were, we were unquestionably upstaged by the finely-tailored suit of the doctor. The drummer, the leader of the band, introduced the doctor to the crowd, and he seemed to have handled his success humbly.

The evening went better than I anticipated. I was able to enjoy myself, and that is an understatement. Between the luscious young female bodies rubbing their flesh against mine and the exhilaration from the Demerara rum punch, all thoughts of Doris and her friend evaporated in the midnight mist. Later on I had to agree with one of my friends who had shouted, 'Love is but the frailty of the mind.' Whatever combination of circumstances conjoined, the cure for my broken heart had begun to take place and soon my torment was dissipated.

A little over one year after my arrival in Washington, I received a letter from Doris. I was at Howard and she had moved to New York. She wanted to get together, to start over. I had heard through the boys that the reunion did not last, that shortly after their second breakup, her boyfriend disappeared into thin air. Nobody, including parents and friends, knew where to find him. She was a beautiful creature, but we were meant to travel different paths. Her offer was very tempting, indeed. She was willing to work so that I could devote all my time to my studies. Upon receiving that letter, however, some words of Uncle Pat's reverberated in my unconscious thought to bolster my resolve. Back home in Georgetown I would visit him on weekends when I was free of cricket obligations and we would talk for hours. Truth is, I would listen most of the time. I used to ask him about women, of course, and since that was his favourite and most knowledgeable subject and I being a neophyte, I soaked up every word like a sponge. It was as if he was rehearsing to write a book: 'What every young man should know about women.' All of my visits to his small neat bungalow in a section of Georgetown called Lodge were unannounced, since telephones in those days were very restricted and only a few homes could boast of that luxury. No matter when I arrived, I never found any woman there since the sudden death of his wife some years earlier. Of course, he always had a couple of bottles of cold Guinness stout to quench our thirst and perhaps that could have been enough reason for my visits, but neither of us thought so.

Guinness Stout was considered to be a tonic for young men as well as the not so young. The older men would endorse its use, whimsically pointing out that it was 'good for the back.' It was for them the Viagra of the times. After the debacle of my relationship with Doris, I naturally headed to Uncle Pat for some commiserative words. "Na worry ma boy," he intoned after our second Guinness and third piece of black pudding. "She gwine come back to you. Ah know you, you soft as sponge, too dam soft for me liking, and you gwine feel sorry for her, but listen heh, na tek her back. Is like trying to use a F.L. more than once. Once is all you can use it."

F.L. stood for French Letter when I was growing up in British Guiana. Today Uncle Pat would probably have said condom. There is some regret that I have not seen Doris since I paid her that farewell visit the day before I left British Guiana those many years ago. From time to time I have thought of her and wondered if she has ever thought of me.

Rethinking all this, I watched Mike and knew that all was not right, even if he pretended otherwise. His sisters had brought him up to be happy and positive, and the way he behaved did not resemble the Mike we had grown to know and love. Only one person could be responsible for his misery.

Alwyn and I concluded that this new attitude must come to an end. We thought his depressed feeling could be contagious. Uncle Pat used to say you have to rub out sadness with gladness and remembering those words, we arranged a party. Its motif was taken from one of the discussions we had at our domino sessions. During those afternoons we solved the problems of the world, theoretically, of course. Here are a few examples: segregation and exploitation of the poor, the accuracy of the Bible—i.e. whether God wrote the Bible as some claim—and of course, being young men of the tropics, the state of our manhood. Pierre was the leader in this particular discussion. He was a native of Trinidad, a town planner who worked for the City of Toronto, and like most of us present, was single and in his early thirties. Pierre posed this question to the group: how many congresses, or to be blunt, copulations with different partners should a young, healthy man in his thirties have had? A few of the players shouted fifteen, thirty, fifty, but most of those present remained quiet for fear of embarrassing themselves by announcing a number that did not meet the standard. Mike shouted: "We give up." There was not a peep from Alwyn.

Since I was a late starter, I remained quiet. Pierre felt overwhelmed.

"I am not saying this is my number," he said quietly, "but my Uncle Cyril, for whom I still have the greatest respect, told me a long time ago that the number should not be less than sixty. That your prostate gland will be grateful to you in later years."

There was a silence that lasted a few seconds as the mental arithmetic went into motion. Then Pierre addressed Alwyn: "Why do you look so bemused? Is my uncle's estimate too insignificant for you?"

"Oh no, Pierre. My criterion has always been not numbers, but ethnicity."

"Ethnicity? What is that?"

Alwyn explained that he had slept with women of East Indian nationality, Chinese women, women from the Philippines, from Great Britain and Ireland, from the United States, and Canada. Both Mike and I knew this was only a fantasy.

Mike shouted, "Is it true what they say about …?"

Alwyn, reading his mind, replied, "Don't be so uncouth."

And so we decided to return Mike to the mainstream by inviting as many representatives of the United Nations as we could muster to the type of smorgasbord he had been deliberately avoiding. The prescription to whet his appetite seemed to work as instantly as WD40. He reverted, on the surface at least, to the Mike we knew and loved. We rarely saw Joy now, since she was no longer part of the weekend crowd, and as I have mentioned, I never saw April after that trip to Buffalo. Mike saw less and less of Joy in his free time and had become more critical, complaining of the little things that annoyed him. What surprised us most was his admission that the passion was oozing from their relationship. At the onset she delighted him by parading her sculptured body every which way and now he had to be content with his imagination admiring the curves under expensive French lingerie during 'le sport' as the French aptly express it. After one time is another time, he intoned laconically with a smile.

So Mike was back on track. After all, this boy was brought up by two loving sisters whose only mission in life was to keep him healthy and happy. His theme was 'Love is the answer' and to this day, I think he was correct. I remember when I was very young in Wakenaam we had a cat we called Miss Neek. If Miss Neek decided to stay out all night, in the morning when I let her in, I had her dish of food ready. I always thought she would be hungry and tired from being awake all night trying to escape the dogs of the neighbourhood, but there she was rubbing her body against my legs and waiting for my assurance of love. She would only eat after I massaged her, stretched out on the floor and had left the room to get ready for school. Sometimes she would jump onto my shoulder—yes, straight from the floor—with a little help from me catching her, and after rubbing her back I would take her to her meal. So Mike was right—love is the answer.

A television preacher said the other day that some surprises could change a person's entire life and then related a personal experience to prove his point. I am not in the habit of agreeing with television preachers, but this was the exception. One surprise that changed our lives were the letters Boogie received from Olive those many moons ago. The first letter encouraged him to apply to Howard University and as a result, his three friends traveled to the United States when such a thought was as remote as flying to the moon. The second letter terminated his plans after she told him of her intended marriage. How ironic it seemed at the time. He was the catalyst that changed our carefree existence and he was the one who stayed behind.

Mike did not have a driver's licence. That's a fact—he never learned to drive any kind of vehicle. He traveled by taxi even when he was a lowly student. Now he had Alwyn or me to motor him around town, or Joy would act as his chauffeur. Of course, the taxi was still his trusted friend. One Saturday Joy called to inquire about the time he wanted to be picked up. "I'm not sure," he replied, "because I'm working on a project that has to be done by Monday. Tell you what, I'll call you when I'm free."

"That's all right, dearie," she said. "Don't forget now."

He was indeed working on a project, but her voice sounded so alluring that he found it harder and harder to concentrate. He rationalized that he could finish the work later in the day or early the next and decided to surprise her with a visit. He called a taxi and on the way stopped in Chinatown to pick up all the greens and vegetables she liked, the ginger beef they both liked, and the fried rice and sweet and sour chicken he liked. In his carrying case he had a chilled bottle of Merlot from Chile, carefully wrapped for the journey. He entered the house as quiet as a church mouse, all part of the intended surprise. This was the first time he was using the key he had made during the renovations and had not returned to the owner of the house.

His senses were aroused by an unmistakably familiar scent. Definitely Mary Jane. It had been quite some time but he had no doubt about the fragrance. His thoughts transported him to Fairmont Street in Washington, D.C.

Yes, marijuana. The aroma seemed to be emanating from every corner of the house. He checked the entertainment room and since there was no sign of Joy, he retraced his steps and proceeded quietly to the bedroom, thinking she could be taking a nap. Lo and behold, two sets of buttocks greeted him, frolicking in bed, lost in the splendour of the afternoon. He was so surprised at the identity of the two lovers that he could not contain a vertiginous feeling coming on—a dizzy moment when he thought he would lose control. He recovered his senses and noiselessly pedaled backward, exited the house and found the energy to run a few blocks before hailing a passing taxi with his goodies still intact. If one surprise was not enough for one day, the taxi driver was the same Chinese man who had deposited him at Joy's not so long ago. For a few moments he actually seemed to be interested more in that co-incidence than in the earlier surprise.

"I was disappointed, shocked, hurt," he told me when he got home. "I felt insulted."

"Boy, you just can't trust these bitches, "I blurted out.

"Amen to that."

"Did you recognize the perp?"

"Perp?"

"Yes, did you recognize the guy?"

"Guy? What guy? On no, never saw him before. Of course, I only saw him for a few seconds. Fat, white buttocks that had never seen the light of the sun. Ponytail and a bald spot on the back of his head. Red blemishes on his backside."

"No shit!"

Mike never did let Joy know of his discovery. His passion and commitment to her had begun to wane and he confessed that he definitely had to abort the relationship for the sake of his manhood. His performance since that memorable Saturday was not very machismo. "It could be classified as pleasure bent," he chortled.

While Mike after an initial soul searching had taken to Toronto as if it was his native village, Alwyn, who had been there longer, was more tentative. Perhaps he was the one who was tiptoeing. After one time? He always brought up one unpleasant racial incident that had happened in Washington, D.C. but which seemed to have stuck in his craw. As he related it to us, he had left the Smithsonian Institute in a mellow mood, when he encountered three men coming toward him on the sidewalk. They stood in front of him, impeding his progress. He was not about to move off the sidewalk and neither were they. Finally he looked them in the eyes and said calmly, "Which f—ing skunt is going to be a martyr today?" He said maybe because they did not understand what skunt meant but knew the meaning of martyr, they decided to let him through after thinking about it for a New York second.

Skunt? Let's say it's not a word anyone would shout in church. We refer to it as a cuss word; only a true born Guyanese would appreciate the word and its sound. It has to be pronounced in a special way. Whenever I visit Guyana and hear that word on the streets I can't express the feelings that engulf me. I am home. It encompasses the whole scene—the people selling their wares, T-shirts, local trinkets and such, the smells, my childhood memories, the sounds—the only place where it is pronounced with such panache, since only Guyanese use it.

I have stated that Alwyn was short but what I didn't say was that he was built like a lighter version of Mike Tyson. All muscle. This was a result of going to the gym from the time he was in high school—not like the fancy ones around now but to a real gym back home in somebody's back yard with only weights. When he arrived in Washington, D.C. he found a modern version where he could work out. We—Boogie, Mike, and I—used to call him Shortman, but I don't remember anyone else using the term. Come to think of it, we only referred to him as Shortman when he wasn't around, such as "Did you see Shortman today?"

Alwyn was the savant among us, though his behaviour in Washington belies that fact. Let's say that conduct was an aberration—a young man free for the first time after leaving the confines of his father's lock and key. In his early teens he had to be home before ten o'clock and after high school and the beginning of his teaching career, the leash was slackened a bit but the curfew never extended later than the midnight hour. There was no trouble on the streets of British Guiana at that time in our history, so there was no reason for this tight security in Alwyn's home. Boogie, Mike, and I lived without supervision and my grandmother used to say "trouble na find you."

I may have given the impression that our lives were consumed with partying and chasing wild women. To the contrary, we reserved Sundays for our dominoes sessions, for our so-called intellectual discussions, a soirée to refine our ideas. Alwyn was definitely in his element speaking of the injustices that engulfed people of African descent all over the world and especially in their own countries of birth. He reminded us all what Georg Hegel, the philosopher, had said more than a century ago: that Europeans thought Africans were mere things whose lives had no meaning.

One of his pet peeves was a particular chapter in African history when King Leopold II of Belgium exterminated more than ten million natives of the Congo because he wanted the rubber growing wild there. A man with an insatiable appetite, he used any means necessary to achieve his goals, including taking women and children hostage to force the native men to harvest the rubber for him. But rubber was not enough and he absconded with all the available art objects. Although Alwyn never condemned all of Europe for having the attitude shown by some, he could never understand the behaviour of some of the participants. He believed Europeans left behind them a legacy, not of democracy, about which they love to lecture, but one of plunder and authoritarian rule. Noam Chomsky has reiterated that there was never a concern for issues of human rights as long as there was a profit to be made. Alwyn was the one who introduced us to the writings of Chomsky.

Alwyn was fond of quoting a Fourteenth-century philosopher who said that the conquered always imitated the conqueror in their crafts, traits, and customs. Look what is happening in Sierra Leone, the Congo, and other parts of Africa today. Africans are chopping off the hands and feet of their so-called enemies—their own people including children—just as Leopold's men did in the Congo. They had leaned their lesson well.

So whatever I have said about Alwyn's behaviour in his early days in Washington, straying from the straight and narrow path can be blamed on youthful exuberance. He was a bird out of a cage for the first time, a kid in a candy store—the United States of America—free drinks, free food for awhile, free women. Can we be blamed for forgetting the code of conduct we left behind in British Guiana—that honour and shame code? I think not. The real Alwyn was indeed a scholar, a thinker, a man who was not afraid to consider the issues that affected us. Recalling those Sunday evenings with Alwyn reminds me of a time at Howard in my public speaking class when I had to give a talk on capitalism and slavery. As fate would have it, one of my transient roommates Mack had some notes on the subject. He was a friend of the author of the book *Capitalism and Slavery,* Eric Williams, then a professor at Howard and later the Prime Minister of Trinidad. My presentation was well received, thanks to this extra background.

I refer to him as transient, since he was not there all the time, but only on his infrequent visits to Washington. He lived there with O.J. a long time before my arrival He was passionate about the subject and was invaluable to my presentation. He was the one who instilled in me the protocol of not asking strangers what they did for a living. Could it be that he did not want to be asked himself? I found out much later that he belonged to the Communist Party of America and held a high position in the organization. He was always well-dressed and never seemed short of funds and had visited Europe on more than one occasion. Whenever he left, men in suits and fedoras would come knocking on the door asking for him. Seems they were always a few days late. When I told them I didn't know anything about his whereabouts, I was telling the truth. In those days, maybe even still today, being a Communist was worse than—no, almost as reprehensible as—having descended from slaves. And being a West Indian Communist without immigrant status was anathema. Alwyn pointed out that in the thirties and for some years after, being a 'Negro' American male was not a healthy existence in the South. One was lynched on the average every four days. Where was the government, any level of government, when it came to protecting its citizens from such terror? The federal government even refused to pass anti-lynching laws for fear of alienating the southern vote. The Communist Party was not afraid to speak out against segregation and the treatment of the poor workers in the cotton fields.

Speaking of communism puts me in a reflective mood. My friend Ulric shared a small bungalow in Nashville with another student from Detroit. Since many of their friends and acquaintances lived in the dormitory on campus, it was not unusual for his home to become a gathering place on weekends. One Saturday Oscar, one of my classmates, arrived with an exotic-looking damsel. She was an undergraduate student from Fisk University and her name was Jenny—a real knock-out. After the introductions Ulric asked me to take care of the new arrivals. This meant serving them a glass of beer, the beverage *du jour*. Jenny declined the beer and requested a coke. As I was in the kitchen getting her drink, I felt her presence close to me. She had heard me speak and my accent piqued her interest. It turned out her father was from British Guiana and had been living in New York for more than a quarter century. We became friends. I cannot recall any exciting heart throbbing dates but I do remember her accompanying me once when a classmate had asked me to babysit his two small children. A boy and girl, and cute little ones at that. After she had given them their baths and put them to bed, we indulged in some smooching and grabbing on the couch. That summer I visited her in New York before my return to Washington and spent a day with her and her parents. Her father was indeed from British Guiana but acted more like a real New Yorker, perhaps because he had been driving taxi cabs for most of his life in the city. Her mother was the first Jewish woman I had the pleasure of knowing. That day was a red letter day indeed. It was the first time I had pasta—spaghetti alla carbonara. Jenny had typed a homemade menu with the lunch and date on it and I've kept that menu pasted in a book through all my travels. After that Jenny visited me in Washington and spent a couple of days there with me. I became the tour guide then, taking her to many places of interest—the Smithsonian, the White House, the Howard University campus, to name just a few.

She transferred to New York University the following school year. This had a dampening effect on our relationship, which eventually petered out. What I really wanted to mention was Jenny's involvement in the peace movement. While still in high school she had joined the marches protesting the death sentence for Ethel and Julius Rosenberg, a couple charged with selling nuclear secrets to the Soviet Union in the early fifties. She and her friends believed they might have been innocent. It did not help, however, and the Rosenbergs did die in the electric chair (the first time for a woman). Jenny was the first person I knew to march for a specific cause.

What I want to convey is that my friends and I were serious at times and were willing to discuss how the past affected our lives. I tried to get both Mike and Alwyn to take golf lessons, suggesting that there is much to learn about a person from the way he plays the game. The obvious example is whether he plays by the rules or cheats. Golf is a good metaphor for life with its hazards, penalties, and triumphs. Alwyn, always the intellectual, would retort with: "How come I have seen you and your friends replay a hole when the results are not to your liking? Or take what you call a mulligan?' My explanation was that we seldom did it, but when we did, it was because we did not practise and prepare before we were ready to start play and only took the opportunity if the course was not busy.

"Wouldn't it be neat if I could replay those lost years in D.C.?"

"No," I replied. "You have benefited from those years. They are part of your experience." And we would laugh heartily remembering the ridiculous situations in which he did find himself.

After one time, indeed.

One Saturday at Alwyn's invitation the three of us went downtown for lunch, then took in a matinee performance at the Towne Tavern. This was one of the few top jazz clubs featuring musicians from the States, many of whom were Afro-Americans. A new group we had not heard before was appearing there and at the end of the session we stayed and chatted with them, as was our custom. On our way home, Alwyn remarked that our shoes needed a shine and suggested we stop at Bay and Bloor and get one. No argument from any of us. After it was all over and we were heading home for the second time, he produced a broad smile and said, "Now you can tell your American friends you had your shoes shined by a white man."

I cannot claim that day at the shoeshine stand was a catalyst for change in Alwyn's attitude toward Euro-Canadians, but there seemed to emerge a difference in his behaviour shortly thereafter. One reason he had given before was "As soon as I think this is a guy I could cultivate as a friend, the watermelon joke or some such joke pops up and reminds me of our difference."

From that day on his attitude seemed to suggest that little things would not bother him anymore and like Mike and me, his circle of friends became wider. He liked German Canadians who, he thought, showed no prejudice. Many had married ladies of the Caribbean. He never did have trouble socializing with their women, though many of them were hyphenated too, like French-Canadians or Dutch-Canadians.

Before we get to know Alwyn as a professional in Canada, I will reminisce a bit. A few months before he left Washington for Canada I was able to get him a job at the Cairo Hotel; one of the regular bellhops did not show up for work and I was doing double duty filling in for him. We had heard of a spate of bank robberies by a 'well-groomed Negro and his beautiful accomplice.' They were able to rob, exit, and disappear so quickly that the police were baffled by their technique. Finally an off-duty policeman happened to be in the bank when they were committing another robbery and almost collared the perpetrator. The robber, however, floored him with a left hook that would have made Sugar Ray envious. The robber and his girlfriend got away but the well-trained policeman was able to give a description of the bandits and as a result, the bellhop became persona non grata and disappeared completely from the Cairo scene. So while he was out making extra money he left a position open for Alwyn. On his second day on the job Alwyn hooked up with a client who was a big tipper and for the first time, he was able to save all his salary and most of his other tips. The gratuity from this client alone sustained him. We called him Diamond Jim. He must have been generous, since money was no longer a problem for Alwyn in D.C.

Some people never seem to grow, spiritually, intellectually, or otherwise. The same cannot be said of Alwyn. Whoever said we carry our past with us was not thinking of him. Of course, he could not and would not erase his past, but for him it was like an iguana shedding its skin and adopting a different attitude.

As an attorney Alwyn was very organized and well-disciplined. Mike and I loved to read detective mysteries for relaxation. Alwyn would read his law books and journals just for fun. The cognoscenti allowed that his profound knowledge of the law and his brilliance in espousing it was a given. It seemed that he had a knack to mesmerize the jury with his eloquence. Mike and I were witness to his oratory when Dr. Gomes, a flamboyant surgeon, was charged with the murder of a fashion model/high-priced call girl. Her surgically-dissected body was found in a dumpster not far from the surgeon's fashionable apartment on Avenue Road. In one of the bedrooms the police discovered in a closet more than a dozen ladies' undies of various colours with matching negligés. The surgeon was often seen squiring beautiful ladies to fine restaurants around town, sometimes two at a time. Although he loved sumptuous dinners, he hardly drank except for a sip or two of wine. Alwyn's defence was as simple as defences go. Although he spoke in his spellbinding manner, the gist of his argument was to challenge the prosecution to prove a connecting link between escorting beautiful women and dissecting them outside the operating room. The jury took less than two days to bring in the verdict of Not Guilty.

Most pundits admitted how fallible their predictions had been in underrating Alwyn's prowess as a criminal defence attorney. How were they to know? Did stereotype influence their thinking? During the trial Alwyn displayed his capacity to stay 'in the zone.' Golfers have told me that for a stretch of time on the golf course they are unbeatable, selecting the right club and reeling off pars and birdies as if some professional was playing the shots. That is how he must have felt during the trial. At least that's how it appeared to Mike and me.

I must mention that the surgeon Alwyn had defended was born in British Guiana of mixed parentage and came to Canada when he was ten years old. His father was of Portuguese ancestry and his mother was the offspring of an Afro-Guyanese mother and English father, who was living in British Guiana. They were Guyanese through and through and sought Alwyn's help when their son was charged. Not too many of the curious at the trial knew of Dr. Gomes's ethnicity or his origins and did wonder why he didn't purchase one of the higher-priced legal experts for his defence. People did not know that George Gomes had been brilliant all his life, first in his class in undergraduate school at the University of Toronto, and among the top ten of his medical class at Harvard. Or that at thirty-five he was the youngest head of the Department of surgery at the Toronto General and taught classes at U. of T. medical school. My grandmother used to repeat this proverb: 'Macaw ask parrot if mango ripe, parrot seh one, one.'

The meaning? One should not tell everything he knows. Leave room for others to find out some things for themselves. Success at Alwyn's first murder case brought more successes. Wherever we went we could feel the stare of the converted and even hear in undertones, "That is the lawyer who ..."

Alwyn had always dated beautiful, exotic women. I have mentioned his penchant for dating women of diverse ethnicity. Of late there was an added criterion that had to be met and I can hear him this minute phoning me to tell me of his newest girlfriend. How tall? That was the question he wanted to hear. Ecstatically he would blurt out her height, which had to be at least five feet eight inches. Because Alwyn was exposed to all this beauty and flattery, we, Mike and I, could see the handwriting on the wall. We were in the process of losing a house mate and the search was on for a house so Mike could put his crew to work. It was not long before the boys found what they were looking for. Once renovations were completed Alwyn became a happy man with his beautiful German/Canadian bride who had measured up to his expectations—svelte, tall, fluent in three languages, and who loved him dearly. This storybook union lasted over two years before it came to an amicable separation. I hope he was into prenuptial agreements (he didn't let me in on everything) because in the space of six years he was married and divorced twice. The second wife was a carbon copy of the first except that she was a French Canadian from Quebec. All his separations were of a friendly nature, but I told him that if he was thinking of getting married again very soon, I would have to start charging him for services as best man. Twice was enough for me.

One evening at a function honouring Dr. Walter Rodney, a well-known Guyanese activist and scholar whose lecture for the evening was 'How Europe Underdeveloped Africa,' I ran into Alwyn's two ex-wives sitting at a table with another woman. I joined them briefly and ordered a round of drinks. Alwyn had commitments elsewhere and Mike remained at the table we were sharing with two young ladies. Alwyn's ex-wives asked about him. "Tell him we miss him," they both said. If you miss him that much, why did you leave? I asked. Almost in unison, as if rehearsed, they blurted out, "Alwyn was beneath us." Laughter from all the ladies.

One day out of the blue I received a call from a young man from Washington, D.C. My receptionist misunderstood the message and for awhile I was crawling up the wall. Turned out it was intended for me to relay to Alwyn. Alwyn had never had a desire to return to Washington since he left, though Mike and I had returned once and looked up Maria, his first landlady cum girlfriend. We had inquired about Amarit, who had moved to a place of her own, and had visited Selma and Coraye.

Alwyn made the call and his past caught up with him. The young man, whose name was Hilson, was the oldest of Amarit's children. Seems she was very ill and, thinking she was about to meet her Maker, decided to tell Hilson the true name of his father. The boy must have inherited his father's genes since he was one of the youngest to graduate from Howard Law School. I don't think the news of Hilson was a complete surprise to Alwyn, but not to worry, he arranged a quick trip to Washington and entreated us to accompany him.

"The first thing I have to do is secure some expert medical advice. I wonder if Jamael (one of his Jamaican friends) is still at Georgetown medical School."

I remembered Jamael very well. Like many students, he and his roommate had only a cot each in the room they shared in a rooming house. They would set the clock at a certain time early in the morning to awaken them to study. Once the alarm went off, Jamael would pick up the clock and smash it on the floor to stop it from ringing. After a few days of this there was a complaint lodged by one of the other tenants and only the threat of eviction changed his habits. I was very surprised to hear that he was admitted to medical school where he was among the brightest in his class. He continued on to become a specialist in internal medicine and now was on the staff of one of the leading medical institutions in Washington, D.C. This was the Jamael Alwyn was about to consult.

We drove to Detroit and had Ulric take us to the airport, then enjoyed the free champagne that comes with traveling first class. Although our visit was short, we packed quite a bit into our schedule, taking a tour of the campus, and of course, Riggs Place. We found to our disappointment a change in the neighbourhood, though disappointment may not be the right emotion. It was more as if we were suffering from pangs of nostalgia. When we left for Canada, 1339 Riggs Place was the only fourplex among the older homes. Now a few more had been erected. Mike's favourite liquor store on Fourteenth Street was no more. When the male guests, all students, attended a party at Riggs Place, a few would bring with them a mickey of cheap whiskey. As soon as they placed their bottles on the table, Mike would uncork the bottles and pour the contents down the sink. He would walk to the liquor store—only a few steps to Fourteenth Street—and replace the cheap liquor with some brand name labels like Cutty Sark or Canadian Club. After a while the message was understood. Do not take rot-gut liquor to Riggs Place or face embarrassment.

The residence for 'Colored Ladies' had also gone the way of the dodo. Gone too was the pawnshop. The owner had become a friend and I bought from him many inexpensive gifts that dazzled the eyes of the recipients. We took Selma and Coraye to a famous seafood restaurant that we could not previously have entered. Everyone thought the trip was worthwhile and we all promised to make more on a regular basis. We were sincere at the time, but all good things, intentions too, are ephemeral, as the ancient philosopher said, and after our short trip we had to get back to reality. Amarit regained her health and was able to live a long, comfortable life watching her son grow in fame and fortune. Like his father, he achieved status in and out of the legal community and is seen from time to time on television espousing sensible views that most of the time differ with the rest of the panel.

Alwyn had paid some of his dues and some of the guilt had been expiated by his charitable deeds in Washington. Back in Toronto life was good. He had two ex-wives who seemed to appreciate him, singly and together, more than when their relationship was conjugal. He wondered why this was so, and I told him, "You don't miss the water till the well runs dry."

"You think so?"

"Of course," I replied.

They would visit him separately and together and sometimes the one who had remarried would bring her husband along. He felt the husband came to show who was the better man.

"What about the free drinks and chow?" I asked.

"Maybe that too," he agreed.

Perhaps he wanted to convey something else, when he said, "Never buy a cow if you can get the milk free." He mentioned that one of his ex-wives wanted to kiss and make up and let bygones be bygones.

"Which one?"

"That's my secret, my friend. Hear this. One Saturday my two ex-wives paid me a visit, one with husband in tow—Renata and Renée and her husband Malcolm. We sat all afternoon, relaxed in conversation and drinking Glenlivet for the men and champagne for the ladies. Malcolm and I were drinking from tall glasses and I poured two ounces topped off with ice and soda for both of us. I told him to help himself after that and he did. He tried to keep up to me, but what he didn't know was that I kept my glass full, topping it with ice, soda, and a tincture of the whiskey and he was replenishing his drink with the original proportions. So while my refill could fit in a thimble, he was proceeding with his doubles."

Changing from Scotch to wine after the Chinese food arrived did nothing to help his guest who was obviously showing the effects of the booze. Not too long after the meal Malcolm was carted off to one of the guest rooms where his snoring could be heard from then on. Alwyn and his ex-wives settled in the master bedroom and I wish I could have been a mosquito on the wall. For the record, it was after this Saturday afternoon that he became philosophical about the cow and the milk. He would never divulge what happened behind the closed door.

Many people I know live in the past. I plead guilty. Sign of advancing age, I imagine, as most young people live only for the now. Alwyn was single again and marriage was not on his radar screen, it seemed to me. He had become pensive, examining his marriages as a failure on his part. He wondered about his penchant for matrimony and why he was not like some of his friends whose motto was 'Love 'em and leave 'em.'

He pointed out to the ladies he squired around town, "I like you very much as a friend, so I don't want to deceive you into thinking our relationship will go beyond what it is—friendship."

"What a speech!" some would say. "What makes you think I don't want the same thing as you? Don't flatter yourself."

Others said: "Whoa, what an egotist. Let's not waste each other's time. Please don't call me again."

He seemed confident he was doing the right thing for although he enjoyed their company, he didn't want to feel any pressure once he took these beautiful creatures out. In spite of our resolutions our lives do not always follow our script and some unexpected excitement entered Alwyn's life at one of the many parties he attended.

She was tall (naturally), educated, had a doctorate in psychology and her own consulting firm in Toronto. Her clients went from businesses who wanted their employees motivated to athletes who wanted to enhance their performances. Fiona was her name and she was very English, cultivating the accent that went with it. She invited Alwyn to elegant restaurants, which he had categorized as A, B, or C. They never ventured to the third and only infrequently to the B group, and she insisted on splitting the bill. She piqued his interest. She loved to eat but her craving did not oppugn her trim figure. He jokingly said to us, "Back home people would say, she got worms." That meant the worms in the stomach digested the food and the person could not gain any weight as a result. No matter what the meal was, she always approached it as if she had not eaten for awhile.

Part of his interest and attraction to Fiona, we told him, were a result of her resistance to his advances. Although she had passed the first phase, 'get her to the crib,' playacting on the couch was as far as they went. He was enjoying the relationship and he was more excited about the chase than the culmination, because, and he got serious—'that's when they think they own you.' She lived on an acreage a fifty-minute drive from Toronto on the way to Hamilton near a little town called Acton. Her parents had a house on part of the property with her brother; she lived alone closer to the highway.

If Fiona was up to playing games, shame on her. It was no sweat off Alwyn's brow. In other words, he found it interesting. Two can play better than one. After a very late night out they ended up at his place on his couch, engaged in the usual manoeuvres. Despite his invitation to stay the night, she rose to leave. "Thanks but no thanks." She had a pet named Peter at home who had to be fed. Alwyn understood. After all, he had a couple of cats named Levi and Bruin, a gift from one of his ex-wives. He had built a special door for their exit and entry.

Mid-morning one Saturday as I was preparing to drive over to his place, he called to say he had a change of plans. Fiona had invited him to a late lunch at her place and he would see me the next day. "No big thing," I told him, although I was disappointed. "Hey, and have a nice day!"

He followed the QEW to the Acton turnoff and found the place easily. He was pleasantly surprised at the beautifully landscaped property with majestic trees and even a one-hole golf course. It was a 2000-square-foot putting green with a couple of tee boxes in the range of one hundred and one hundred and forty yards respectively. Now he wished he had taken up the game, as a few of her guests were having what seemed like a jolly good time trying to see who could hit the ball closer to the pin. There seemed to be some wager over the contest. And there was the swimming pool, big, not quite Olympic in size but quite grandiose with attractive people in swimming attire milling around with drinks in their hands. They all seemed to have English accents. Among the guests were Fiona's brother his live-in girlfriend and the only person Alwyn knew was Peter Appleyard, the English Dave Brubeck who played frequently at the lounge of the Park Plaza Hotel located at Avenue Road and Bloor in Toronto. He and his wife were my patients and Mike, Alwyn, and I used to drop in from time to time to be entertained. Small world indeed. Alwyn later remarked that the English never seem to lose their accent. Fiona and her brother Trevor arrived in Canada as youngsters and they sounded as if they just got off the boat. Alwyn found the afternoon swimmingly delightful. He was glad he was a relatively good swimmer, thanks to those early morning sessions at the Sea Wall when the Atlantic Ocean was bombarding the shores of Georgetown. 'Skulking' or skipping a class or two to go to what was called during our youth, the 'back dam' or 'punt trench' was one way of learning how to swim, and for the older boys, a way of enhancing their prowess. Of course his early training started at the punt trenches. The trenches had been created for the sugar estates so that the cut cane could be transported to factories where it was converted to sugar, molasses, and rum. Punts were flat-bottomed metal boats about thirty feet long, propelled manually by workers with long poles, stationed at the bow and the stern. The trenches were free of debris and deep enough to afford smooth sailing. Cane was moved to the factories and the refined products were shipped back to the estates in this way. The factories and estates were in different locations.

One of my cousins was visiting with us for a few days. His mother, who was a nurse from Wakenaam, was interviewing for a job at a privately-owned hospital. Of course we went skulking, cutting two of my afternoon classes, and we were not attentive to the time. We were having too much fun with the other boys from Central and other schools. We hurried home as fast as our bicycles could take us once we knew we had missed our departure time. My mother was ready for us, as she opened the door.

"Don't tell me you were in detention," she said to me, ignoring my cousin whose name was Brap. That was his false name, what his friends called him. At home he was known as Patrick but after all these years he is still called Brap.

"No, Mom."

"What then? And you better don't lie or else."

'Or else' meant 'I'll tell your father.' And to 'tell your father' always brought out the true confessions. My father had never dispensed corporeal punishment but the fear of the unknown was always enough to keep me in check. I was never sure when that first time would be and although he was known as the village practical jokester, I never saw that part of him. He was a man of few words and sometimes he had a look that made me not want to take the Russian roulette chance of getting his thick belt across my body. I was glad to take the few lashes administered from time to time by my mother to avoid my father's discovery of my misconduct. This time Mother was able to take one look at our red eyes and chalky faces to know what our activity for the day had been. Because of my cousin's presence I was spared the rod.

Let's return to Fiona's party. All the visitors were preparing to leave and Alwyn began making the moves of someone ready to bid good-night, though his heart was not in it and tried to telegraph his message to her. He was hoping Fiona would read his mind. He listened as people promised to get together soon, thinking of our mutual friend who would, while taking his leave after a night of drinking, issue invitations to his place for the next day only to regret it as soon as he woke up. Fiona must have tuned in to his thoughts, since she went over and asked him in a whisper to stay for supper.

His imagination went to work conjuring up a vision of what surprises lay in store for him. He realized he hardly knew his hostess and decided to relax and follow her cues. No point interpreting her invitation to supper as something else, though his heart rate was doing the opposite. When all the guests had left she led him to the house and directed him to a shower next to the den with a TV, bar, amplifier and speakers, which were also the source of the music around the pool.

Just as he was toweling himself dry, she appeared so quietly she startled him. His lascivious thoughts, he reckoned. She was wearing a short Japanese kimono and handed him its twin. "I took the liberty of putting your things in the washer. I thought you would want fresh clothes for tomorrow."

All he could say was "Muchos gracias." She led, he followed into the den where a smorgasbord of Chinese food, a chilled bottle of white wine, chilled wine glasses, and a bottle of Scotch waited on the bar. She was definitely in charge, opening the bottle of wine and pouring it into the glasses.

"Just relax," she said, reading his mind. "Your wish is my command. I am here to serve you."

And why not, he said to himself. He was reminded of a friend who never accepted an alcoholic drink when he visited friends. Everybody was of the opinion that he was an abstainer, a teetotaler. It was not until after the divorce that the wife let the cat out of the bag. He only drank at home, but then heartily. The day he was off from work, the drinking started early and lasted until half of the bottle was consumed. So Alwyn was really getting into the mood, hoping that his hostess was of the same mindset—that she only played at home.

They enjoyed the Chinese delicacies with the wine, then continued with the Scotch. If music is the food of love, then they were relishing that too. They started to dance, first with kimonos tied, then with kimonos untied. Fiona stopped the music, turned off the lights, grabbed his hand and led him to her ornate bedroom where the dim bulbs like Christmas tree lights contributed to his dry mouth. Here they were on the biggest bed he had ever seen, custom-made most likely. He could not believe the passion exuding from this lady. She was an equal opportunity participant, no dormant partner here. He loved the reverberations he was experiencing from her unladylike behaviour. What a surprise! The villagers in Fredericksburg had a saying 'Quiet waters run deep.'

It had been a long time since he felt this ecstasy, perhaps since he was an inexperienced youth with Amarit. She confessed she had not had a man in ages. Live and learn, he reflected, when he suddenly felt something cold on his toes. How could this be, if she is caressing his face? Then he felt a nibble, followed by the unmistakable sound of a grunt. Fiona must have heard it too, because she raised the upper part of her body and rested on her elbows. "Oh shit," she shrieked, and turned on the lights.

What did he see? A black pig, still trying to get at his feet. At first he thought the mixture of wine and Scotch had caught up with him, but when he realized the well-groomed animal was a reality, he lost his cool. "Wha de ras?" he shouted.

Fiona didn't understand his Guyanese but his tone of voice made her want to reassure him. "Don't be alarmed, Al, it's only Peter, my pet."

"Who?"

"Peter. Don't you remember me telling you about him?"

"I don't recall you telling me Peter was a pig. What's he doing here?"

"He sometimes sleeps on the floor. Tonight I did not see him and to tell you the truth, for once I had forgotten him." She escorted Peter out. He was well trained and followed obediently. Where? Alwyn didn't know and said he didn't care. Fiona returned with two snifters of brandy, which had a calming effect on his nerves.

This was the way he recounted his day and night to me, so I shall continue the way I heard it.

"She must have read my mind. The drink had its intended effect and we were entwined again. Fiona may have lacked practice but she proved the point that once someone learns to ride a bicycle, she never forgets. How can someone who displayed so much passion turn the switch on and off so easily? I tell you, this woman can sweat—I mean perspire. At the end of our session the sheets were soaking wet. Talk about letting off steam."

Alwyn had come to our house directly from his night out. We had an early lunch, a Latvian herring salad, first introduced to us by one of my assistants, washed down with a Guinness stout. Mike suggested we change our greeting from 'Where's the pawty at?' to 'Seen any pigs lately?' Nah, we decided to stick with the old.

I have to say Alwyn was not content with the status quo. People still recognized him wherever he went, and sometimes he was unpleasantly surprised when an old woman would wag her finger at him, saying "You had no right defending that murderer." Since those confrontations were rare, he was philosophical: "You have to take the bad with the good." But he was always trying to grow as a person. Probably that's what I meant about his living in the future. At least one hundred people in Toronto claimed him as a personal friend, and since many of them were of different political persuasions, he was besieged with enticements to enter the political arena. If the truth be told, his respect for politicians was as low as was his esteem for some members of his profession. This opinion he safeguarded, sharing it only with us.

With all his financial and related successes, Alwyn seemed to be in search of a piece of the puzzle that was his life. He was looking for that peace of mind that eludes many of us in a lifetime. He thought he should be able to contribute more to society, to be more useful. Don't misunderstand. I don't think he regretted his romantic episodes, but wondered why he could not be of more personal help to people in need, beyond donating to the usual charitable organizations. After much consideration and mindfulness he opened a legal office in the College and Bathurst area catering to the needs of mostly new immigrants from parts of the world where their rights had been abrogated, and get this, disabled people. There was a one-time registration fee, some small amount to keep out the frivolous, and after that, a nominal fee for work that had to be done. He had one full-time receptionist, a retired person on a part volunteer basis, and a few attorneys who also volunteered a number of hours a week. He claimed he was helping to build democracy and wanted to do one good deed a week.

"That's a very ambitious undertaking," Mike interjected. "What do you see yourself accomplishing in five years?"

"That's too far into the future. I'm not one of those people with a crystal ball. One, one dutty build dam."

As you can guess, he was a busy person. Since that weekend with Fiona he had gradually allowed himself a little space. Perhaps his energy could only extend so far, for he had become more reflective again. Mike teased him, "I thought you liked pigs." His reply: "Only the two-legged variety." He could have continued seeing old friends, even continued the relationship with Fiona, but maybe the thought of that pig had more effect on his ardour than he was willing to admit. Mike told him it could have been a snake, as he had heard some women have snakes as pets. And we knew how he hated snakes.

But after awhile it looked to me that Alwyn had to be in love, or to think so anyway. He needed his nose to be wide open, as the young men at Meharry used to say. There is that saying "Better to have loved and lost than not to have loved at all." That was Alwyn.

One Wednesday afternoon he dropped in for a late lunch. He knew I worked through the lunch hour so I could take off a bit early. He happened to arrive at the same time as my last appointment and stepped back to open the door for her. This was a new patient, though I had met her father at one of the Caribbean golf tournaments. He owned a restaurant/nightclub on Eglinton East and his restaurant became the tournament headquarters—a golf club without real estate or club facilities; in other words, they played tournaments on various courses throughout the city. I had played well that day and was the recipient of a prize. Later we exchanged stories and became good friends. He was from British Guiana and looked to be a mixture of the various racial groups. His wife seemed to be a blend of African and Portuguese. Both were tall; he was over six feet and heavyset while she was a thinner, well-proportioned version. Ordinarily, Alwyn would have retreated to my private office, but this time he waited in the reception area, pretending to be a patient while engaging my new patient Betty in conversation. Of course, she immediately passed his height standard and was quickly fulfilling all his other criteria. She had grown up in B.G. and had won the premier scholarship before her sixteenth birthday when she left with her parents and younger sister for Canada. That was ten years earlier. She attended the University of Toronto, majoring in mathematics and had set records for proficiency before moving on to Seton Hall in the United States to do a PhD. in Computer Science. This was the time when computers occupied a large room, many years before the World Wide Web and the proliferation of the computer industry.

Later when I proclaimed this daughter of B.G. to be beautiful, Alwyn raised his hand as if he was about to stop traffic at Bloor and Yonge.

"'Beautiful?' No, no, my mother is beautiful. This creature is ah, exquisite." I had to agree with him. As I said, Betty was at least five feet eight, had beautiful long olive legs and of course, a firm African behind. She met Alwyn's 3 Bs requirements: brains, boobs, behind. She would also meet the requirements for what my mother called ladylike—a soft, quiet way of speaking, mannerly, legs crossed in a becoming fashion when she was seated.

As you can guess, he was getting into a frenzy about meeting Betty again. That soft whisper reminiscent of Marilyn Monroe echoing in his mind from the waiting room was enough to derail Alwyn from his resolve of doing good deeds, if only temporarily. He had to see her again. When we pointed out that Betty was a distraction from his nobler aims, his answer was not worth repeating. All we could say was, "If you want to be like a yo-yo with your life going up and down, you are intelligent enough to see it for yourself, so why should we fight about it? It is your life." Making excuses to delay the inevitable was like trying to hold back the dawn. All of Alwyn's conversations led to Betty. Betty this, Betty that. "You sound like a school boy smitten," we told him. "Are you in love again?"

"What's love got to do with it?"

Betty's name was a contraction of Elizabeth, the same as my grandmother whose friends and relatives called her Pet. She was my mother's mother; my father's mother died before I was born. Betty, or Elizabeth, was named after royalty and that piece of knowledge became the subject of our debate.

Alwyn wondered whether the significance of a name can fulfill its prophecy. I told him the thought has occurred, as the people in Wakenaam are fond of saying, at the back of my head. I think of Tiger Woods and there is Champ Bailey, who as an NFL rookie for the Washington Redskins broke records in just a few games.

Mike tried his best to point out to Alwyn that a girl like Betty was not out for some frivolous relationship. She would be in it for the long haul. Then he reminded him how bitter he had become after his second divorce. We had to listen to his tirade after their early uncoupling. During the glory days of sunshine and blissfulness he was obsequious to her every whim. A new car as soon as there was a notable change in the model as well as new expensive furniture. She was a delight to the owners of her favourite boutique, one of the privileged few to be notified of new collections. Also a membership in the new gymnasium club for women. This ex-wife later married one of the men who worked for Mike. She had no problem moving in with her mother-in-law, since her husband had never left the nest. They lived in a two-storey older home in a quiet neighbourhood near Hyde Park. When her husband was still in high school, his father went to Montreal for a bowling competition and never returned. His mother was the bookkeeper for a Jamaican immigrant family who owned a few corner stores and she supplemented this income by renting rooms to students from the University of Toronto.

If I convey the impression that Alwyn's separation from his wives was not amicable, then I am doing a poor job. Both separations were done in a friendly, businesslike manner and his outbursts were not characteristic. We teased him. "Good for you, blowing off steam like that." Although he was not heartbroken, he was not a happy hombre when love took a walk. But all our powers of dissuasion to end his obsession with Betty proved to be useless. The last straw came when he dramatically announced, "She is not just any woman, you know."

Mike snorted, "Weh I hear dem words before?"

"I surrender, we surrender," I rejoined.

We capitulated and invited Betty to a little gathering at our home. She accepted without any palaver on condition that her sister be included in the invitation.

It was an informal affair with in-house snacks prepared by our girl Phyllis. We served our homemade ice cream too, so good that we were talking of marketing it. The arrival times for the guests were staggered. We had some couples come at seven o'clock, and others an hour later, the later being the known romeos and single ladies, so as to give Alwyn a head start. Before long it seemed our strategy was paying dividends. Betty and Alwyn were taken with each other, if the laughter emanating from their corner was any indication. Betty's younger sister Sharon was enjoying herself as well. Shorter than Betty and not as slim, she was nevertheless very attractive. Epaisse, as the boys at Central would have called her; big-boned my grandmother would have said. All the other young men in British Guiana, regardless of education or class, would have said "Dat girl is thick," which meant she had sex appeal, was desirable and alluring.

Mike had rehearsed his joke for a week.

"A duck went into a country store and asked the salesman: 'Do you have any duck feed?'

The reply was: 'No we don't.'

The next day the duck went in and repeated his request. 'Do you have any duck feed?'

The salesman politely said, 'No, we don't. We never carry duck feed.'

On the third day the duck went back and asked the same question. This time the clerk was really irritated. 'Look, I told you before and I'll repeat myself, we don't have duck feed and we don't intend to have any. Furthermore, if you come back here again, I'm going to nail your webbed feet to the floor.'

The following day the salesman looked down and there was the duck. 'Do you carry any nails?'

'No,' said the man.

'Well, do you have any duck feed?'"

Mike wanted to tell it to illustrate Alwyn's persistence and perseverance in meeting Betty, and although most of the guests did not appreciate its significance, the joke evoked outbursts of laughter.

It was one of our most enjoyable parties. Although it was more or less impromptu, the mixture of guests generated a certain chemistry that was hard to define. Strangers and old friends alike seemed to hit it off and before long it seemed everyone had known one another for decades. Even as hosts, we were swept into this collective camaraderie, and when it was time to halt the festivities, no one wanted to call it a night.

I remembered the routine my father used when he wanted to end an evening of music and dancing and no one wanted to leave. At a certain time after midnight, he would open the front door, look up at the skies and proclaim loudly, "Boy, if I was at somebody's house at this hour of the night, I certainly would be heading home." Whenever he did this, loud laughter ensued and everyone took the hint gracefully.

My father's workday started very early. His launch service was between Wakenaam and Leguan and the first scheduled trip for the day was at five in the morning with connection to the government steamer at the other end of the island. Although he had at least two of his nephews working with him, he had to be there early enough to make sure no one had overslept after a night of carousing. These were young men, unmarried, and like many young men before and after, they thought of one particular subject every sixty seconds of their natural born life.

On the night of our party in Toronto no one wanted to interfere with the magic formula. Of course, Alwyn was really bewitched. His nose was as wide open as the koker where we first learned to swim. Betty seemed to have inhaled some of the intoxicated air as well. She was charmed by it all and could not avoid noticing how popular Alwyn was and how he was treated with such love and admiration. He looked like a short version of Michael Jordan with short hair trimmed by his barber who went to his home once every fortnight.

As the evening progressed and the wine tasted even better, we danced the night away. We were still in our North American mood and Sam Cooke and Sinatra were two of our favourites. I was a Ray Charles fan, perhaps because every time he appeared in Nashville my friend Norm and I would go to hear him. I still remember a building on Meharry Boulevard where the working people of Nashville gathered to dance to his music. Norm and I would become non-students and enjoy ourselves thoroughly. Oh! I almost forgot to mention that we played Dinah Washington's music, someone we had met in Detroit through Ulric. Of course, we had to play Jackie Gleason's *For Lovers Only* to send everyone away with the right feeling. Now I am back to my roots, playing Bob Marley, the Tradewinds, my cousin Mark Holder, Burning Spear. There is that saying: 'After one time.'

Betty was feeling self-conscious. She was meeting strangers for the first time and was enjoying herself more than she imagined and staying longer than she intended. She was about to cop a Cinderella. She signaled her intention to leave and was genuinely surprised when everyone coaxed her to stay. "Okay, but only for a bit longer."

When she and her sister were finally ready to go, Alwyn volunteered to drive them home. He was back in a jiffy.

"Back so soon?" Mike wanted to know with a hint of sarcasm in his tone.

"What did you expect? Me spending the night?"

The next few weeks occupied our time and talents in different ways. The Prime Minister of Guyana (remember, it was still British Guiana then) was about to visit Toronto and a reception was being planned to welcome him. Although Mike, Alwyn, and I were not political, we were invited to join the inner circle planning committee because of our status in the community. An election was to be held in British Guiana and overseas voting was allowed. This meant anyone born in British Guiana, including children of voting age even if born outside the country and with no intention of returning to live there, could cast a ballot. Alwyn became very involved and coerced Mike and me to attend strategy meetings, some of which were held at the Royal York Hotel as well as his home.

On the day of the dinner reception we found ourselves in the receiving line waiting for the Prime Minister. Mike and I were there with our dates along with other Guyanese, some of whom we were meeting for the first time. Alwyn, as master of ceremonies, was already seated with Betty at the head table. I must mention a peculiarity of the Prime Minister as he stood in line to greet his expatriates. As each guest in the receiving line was introduced by a member of the committee, the Prime Minister would be shaking his hand but not looking at him. Instead, he would be staring at the back of the line. He continued to look away, even as he shook my hand, despite the fact that I had met him before. Alwyn displayed as much eloquence as the Prime Minister in his speech, introducing him as a man "with thoughts that breathe and words that burn."

If there was any fire between Alwyn and Betty I could not say. Of course, I had no way of knowing what went on behind closed doors. I spent time with them whenever they wanted to review the bands at the Towne Taverne or the Colonial downtown. Since Sharon and Betty were like nuns in that they were rarely seen alone, I was occasionally asked to fill in. I didn't mind, if I had nothing else to do. I liked both sisters and it was always a relaxed atmosphere with these two beautiful women.

During those times we saw a young Bill Cosby and just about any other big name who performed in Toronto. We knew Cosby bought his clothes from a certain haberdasher on Yonge Street and we would patronize the store. Although Mike and Joy would join the group from time to time, their visits were few and far between. One event we did all attend together was the inaugural season at Mosport, the international circuit for race cars. It was the only time we went and we made a day of it, taking picnic baskets full of lunch and wine and later returning to our home to finish the party.

It occurred to Mike and me that Alwyn and Betty were always surrounded by company. Almost as if by mutual consent, they were afraid to be alone. Lunch or dinner in a public restaurant did not constitute seclusion.

Betty always had some excuse not to visit him at his home, he later told me when I confronted him. I knew the thinking at the time was to get your date to the 'crib' and his was a beauty—his house, I mean. Boys will always be boys, regardless of age, so we would ask him, "Have you been consumed yet?"

To explain the meaning of that question I have to return to the village of Fredericksburg where the men told this story to young men approaching manhood. After the sexual act, the female praying mantis ends the affair by consuming the male as a meal. Hence the question. Alwyn's supercilious smile said it all—he was spending his time on more important matters. It was true he was busy with a prospering law practice as well as his advocacy shop on Bathurst; he also found time to advise his junior staff. When Mike decided to take up the guitar, Alwyn also wanted in, and they had an instructor from a school on Yonge Street come early every Saturday to Alwyn's house to give them lessons. Of course, I could get neither of them to develop an interest in golf.

The courtship of Miss B did not seem too fiery to two keen observers. There was not that passion that made reason take a holiday. Of course, the pursuer saw it differently. After all, here was a man who of late was beginning to think the world was his oyster. He was not arrogant, but confident. He would recite Churchill's famous speech from time to time: "We shall not flag or fail, we shall fight in France, we shall fight in the seas and the oceans, we shall fight with growing confidence."

One Friday evening I was determined to make a night of solitude for myself. Mike had checked in with me while I was still at the office and he knew my intention was to relax at home. He had planned to hook up with Alwyn later on. I settled down to some black pudding our cook Phyllis had left for us, washing it down with a chilled bottle of Guinness, backed by a new recording of Miles Davis purchased that day. Life felt great. I was very relaxed. Then the ringing of the telephone broke the spell. I decided not to answer it. After about ten rings, silence followed only long enough for the person to dial again. I answered on the fourth ring. "Yes?"

"Are you deaf or what?" It was Alwyn.

"What can I do for you, my man?"

"What can I do for you? Is that any way to speak to a friend?"

I didn't like the tone of his voice. Not at all. "Sorry, bud, I must have fallen asleep."

"At this hour? Never mind. If your Highness can hightail it over here toute de suite, I'd appreciate it. No time to explain now."

After the way he spoke, I dressed as fast as I could and broke the speed limit to get to his place. I entered the house, using my key, and found him pacing up and down his living room. There was a fire going and, to my surprise, Betty seemed to be asleep on one of his expensive imported sofas. I could hear her loud snore long before I knew from where the sound was emanating. She was covered from the waist down with a blanket.

"Did you bring me here to hear a woman snore?"

"Don't be silly, it's more than that. I want you to examine her, see if she is all right."

The tenor of his voice made me look at him, then at her. I checked her breathing, opened her mouth even while she continued to sleep, and placed a pillow beneath her head. "She seems to be in a deep sleep. How long has this been going on?"

He recounted the situation in his own words:

"We were to go out this evening but she called earlier and with the least bit of coaxing she decided to come over. She caught a cab and it was the first time we were alone here."

'What is your pleasure?' She looked puzzled. 'What do you feel like doing?'

'Oh. Can't we just relax? Listen to some music?'

I put on the reel-to-reel—Ella, Nina, Miles—and asked Chandra to fix some sandwiches (Chandra was his housekeeper). Instead of tea, I opened a bottle of champagne for the maiden visit and after a couple of glasses, we danced. Betty was in a mood I had never seen before. Very playful and relaxed. Dancing led to slow dancing, then to kisses. To make a long story short, before you could say 'boo,' we were in the guest room and we copulated."

"Say what?"

"Yes, we fooped, and all affectations went down the drain."

"I hope you were prudent," I remarked.

"Does Goodyear make tires?" he replied before continuing. "We took a bath, got dressed and returned to the couch, holding on to each other, enraptured. We remained quiet as a burglar, still enthralled by the ecstasy of what went before, afraid to break the spell. Then Betty said in a low, sexy voice, 'Some wine, please.' I complied, we touched glasses, and in almost a whisper, she said, 'Betty bad.'"

"I was not certain what I thought I heard and so I did not react. But then, there it was again, a little louder.

'Betty bad.'

'Pardon?' I could not pretend not to hear her any longer. It was a plaintive, childlike refrain that got my attention. This is purely A.F. I said to myself, when the phone rang.

"It was Mike on the phone calling from some place far away on Eglinton East, saying he and his girlfriend were on their way. When I returned, Betty was spreadeagled on the sofa, snoring away. I let her sleep for awhile, then decided to move her to the bedroom where she could sleep in comfort. I did not want Mike's girlfriend finding her in this condition. When I tried to awaken her, it was as if I had a drunken sailor on my hands. Although she was breathing freely, it did not seem normal and that's when I panicked and called. I have forgotten to thank you for your alacrity."

We decided to let her be, checking her breathing from time to time and making sure she remained warm.

"You hungry?"

"Well, I have not—" was all I could say, as he disappeared and returned immediately with a bottle of wine, a couple of glasses and some roti and curry, which we devoured.

Alwyn mused, "'Betty bad?' I can't imagine her being bad at anything. Could bad mean good? Remember what those Americans said to us at the carpet-cleaning outlet? No? Because we worked so hard for the few weeks we were there when they were behind in their schedule? Of course you must. They repeated it so often: "You are some baad motherfoopers." How could you forget that?"

"Yes, yes, I do remember now." I hoped my admission was helpful to his rationalization.

Little by little, the snoring became more subdued, and not long after, the sleeping beauty stretched, yawned, put her hand to her mouth, rubbed her eyes, and in an imperious tone, queried, "What's with the blanket? How long have I been asleep? What happened to Sharon?"

A lot of questions and not many answers.

Alwyn led her to the bedroom to arrange her face, supplied her with a new toothbrush and used the time to tell me that Sharon and her escort were due at any moment. While Betty was indisposed, Sharon had called to say they were delayed because her friend had inadvertently locked his key in the car. Lady Betty re-entered, looking as beautiful and dignified as ever. She seemed amnesic of the Betty Bad episode and it occurred to me she could also have forgotten about the dalliance earlier in the evening.

Sharon and her escort Karl, German by birth and accent, arrived a few minutes before Mike and his date. When Mike introduced her, I knew immediately she was from my homeland. Her accent was unmistakable. Her name was Bibi and she was attached to the Consulate. When Alwyn took her to be introduced to the others, Mike turned to me as if we were conspirators and muttered in sotto voce, "She's half Chinese, you know."

"Really?" I retorted, wondering if he felt the sarcasm I was trying to convey. Of course, I saw she was part Chinese. She was part East Indian too, an exotic mix if ever there was one. Her father was born in British Guiana to Chinese immigrant parents who owned what we called shops, and what are referred to as grocery stores. Shops that sold everything from meat to nails. Her mother was of East Indian ethnicity and boasted deep roots embedded in the country. Bibi reminded me of one of my favourite movie stars, Betty Davis, in her younger days—the way she walked, her pose when she stood, even to the way she inclined her head.

When we joined the group, Sharon, Betty and Karl were sitting on one of Alwyn's beautiful sofas and Alwyn and I occupied single chairs opposite them with a coffee table between us. Mike found a love seat where he and Bibi could be comfortably ensconced, or perhaps joined at the hip would be a better description. Their position created a triangular seating arrangement and for a few minutes it looked as if we were at a wake. At least two people in the room knew the reason for the quietude, but I knew Mike was wondering about my presence there, particularly when I had been so emphatic about wanting an evening of tranquillity. I watched his body language convey his unease with the formality of the situation until he decided to remedy it.

"Whe the pawty at? Leh the pawty begin rat now." He began taking orders for everyone's favourite beverage and made sure refills followed in quick order. Within a short while the atmosphere changed along with the music, as Mike replaced Mantovanni with the Trade Winds, a Guyanese band resident in Toronto. You have to remember that each of us had keys to the two houses and felt equally at home in both. Alwyn still had keys to our Walmer Street home where we had settled after a couple of moves following renovations.

Mike's prescription must have worked, since Alwyn was back in form. He had recovered his cheerfulness and took charge ordering some food when no one seemed eager to go out. Even Miss Betty was in good humour, telling some gossip about some of her clientele without mentioning any names.

What happened after that evening? Betty and Alwyn continued their relationship as if that Friday evening was a part of a Twilight Zone episode; in other words, it was almost like a dream, from which you awake just at the moment it was about to become too terrifying to endure. Alwyn was convinced Betty was amnesic about the early part of the evening and I had reason to believe him. When we lived in Washington, D.C. we had a friend whose behaviour sometimes crossed the boundaries of decency when he had too much to drink. We found out it did not take much to get him to that stage. When confronted the next day, he was always full of remorse and apologies, as he had no memory of his conduct. After a few reminders of his intoxicated actions, he decided to change, and quit drinking completely. He was a decent chap and thought his alcoholic amnesia was not a sensible way to go through life. It must have worked, because he became one of the renowned legal authorities in the D.C. area and remained a lifelong abstainer.

Betty and Alwyn continued to date, and Sharon to double date with them, rarely bringing the same escort twice. I was not considered part of these statistics if I happened to join them. But Betty never did set foot in Alwyn's door again.

We had become friends with an American musician who visited Toronto on a yearly basis. His name was Earl Grant and we were introduced to him by Ulric. He had been encouraging us to take in one of his performances in Detroit for some time, and when we found out he was performing there again, we decided to surprise him with a visit. We piled into Alwyn's car—all six of us, Betty, Sharon, Mike, Bibi—and traveled to Detroit by way of Windsor and the tunnel.

It was a marvelous occasion with dinner at the club with Ulric and Earl and two of their friends. Earl was a triple threat performer—piano, organ, vocals—whose song *The End* had hit the top of the charts in 1963. Unfortunately, he was killed in 1970 in a car crash at the age of 39. We were really enjoying the evening—at least the men in the group were—when a pall of discomfort seemed to be hovering over Betty and Sharon, and then

Alwyn. Shortly thereafter, we knew the cause. Betty had been indicating to Alwyn and Sharon that she wanted to leave Detroit early the next day. That meant leaving the club and returning to our temporary quarters. Ulric owned a couple of apartment buildings and kept a suite available for guests or business conferences.

The sleeping arrangement: it was what we call prosaic. The sisters occupied one bedroom, Mike and Bibi another, and Alwyn and I the master bedroom. Although the cupboards were well-stocked, these non-North American damsels had picked up the ways of their American sisters in this instance. They refused to enter the kitchen. They were on holiday, they told Mike when he broached the subject. We decided to have breakfast/lunch in Canada and an hour outside Windsor, we pulled in at a wayside restaurant and had our meal. Everything and everyone seemed copacetic—no tension in the air, no carryover recriminations from the previous evening. After all, the sisters had occupied the same room and Mike and Bibi were still holding hands. What I did notice were the frequent trips the sisters were making to the ladies' room.

When we were students in Nashville, my friend Norm and I would sometimes leave the fraternity house on a Saturday evening and visit one of the popular watering holes where students from the nearby colleges would gather. Once we had decided to stay at a selected spot we would call the frat house and have them page us at a given time. If we were able to charm a couple of coeds to join us at our table, our pre-emptive plan was set in motion. The idea was to invite them to our fraternity house where there was always a party in progress. If there was an inordinate number of trips to the ladies' room, we would suspect the ladies were hatching a plan of their own. When we do pop the question of visiting the fraternity house and if the answer is positive, we all leave. If the reply is negative, we pretend we are not disappointed and we wait for our call. When the call comes for Dr. Norm or me, we make profound apologies and explain we have to return to the hospital. Although we were not doctors yet, the deceit seemed inconsequential. These frequent trips of Betty and Sharon reminded me of the past and warned me that some scheme was afoot.

Back in Toronto, we drove to our home and started to get ready for our weekly contest of dominoes. The enthusiasts would be arriving in a while. Mike could not wait and decided to have a game with me. Alwyn and the sisters sat quietly in one corner of the room and Bibi was busy in the kitchen, intent on fixing something other than Guyanese food. Gradually the pieces started to fall into place. To our surprise, Sharon became the quarterback and announced their impending departure. Something like "We have to be going very soon," when she was usually the one who wanted to stay longer. Alwyn offered to drive them home and was gone for quite awhile. Upon his return, when he was settling down with a cup of bush tea, Mike said with a broad grin, "Boy, that took a long time."

"Since when are you monitoring my goings and comings?" retorted Alwyn so seriously that it threw Mike off guard.

"Look, buddy, you don't have to bite my head off. Sorry I said anything."

"Let's forget it."

Bibi decided to go upstairs to be with some friends, referring to her books. We opened three bottles of Guinness Stout and nibbled on some chicken Bibi had prepared. Everyone seemed relaxed now. Alwyn decided to explain the reason for his foul mood after he had returned from driving the sisters home. He was embarrassed by his outburst, which signified he was not in control of his emotions, his thoughts, his actions. Whenever we reminded him about his days of wine and glory with Amarit and others, he always dismissed that behaviour as an aberration.

To put a lighter touch to that particular discussion, I always maintained that my inept behaviour was a result of falling from our kitchen door to the ground below at age two. In those days larger homes were built high above the ground to avoid the effects of flooding during the rainy season. I fell twenty steps from our kitchen door and by the time my mother reached me after hearing a scream from the cook, a scream that was capable of raising the dead in the nearby cemetery, I was bleeding more than the pigs my cousin Buddy butchered every holiday. The cook had the rare prescience to take pieces of the sheet she was ironing to my mother who used them to suppress the bleeding on the frontal part of my head. My grandmother, who was always present, retrieved some leaves from her garden nearby and promised she would staunch the bleeding with leaves compressed in a piece of sheet. My brain, I told them, was never ever able to recover from the insult of the injury. The indented part of my forehead still bears testimony to the life-saving efforts of three women working together. I truly believe that injury has had a lifelong deleterious effect on my thinking and emotions. Because of that trauma to the frontal lobe I agree with Woody Allen who claimed that his brain is his second favourite organ.

Talk about recessed memories! I had forgotten the following incident until I recalled my injury. My mother had taken me to visit my father at the stelling. It was high tide and only the artificially-built up land and a concrete facade kept the river from overflowing into the village. My father was working on his boat and my mother left me for a few minutes in the shed where the passengers usually sat and waited. She walked to the end of the stelling where the boat was moored to tell him that he had company. She had not gone very far when I became disobedient and adventurous. I was three years old and was curious to see why the water and the waves were splashing against the embankment. In the meantime, my dad had seen my mother and started down the pier to meet her. Of course, I fell into the river, as they stood watching. Both reacted simultaneously. My mother screamed loud enough to scare the children playing in the schoolyard nearby and my father broke the record for the 50-yard dash, jumping in to save me with his boots and all. Just as I was going under for the second time, he grabbed me and swam ashore. My father held the only record for swimming across the mouth of the Essequibo River from the pier at Fredericksburg to the stelling at Leguan. This was the journey of his thrice daily trips ferrying passengers between the two destinations. I was saved by each of my parents on at least those two memorable occasions and am reminded of them daily by that indentation in my forehead. Especially now that my hair is receding.

This is what Alwyn had to say after he drove the sisters home:

"When I got to their house, Betty invited me in for a drink, but I asked for tea instead. While Sharon was brewing it, Betty excused herself to get into something comfortable. When she returned with a glass of wine in her hand, she pulled up a chair facing me. She looked very intense. Here comes the explanation of the frequent trips to the washroom, I thought.

'I don't know how to start,' she muttered.

'Start what?' I asked. 'Always start at the beginning.' I tried to be flippant.

'I want to tell you something and I don't want to be interrupted. No cross examination either, since I am not on the witness stand.'

'Okay,' I said quietly, while thinking this lady must have three seeds, giving orders like that.

'I am a little embarrassed telling you—not by what I am about to say but by the fact that I should have told you before.'

Here comes the Betty Bad explanation, I told myself.

'I am going to be brief,' she continued. 'I have decided not to go out with you any more,'

'Just like that?'

'Didn't I just ask you not to interrupt? You are making this very difficult. As I said, we will not date anymore, but I would like to remain friends. I have always liked and admired you but a relationship needs more and I cannot go on pretending any longer. I am a lesbian.'

'Say what?'

'I repeat, I am a lesbian.'

'When did you realize this? On our return trip from Detroit?'

'No, no, I have always been.'

'No shit. You certainly pulled the wool over your eyes.'

'My eyes?'

'Yes, your eyes, my eyes, the eyes of my friends.'

Since this sounded like A.F. to me, I thought it was time to leave. Be calm, breathe in optimism, breathe out despair. I was able to say, 'Thanks for telling me now, Ta ta.' I could not think of anything else to say, so I pulled my tail between my legs and left. As I was driving back here, I decided my assessment of her was wrong. Instead of her having three seeds, she had to have a goadie."

Seed is the equivalent of the American balls. Like that guy had a lot of balls to rob the bank when there were so many policemen around. Seeds or balls mean testicles. Goadie is when the testicle becomes enlarged by a sac of watery fluid surrounding it; the medical term is hydrocele—goadie is strictly Guyanese.

As Alwyn regained his composure, I tried to console him. "That's life, my friend. Better now than later."

"We weren't engaged, you know," he replied.

"I thought you were so much in love."

"Wha' luv gat to do wid it?"

Mike, who was quiet during all this, piped in with "What a waste!" He was referring to Betty's beauty as if lesbians don't see beauty in each other.

Alwyn must have agreed with Mike's sentiment, because he quickly rejoined with: "Ditto."

Over Guinness stout we became psychologists analyzing Betty, from her Betty Bad behaviour to her latest confession. After awhile Alwyn seemed to relax. Our conversation became less specific to one woman and turned to a generalization of women. We were glad to see our friend was handling things in their natural perspective.

"May you live long enough to be rejected many more times," I said and could see that my low level psychology was working. So I added, "If I had a dollar for every rejection I have had I'd be a rich man today." Everyone laughed.

After that the days and weeks seemed copies of sameness. We would get together on weekends, mostly at our place, although we would see Alwyn during the week, either downtown or at his place after work. One weekend he came over with a proposal. He must have been thinking of it for some time, although the project, as he called it, was very simple.

"You know, friends, you have to admit that we have been blessed beyond reason."

"Amen," I chimed in.

"We were not the smartest of the smart."

"Speak for yourself," Mike interjected.

"No interruptions please."

"Yes, Betty B."

"Have your fun, but as I was saying, you were not the brightest, but here we are enjoying the good life. This project will give you a chance to sow good seeds. You want to grow, don't you?"

"You bet," we said, trying to humour him.

The proposal was that we travel to Guyana and set up a scholarship fund for students from our original public schools to allow them to attend Central High School in Georgetown. Mike's alma mater was no longer in existence. Remember, in Guyana high schools are private with tuition fees. He had already thought of the name of the fund and the choice was a welcome one. We named it after a group of us who used to meet informally after we had graduated from high school. The name was Les Amis. We competed in dominoes against other groups in the Georgetown area, played cricket, or got together to go to dances on weekends or just listen to the big bands that played every weekend at dance halls. We sat on our bicycles outside the building and enjoyed the sound. We watched the dancers—men in suits and ties and the women dressed to kill. Sad to say, those dance halls and big bands are just a memory now. Suits and ties, I'm afraid, are now reserved for weddings and funerals.

We put some thinking and planning into our project, wrote some letters to friends in Guyana with the proposal and had most of our work assigned, so we would not spend time on the small matters when we got there. We still remembered that everything moves at a slower pace in the tropics and why not? The heat saps the energy.

The day of our departure arrived. I remember it being around the end of March, the snow and cold still with us when we boarded our plane, and when we landed in Guyana, the heat felt as if it were steaming out of the earth. We were dressed in a suit and tie, so we immediately tucked our coats under our arms and loosened our ties. Times and fashions do change. After one time?

Remember Boogie who was inspirational in changing the direction of our lives? I mean, Mike, Alwyn and me. Although he was the first to apply for admission to Howard University in Washington, D.C., he never arrived there. Instead, he went to the United Kingdom much later. He took his medical training in England and Ireland and I have a feeling that to this day, although he is a well-traveled person, he has not visited Washington. My grandmother had a saying: 'Na every crab hole get crab,' meaning that things do not always turn out to be what you expect them to be. I suppose that's the reason he is marginal in this narrative. Boogie was there at the airport to meet us and drive us to Georgetown.

Mike, the all-American on seeing Boogie, shouted, "Hey you, motherfooper, you're still ugly."

Boogie, with a smile, retorted, "You're still a character, Mike, only a louder one."

Did I detect a trace of an English accent in Boogie? Why not? All of us were sounding quite different from the way we sounded many years ago. But wait, after a very short while, we were all sounding like Guyanese of old, almost as if time had stood still. Maybe the sounds emanating from the streets resonated in our ears and the unconscious took over. I have to say that, when I heard some of the slangs and words (cuss words, we called them) coming from the street people, my being felt encompassed in rapture, that this was truly where I belong.

The drive from the airport was about twenty-six miles in distance but the narrow roads and the mentality of the drivers made the journey interesting and sometimes hair-raising. We passengers had forgotten that vehicles had to compete with stray dogs and cattle graciously taking their time to cross the road or simply to rest there, with cyclists and pedestrians, not to mention competition with hell-bent motorists and truck drivers who had not the least concern for anyone else. In the course of our journey we saw the evidence of two accidents. Boogie was a careful driver and we arrived at our hotel without incident. Boogie, of course, was disappointed that we opted not to stay with him at his more than spacious residence. Staying at the hotel allowed us more freedom to retire at our leisure without imposing on his time. Probably the real reason was that Boogie had Rottweiler dogs guarding his premises and with that came the encumbrance of having someone always there to monitor our egress and entry. My feelings about guard dogs are well known to my friends. Once bitten, twice shy. Boogie looked successful and why not? He was not only the personal physician to the Prime Minister of the country but was also the Health Officer for Georgetown, the capital city. In addition, he had a very busy private practice. Success seemed to have touched us all.

The Tower Hotel was very central. To the south was the Public Library. As a student I spent many hours there boning up for those external examinations from the United Kingdom. Sometimes I would skulk, and instead of going to the punt trenches to swim, I would settle in there for the afternoon. Across the boulevard was Bookers, a store owned by an expatriate company. This company, to a large extent, controlled the sugar industry of the country and its power was said to exceed the government of the day. When I was preparing to leave the country as a student, I had Mr. Griffith, who was the head tailor of the store, make me two suits of the finest English tweed to take with me to Washington, D.C. Mr. Griffith had made my first long pants, or slacks for my thirteenth birthday. Up to that time I wore short pants, or shorts. When I was sixteen, he made my first suit. It is almost painful to recall how proud I was of my brand new tailored suits when I first arrived at Riggs Place and how critical O.J. my countryman, was of them. As soon as I was able to afford replacements, they were relegated to the back of my closet.

On our first day at the Tower we decided to go for an early morning walk. We crossed the boulevard on Main Street and entered Bookers. We were impressed with the inventory in the men's wear, with the modern book department, a pharmacy that stocked expensive perfumes among other items and a lunch counter that reminded us of North America.

Continuing west through Bookers, we found an exit to Water Street, and as the name implies, we were close to the Demerara River. We ambled our way south on Water Street, slipping through the crowds where every square inch of the sidewalk seemed to be occupied by a vendor selling the same merchandise as his competitor. It was as if some established merchant had a warehouse and all these budding entrepreneurs would arrive every morning, collect their basket full of goodies and assemble in the same area of Water Street to attract the attention of the few shoppers who decided to buy that day. It was hard to tell who were the successful salesmen, seeing them all together selling identical products—t-shirts, dresses, socks, to name a few.

We then headed to an area that held special memories of my tender years. These were my pre-school years when I would accompany my mother to Georgetown whenever she decided to go shopping. She made more frequent visits at certain times of the year, like Easter and Christmas. Apart from her visits to the Salvation Army Tea Room where she would meet one of her friends for tea and crumpets and I would indulge in cake and ice cream, there is only one other place that stirs up such nostalgia. I am referring to Stabroek Market. It was named the Big Market to distinguish it from the other two in Georgetown. Size could have been one explanation, but the concept of the market itself could have been the real reason. Without any empirical evidence I would hazard a guess that the Stabroek Market is one of the first malls built anywhere. The blueprint is still the same—a variety of stores housed in one enclosed area. Built by the Dutch in 1880, it is still as busy today as it was those many, many years ago. Its original structure of wood, concrete, and iron is still there and its famous four-faced clock is still functioning and stands like a beacon from a great distance. The back of the market opens up to the Demerara River and this allows fishermen to bring their catch to be sold to very early risers. In those bygone days, whenever I visited Georgetown with my mother, a cousin about my age would join me, while she was shopping. We would spend an exhaustive amount of time playing what we called ketch-a-coup or what many refer to as hide-and-seek. There was a store for everything—imported rugs from India, garments from Africa, drugstores, and food stores. Homemade sweets, cakes, drinks, furniture, sold by individuals as well as family enterprises were all represented in that market.

A wave of nostalgia completely engulfed me and I suggested we abort the Big Market with plans of returning and spending more time there. We went back to the hotel and found accommodation poolside. Some fellow countrymen and others who looked like tourists were having fun playing a game with a beach ball. While we were enjoying some cold local drinks after the bustle of Water Street and the heat of the tropical sun, Boogie arrived looking like an expatriate. Dressed in what was known as a shirt-jac, he appeared very important. The shirt-jac is neither a jacket nor a shirt. It looks like a combination of the two: a stylish shirt, loose fitting garment—in his case, tan linen—and worn like a jacket. We admired his so much we went across to Bookers and we each bought three.

Boogie drove us to his home and we met some of our friends from our original group. One of them was the manager of one of the local banks and he and the others had consented to be part of the committee which would administer the scholarship funds. There were still i's to be dotted and t's to be crossed but Boogie had taken care of the groundwork so assiduously that there was not much more to be done. Now that the main purpose of our trip was all but accomplished, we were free to roam with a clear conscience.

The next day we were up early. Around four thirty the streets become extremely busy. Entrepreneurs from the countryside, some in horse drawn carriages, some in trucks, some in donkey carts, bring their wares to the city to be sold alongside city vendors. Others are already on their way to work at the wharves and markets. We decided to head to the Sea Wall, hoping the tide was up. It was, the waves beating against the Sea Wall once more. We remembered going there for a swim many times when we were very young and the sea was in its element. It was always a beautiful time of day, this early morning.

Not much had changed. Maybe there were more people out, exercising, jogging and of course, battling the waves. We watched all this activity, now more mindful of the advanced engineering feat of the Dutch back in the eighteen eighties. When we lived in British Guiana previously, we took all this construction for granted. In their highest splendour the force of the Atlantic could not move its water over the walls and onto the city. The city is below sea level, which meant the walls were the only protection from the flooding of the city.

Still reminiscing, Mike said, "Want to bet we'll run into one of the boys from one of the other groups?" Of course the answer was a resounding "No!" and we did not.

From the Sea Wall it was a short walk to the Pegasus Hotel, the hotel that was new to us. We had brunch outside overlooking the swimming pool. After a meal of local vegetables and fish we were ready to brave the sun in all its radiance by walking back to the Tower; perhaps we only wanted to prove we had not been softened by life in North America. Following a midday nap at our hotel we visited Alwyn's family where we enjoyed a hearty dinner of chicken curry. He had seen them on several occasions since his arrival but this was a first for Mike and me.

The next day it was Mike's and my turn to visit our family and Alwyn decided to move back home while we were away. We had to cross the mouth of the Demerara River on a government steamer called the Queriman, still going strong after all these years. I remember traveling with this ship on many occasions before leaving for North America. Vreed-en-hoop was just a 20-minute ride across the mouth of the Demerara River and since we had arranged for a taxi to take us to Parika after disembarking, the driver drove his vehicle on board while we sat above on deck. We joined him when the boat docked and discovered he was a gold mine of information. He told us the vessel could carry close to one thousand passengers and about forty vehicles and judging from the number of people getting off, we had no reason to doubt him. Vreed-en-hoop to Parika was a distance of about 35 miles on a road in need of repair. There were many other vehicles traveling in our direction as well as children on foot on their way to school, pedestrians going to work, cyclists trying to do the same, donkey carts, dray carts and of course, the ubiquitous animals—dogs and cattle stopping for a rest or a nap in the middle of the road and even ducks and ducklings taking their own time to cross from one side of the narrow road to the other.

With all these obstacles you would expect our driver to be traveling at a tortoise's pace but this was not the case. Instead, as soon as there was an opening in the traffic he would go as fast as possible and slow down only when it was foolhardy not to do otherwise. It was during this period that we were able to see some of the signs indicating our location. They were very imaginative indeed. Here is one I can never forget: 'You are entering Rotterdam.' Some others were Greenwich Park, Israel's Delight, Harlem, and much more. I repeat that they were original names, not to be found anywhere else in the country or in the council records. This was the first time Mike and I were seeing the names of the villages, since we had never traveled this route before. Previously we had taken the train from Vreed-en-hoop to Parika, our destination that day.

Parika is situated at the estuary of the Essequibo River and from there the government steamers had routes to different areas along that river. Our route took us north to Wakenaam, the largest island, then continued to its final destination to the Essequibo coast. There are at least one thousand islands in the river, most uninhabited. You could easily live on one and no one would be the wiser.

Mike and I disembarked at Wakenaam and his sisters were there to meet us. We walked the short distance to their home and were welcomed with a delicious country lunch of fried fish and other delicacies, followed by iced coconut water. They arranged for their neighbour to drive me to Fredericksburg, a distance of four miles, where my mother, grandmother, beaucoup cousins—the entire village, in other words—were waiting for my arrival. My father had died the year after I left for the United States. During my two-day stay in the village I visited every house, spending time with young and old alike, meeting some cousins for the first time. I was also determined to explore some hidden fears of my childhood. I was about four when my grandmother started taking me to a farmer's market in another village, Noitgedacht, about a mile away. The market was always held on a moonlit Saturday night as there was no electricity on the island. Each merchant supplied his own illumination as nightfall approached. We would get there early in the afternoon, around five, and leave for home not later than seven. It was a good time for us, the little ones, as we played hide-and-seek and partook of shaved ice covered with syrup, sugar cakes and all the delicious stuff that played havoc on the teeth.

Once the festive reason for the trip was over, we had the daunting task of walking home ahead of us. We had to walk past the cemetery. I remember instinctively holding on to my grandmother's hand, twisting my head to the left, as the cemetery was on the right. As my steps became stiffer and my grandmother sensed my fear, she would hum a familiar hymn. As soon as we arrived home she presented me with a sweet treat she had bought at the market, and called the servant to make sure I took a shower and brushed my teeth.

As I advanced in age, I would enter the cemetery during the day and take the short cut through the back of the churchyard to the stelling. My father would use that shortcut no matter what the hour, even two or three in the morning, if he had to change the moorings of the boats due to the tides. He had to do it if his helpers were out late dancing in a neighbouring village; he loved to dance himself, so he understood.

The night before my return to Georgetown on this most recent trip to Wakenaam, I wanted to test just how much the early imprinting had on me. I had grown up listening to relatives speak of their encounters with jumbies and ghosts. Even my grandmother confessed that yes, she had seen at least one; it was her turn to nurse a high fever I had and she was looking out of my bedroom window early one morning after re-soaking a bandage in Limacol to keep my head cool. She saw a strange woman in a long white dress, bare feet and with a rose tucked into her long braids. She was of East Indian descent and was not from miles around or she would have recognized her. She had an eerie feeling and went out on the balcony to see what was going on. When she looked again, the woman had disappeared and my grandmother knew she had seen a jumbie, because there was only one road leading to the house and she would have seen someone walking away.

My grandmother had no fear of man, beast, and certainly not of apparitions. She would visit the school and confront any of the bullies who tried to push me around. I did not have to tell her, but some of my cousins did, for the sole purpose of striking fear in the hearts of those who were bigger and stronger than we were. She carried a stick and was not afraid to use it. She read the riot act to a teacher who strapped me for talking in class. When I put my hand to absorb the blow to my backside, the cane landed on my fingers and caused one of them to swell. I did not tell my parents at first, but showed the finger to my grandmother who was not amused. I did not have to be concerned about that teacher again. I had always thought my behaviour had been exemplary until then anyway.

So when my grandmother told me she had seen something unnatural, there was no doubt in my mind that she had.

The night before my departure I thought it would be the right time to test my sophistication. After all, I had left a village without street lights and had been living in the so-called developed world for many years. It was very dark outside.

"Mom, I think I'll go for a little walk. I feel sluggish after feasting on your delicious meal."

"Dis time o'night?" my grandmother piped in.

"It's not that late," I said, looking at my watch. The sun sets precipitously in Guyana around 6 o'clock. There is no foreplay.

"Well, watch out for the Old Higue now," my grandmother teased.

There used to be a woman who lived not too far from us, the first house I had to pass on my way to school; the rumour in the village was that she was an Old Higue. Old Higues only took their form very late at night, after midnight when everyone else was asleep. Their victims were always little children. The Old Higue was able to shed her skin, the legend tells us, and turn herself into a ball of fire and suck the blood of her victims. To protect their children from such a monster, parents had to leave rice scattered by the door where the Old Higue must enter. Each grain of uncooked rice had to be picked up individually and counted before sunrise, as she was only able to operate during the darkness. What a daunting task it was!

I took my leave, content that I would not see the Old Higue—she was too old now and I was no longer a child. The darkness was formidable. I walked briskly, determined to cast aside any fear and get to the stelling as my father had done—early in the mornings or late at night, always walking through the burial ground. I felt no fear as I approached the entrance of the churchyard and it seemed I had reached there faster than I anticipated. Maybe I was walking faster than I realized or was it because distances seem to shrink when we return home as adults. There was a path that led from the road to the steps of the church and I followed it. About ten steps along the path and another ten steps to the left was my father's tombstone. I had paid him a visit the previous day and confirmed my position by daring to use my torchlight—or flashlight—which I had brought. I continued walking forward until I reached the lowest rung of the church steps. So far so good. All I had to do was take a few steps right and get on the path that would take me to the Sea Wall behind the church. Once again I used my light and saw that I was on familiar ground as I proceeded to the Sea Wall and the mangrove trees behind the wall. The Sea Wall, as the name implies, is a wall built along a specific part of the coastline to prevent the tides from encroaching upon the land.

Mangroves usually grow in swamps. The trees have long legs, which are their roots, shaped like large prehistoric spiders. The legs are above the ground and are covered when the tide is up and are exposed when the tide recedes. These roots act as a bulwark against the ravages of the water and the waves. The mangroves looked tall, dark and foreboding, but I was familiar with that area, at least during the day. Every year when we became old enough to be adventurous, about eight years of age, my cousin Willie and I would visit that area around the middle of July to harvest crabs. During the span of three days we would get wicker baskets and scoop the crabs up, as they came floating ashore with the tide and waves like manna from heaven. Just as their appearance was sudden, so was their disappearance. For that short period Willie and I would be dispersing crabs in the village. Boys would come to our yard for a cook-up, some of them having scrounged some corn from a neighbour's field beforehand, and an enjoyable feast would follow one more time. Naturally memories started to make me feel relaxed and I am sure there was a smile on my face. I was back to my childhood happy days with not a care in the world. I had not even dreamed of attending Central High and the move to Georgetown. I was master of all I surveyed.

So here I was less than fifty yards from the familiar mangrove trees, feeling confident, when out of the darkness I thought I heard what sounded like a grunt or cough. I used my torchlight, keeping it on the path close to me, then extending the beam toward the Sea Wall where I saw a man in a khaki suit with a jacket to the knees, a white helmet on his head and smoking a pipe. I could even smell the tobacco. No one dressed like that anymore in our area. For a brief moment I thought: 'There goes my dad pulling a stunt like this,' until I reminded myself that his days of practical jokes were over. The man looked familiar and foreign at the same time. I did not wait to verify what I was seeing. I backed up, said to my legs as that comedic character Stepin Fetchit in the movies said, "Feets, don't fail me now," and I was home before you could say 'Boo.'

"Back already? You look like you just saw a ghost."

I could never fool my mother.

Those two days in Wakenaam were the shortest I had ever spent in my life. It was better than a good feeling to return to a place where there is no pretension, where you are loved, not because of what you have become, but because of who you were, where the memories are always pleasant, and where the roots will remain buried and the trunks get larger and stronger.

My mother would travel back to Georgetown with me and stay with her brother. "Why waste money when I can stay with Uncle Pat?" she replied, when I encouraged her to stay at the hotel with us.

The next day Mike, Alwyn, and I became tourists, walking leisurely to Central High School and through the old neighbourhood, then continuing our stroll to Stabroek Market where we picked up some delicious fresh pineapple. From there we walked along Water Street until we reached Regent Street and found ourselves in front of a restaurant. Alwyn suggested we stop and have a cold drink. We were in the tropics and had worked up not only sweat but a thirst. We had to walk up some steps and as we reached the restaurant floor, I knew I had been there before. On our left was the cash register and bar, and to the right, the dining area. It was déjà vu all over again. To our surprise the owner was not only from Wakenaam, but a relative from my area. This was our lucky day. He insisted that we eat and drink at his expense. He was genuinely glad to see me and we accepted his invitation.

That visit to the restaurant rekindled adolescent memories. Many years before, still in high school in Georgetown, I went home to Wakenaam for the weekend. Performing at my old school in Fredericksburg that Saturday night was a young magician named Vernon doing tricks and entertaining the country folks. Sunday morning about five o'clock the magician and I met on my father's launch on our way to Leguan. We had to travel on a small bus to the other end of the island, where we would board the government steamer for Parika. From Parika we took the train to Vreed-en-hoop and another steamer, the Queriman, which I have already mentioned, to Georgetown. Vernon saw me steer the launch from Wakenaam to Leguan and sat next to me in the bus, owned by my father's first cousin Jas. Vernon regaled me with tales of his visits to the schools all over the country and I must have been hypnotized by his eloquence as I invited him to travel with me in the first class sections of the steamer and train to Vreed-en-Hoop. As I have mentioned before, I knew the captains of the steamers and the pursers who collected the tickets and all I had to do was signify that Vernon was with me. Although my father's launch service was a private enterprise, he was known by everyone working on the steamers and trains and they in turn knew me. All I had to do was mention my father's name. I suppose I was well connected then. I was almost fifteen when I met Vernon and although he was no more than twenty-two he was well-traveled and was already a man of the world. Guyana was a colony then and there was a class distinction. The cost of travel distinguished the first class from the third.

Before Vernon and I said good-bye, we had agreed to meet the following Saturday evening at this very place, which was not this mundane restaurant but a dance hall with a band and beautiful young women for partners. I left home early that evening, telling my mother I was going to visit a sick friend, did my trick with the clock by turning it back one hour, and was out of the house. When I arrived, I leaned my bicycle against the wall and excitedly went upstairs. In those days everything was safe. Now all the windows and doors have safety bars and most people have Rottweiler dogs to protect their property. Luckily, Vernon was there. He seemed to be a regular, popular patron, surrounded by young beautiful ladies, a showcase of the ethnicity of the country: African, East Indian, Amerindians, Portuguese, Chinese, and mixtures of all of the above. He gestured for me to join him and introduced me as if we had been buddies forever. I was overwhelmed. I had never been in the company of such beauties before. I suddenly became their friend and each took her turn inviting me to the dance floor. These girls did not seem much older than I was. The average age was probably 18. There was one girl, tall, slim, erect and dark, whom I was particularly attracted to, especially since she was paying more attention to me than any person of the opposite sex—not including my cousins, of course—either in or out of school had ever done before. Dressed in black with black stockings and black shoes with just the right height heel to make her look regal. As exhilarating as the evening was, I knew I had to be guided by the clock. "Do you have to leave?" she whispered to me, when I announced my departure. I promised to return sometime soon.

Of course, I could not be visiting sick friends every Saturday night. Mother was no fool, even though I believed I had the clock trick down to an art form. As soon as I came home I would turn the clock back to its correct time after she had noted my time of arrival. Years later I realized what a Supermom she was. She let me know that she was aware of my deception. She also knew I was too cautious to get into trouble. Two weeks after my first visit to the dance hall, Mother had to make a quick trip to Wakenaam to see her mother who was under the weather; and since I had a serious cricket match that Saturday she had to go alone. My uncle Pat was supposed to look in on me; I told him I was going to the movies—the late show—with some friends and I would be home about eleven.

You know what happened. I rode my bike to the dance hall and walked in like a regular patron. My magician friend, I was told, was away on a trip to Berbice and would be gone for another week.

"Did you come to see Vernon or did you come to see me?" This came from the girl in black, who then pulled me onto the dance floor and we did our steps. Her name was Barbara. I was excited again. I was truly flattered she was spending all her time with me, telling the men who were asking for a dance, "Not now, Hector; come back later, Ovid." I found out that she had a sister in England who was sending her outfits. She was pleased to have the black nylon stockings because they were a scarce commodity then. Those were the days when ladies, or those who aspired to be, never went out without their stockings. That was the benchmark then. The more ordinary ladies rubbed their legs with coconut oil.

Her sister was reserving a passage for her and she would be leaving soon. I almost said "Don't go," but the words that came out were: "Will you write?" When my friend in black excused herself to go to the ladies' room to freshen up, I was brought back to reality by someone grabbing me by the shoulders. "Wha' you doin' hey, boy? J.D. know you come hey?"

People from our area on the island referred to my father as J.D. and I recognized this man. He had moved to Georgetown and now I had discovered he was a bartender at this place. I was getting nervous. Outwardly, I was not committing a crime, but inwardly, I knew I was breaking some rule. I was having too much fun keeping my blinkers on that I only perceived what I wanted to see. Every time my father paid a visit he would always take me to the late showing of a movie, but the bartender was right; I knew he would not bring me to a place like this. I tried not to show my concern. "What do you mean?" I asked defiantly.

"What do I mean? You na know wha place did is? These women, don't let them fool you wid dey youth and good looks; all ah dem are prosti, limers. Nothing is free. Better not come back hey."

I thanked him profusely, hoping he would adhere to the bartender's code of See No Evil, Hear No Evil, Tell No Evil. Above all, I hoped the news would not travel to Wakenaam. When my lady friend returned, I was expecting her to look different, but of course she didn't. In my young mind I was convinced bartender Eddie had made a mistake in this instance. After all, she was buying me sweet drinks, roti, and curry. I stayed a little longer, then left, and I never returned to that house of ill repute, as one of my friends called such places. Never, that is, until that day with Mike and Alwyn.

Barbara did travel to London where she soon married a rich Englishman and made him very happy. Sitting in the restaurant that day took me back to a time when people were very thoughtful. Compassion ruled and innocence was bliss.

The next day we had a trip planned to visit a friend on the east coast. He was not only a friend but he was part of that special group Les Amis to which a dozen of us belonged. We were young and sentimental.

Our destination on the east coast was a place called Ogle, less than 30 minutes by car. By 11 o'clock we were on our way in a hired car heading east along the Sea Wall. Our trip took a little longer than we had anticipated, because there were more vehicles on the road than when we left those many years previously. It gave us time to read the names painted on some of the trucks and cars, names like Ah We Own, Happy Landing, Just In Time, Sexy Baby, You Can Never Trust A Stranger. Our friend George, a judge in the court system, had grown up in this area and the location of his property was as lovely as the day. The judge's house was situated between the highway and the Atlantic Ocean with the Sea Wall or embankment guarding his property at the back from heavy waves. The front was protected from the public by a high fence and a number of coconut trees, which hid the house from casual view and dampened the noise from the traffic on the road. Inside the compound was a guard house manned by a friendly armed police woman, a tennis court (I remember our friend being a tennis enthusiast) and the main house. The house had three storeys, built along colonial lines with shutters that opened outward. Part of the ground floor housed servants. We were escorted to the entrance by the uniformed guard and a maid was ready to take us to a cozy room. Shortly after we were seated, we were offered glasses with ice and invited to help ourselves from a very well-stocked bar. A chilled bottle of coconut water was nearby. There was a whisper that the Prime Minister was said to have the best assortment of liquor in all of the Caribbean and we wondered if there was a contest among our friends to see who could outdo him. Everywhere we went, we were surprised at the variety of the booze. As we were enjoying our refreshments, the maid appeared again, bowed as the Japanese used to and said, "The Judge soon come."

She also brought us what is called the jelly of the coconut. After removing the top and saving the water, the shell is cut in half and there is the jelly. Delicious. Looking out the windows, we could see a swimming pool with a workman toiling away. The tide was high and its waves were testing the Sea Wall one more time. An overhead fan competed with sea breezes from the ocean. After two servings, our twenty-year-old rum mixed with coconut water began to taste like nectar from the gods. When I thought the feeling that was encompassing me was a personal one, I glanced at my two friends and they seemed to be in the same state as I was—that relaxed hypnotic feeling that makes you have to pinch yourself to realize where you are. A state of unmindfulness, Uncle Poo would have said. Mike broke the spell by voicing under his breath what I was definitely thinking, "This could be the life," and in the same breath, whispered, "Here comes the Judge."

The Judge appeared, looking frail at first glance because we had not seen him for so many years. Thin in the face, as we still say in Guyana, very flat stomach, he was all in white—white long-sleeved cotton shirt, buttoned to the top, white slacks, and white yachtings; I mean tennis shoes with matching socks. He was helped by a woman whom we presumed to be another maid, although she was not dressed like one. She seated him in a comfortable Berbice chair and departed without fanfare. Although his face showed illness, his smile was as radiant as the tropical sky.

"Wha' happening, banna?" He greeted us with a wide grin, showing even, prominent well-kept teeth.

Pleasantries were exchanged, as each of us went up to him and gave him a hug. He used to be a very big part of our extended group. We explained the purpose of our trip. He wanted to tell us about his illness and his battle for recovery. This was his story.

About six months previously, as he was about to leave the country on holiday, he suddenly became ill. For him this was unusual, as he observed good healthy habits, eating well, exercising every day, playing tennis regularly. He was never ever sick. Unexpectedly, he began to feel dizzy at intervals and then everything seemed to be collapsing. Loss of appetite and taste for his favourite Scotch was bad enough, but worst of all, and he smiled when he said this: "I hope it never happens to you, banna, but the boy was dead as a coffin nail."

Consultation with the medical community including specialists, and a visit to Trinidad to seek advice from more specialists didn't help. Neither did the medications. He resorted to prayer, and quoting Charlotte, he said: "The Lord doesn't always come, he sends." She had been with his family almost from his birth, and he had then inherited her from his father after his marriage.

As if on cue, there was a knock, and an older woman, whom I immediately recognized from visiting him at his parents' home, entered the room. He introduced her, since she was more than a servant. She was Charlotte.

"Ah done hot up de tea," she said, handing him a steaming cup of what looked like green tea. He sipped the hot liquid as he continued his story.

Charlotte had suggested he see a woman from Plaisance, which is a nearby village within walking distance. "She see far," Charlotte told him. "She very good."

I have to explain that 'see far' means that she has psychic ability. He continued his story, admitting he could not afford to be a skeptic; the way things were going, the medical gurus in the region were no help. At least this woman's treatment would not produce side effects, as some of the drugs he was taking did. He remembered what his father used to tell him in an effort to motivate him. He had it written on one of the walls of his bedroom. This was at the time when George was trying to show some adolescent independence. His father was a leading attorney in the country and like most fathers had his son's best interests at heart, although the son thought otherwise. The saying went like this: If you don't know where you are going, any road will do.

George said he saw a different interpretation of those words this time around. Now they meant he had tried the best in conventional medicine and was losing the battle, so why not try other routes? Charlotte took the initiative and brought this healer to the house, and the woman, known as Granny Holder, took charge. After she had talked to him and inquired about his medical problem and his feelings, she held his hands, looked into his eyes and asked him why he thought he was ill. "Was it juh-juh?" she asked.

Juh-juh means bad luck and I suppose she must have meant whether his bad luck came from his doing or from his enemies. Many people still believed in obeah men, men who practised some form of spiritualism or witchcraft and are supposed to have powers to hurt or heal. Maybe some enemy had worked obeah on him. He didn't know. She promised she would return early the next day. And early she was. Since he had become very ill, he had moved into the guest bedroom, not wanting to inconvenience his wife. There Charlotte could check on him and not disturb her. Of course, his wife was very attentive too, but since his care demanded so much energy, they had agreed to spare the wife much of the turmoil. She still had the household to run and children to oversee. Children? Twin boys, about ten years of age.

Granny Rogers arrived early and with the help of Charlotte placed him in the tub. At this stage he could hardly walk. A hot blue bath, as hot as was bearable. Granny would not explain the blueness to anybody. After the bath, she placed a blanket on the floor and dried him off, massaging him, even the boy, with special oil she had brought. This was followed by a special tea which she prepared in the kitchen. Bush tea, she called it, brewed from bushes on her property. It was to be taken five times a day. His dietary habits, as you can guess, had to be changed. No meat, some kind of fish soup, and of course, the popular lentil soups, especially split pea with some shrimp thrown in. Twice a week he would have foo-foo added to the soup. I had my share of foo-foo when I was very young. Whenever my mother had to be away, she left my grandmother in charge of the household and we had foo-foo soup every day in her absence. Foo-foo is made from plantains pounded in a mortar with a pestle. Imagine a block of wood with a part scooped out. That's the mortar, and the pestle is a cylindrical-shaped piece of wood with a rounded end. Once you have pounded the boiled plantains into a cohesive mass, you separate it into small rolls, and drop them into the soup like dumplings. After three weeks of baths, massages, and soup she asked him not to take his medication anymore.

"Should I throw them away?" he queried.

"Ah don't care what you do, jus don't take them anymore."

Shortly after this he started to feel some improvement but didn't tell anyone, including his wife. Charlotte had moved a cot into his room and was awake the minute he was. She had the instinct to know when he was awake and when he was sleeping. Charlotte was like a mother to him, having been with him all those years. His own mother had died shortly after he was born. Within a month of his alternative treatment he was sleeping soundly for long hours and feeling a profound sense of relief. Charlotte removed her cot and had an electrician install a bell for communication.

Granny must have been wiser than he had ever imagined. Although she continued the regimen of hot baths and massages, she avoided massaging the penis area. Her name may have been Granny, not because of her age but because of her knowledge. She was not much older than the Judge, and was tall, slim, and very attractive. He was glad she was so intuitive, because he did not want to be embarrassed. He knew he was improving—the boy was letting him know. The Judge paused in his narration to allow Alwyn to go and return from the washroom and before resuming, explained that his wife was away in Georgetown attending a parent-teacher interview. She would be home shortly.

"I am back, I am back," he shouted, referring to his road to recovery. Within minutes Charlotte was there with more ice and fresh glasses. He offered us some Scotch, but we preferred our twenty-year-old rum. Charlotte poured him a half shot of Scotch from an unfamiliar unopened bottle after dripping a little on the floor as a deference to the spirits of the dearly departed. He made a toast to our health and vigour, then took a sip, the first and only one since his illness.

"Hope you hungry, bruddahs." This remark from Judge George was good news; we had not eaten in awhile. Then: "How does hassa curry and guana sound?"

My mouth was watering. Hassar is a fish found in the trenches, not rivers, and guana is iguana, a very large lizard that lives in trees and eats only leaves. Growing up in Wakenaam, I had my fair share of both. As a boy we would catch the iguana—or more truthfully, my friends would do the catching—and have a cook-up at a friend's house when his parents were away. The iguana is more delicious than any meat I have ever tasted. It was a hearty and delicious feast and we returned to our breezy front room and fixed ourselves a fresh drink of rum and coconut water. Not only is the taste commendable but the combination never leaves a residue in our system. Translation: no headaches, no hangovers. I wish I could bottle that combination like the British have done with their shandy.

"Now that you have a full belly," the Judge continued, "I want you to meet the person responsible for my recuperation. I want you to meet Granny Holder." There was a rap on the door and in walked a woman who did not look at all like any of our grandmothers. She was above average height, well-built in almost athletic proportions, olive complexion, long curly hair drawn back in a bun at the back of her neck and a granny scarf over her head. No makeup, but she didn't need any. We knew from her features (and this was confirmed later) that she was a mix of an African Guyanese father and one of the indigenous peoples of Guyana, the Arawaks. Granny's voice had a soft, hypnotic sound. The Judge told her he had sung her praises to his sophisticated ex-Guyanese friends who have been in an alien culture too long. He wondered why we would choose to live elsewhere as second-class citizens. He said this with a wink and a nod and she lowered her head, showing a radiant smile. After he had finished his praises of her, which seemed to embarrass her, she started to say good-bye. Before she could finish, the Judge interrupted, looking at each of us: "Banna, anything you want to ask Granny?"

In unison, Mike and I shouted, "No man," but nothing was heard from Alwyn. All eyes were then naturally focused on him and after a few seconds he shifted in his seat and said in almost a whisper: "Maybe."

"Maybe or yes?" asked the Judge.

"Why not? Yes."

Without hesitation, she pulled her chair closer, facing him, then took his hand. In a gentle voice she told him to think only of the one question he wanted answered, and she would try to comply. Did he want to hear the answer privately or in front of us, his friends. He chose the latter. She continued to hold his hands and I can still hear her voice after all these years.

"Very well, then. Close your eyes and take a deep breath and listen to me. You will hear my voice and it will become the voice of your mother. You will be a little boy again and you will be relaxed and happy."

She placed his hands on his legs, then moved her hands to each side of her head and after a few moments, her hands dropped. I mean they really dropped in her lap, and at the same time her head began to bow until it touched her collarbone and her eyes closed. In a deep, low voice she began to speak to him.

"Because your father told you many years ago never to get married, you believe you have insulted his memory by doing so more than once. You find yourself in a quandary, not knowing if you married for love or because you wanted to prove your manhood by disobeying your father. Perhaps he did not mean never, which is a long time, but only until you gave yourself time to grow. Because your mother brought you up to be kind and compassionate, you could never misuse those women you chose to marry. To find the peace and understanding you seek, find the woman without seeds. She will seek you out and you will recognize her because she speaks like you. You might forget what I have said here today but in due time it will come back to you."

Suddenly there was a remarkable change in her voice and speech when she gave Alwyn his final piece of advice: "Na brace em, na tase em fuh six weeks." Her breathing changed, she opened her eyes, looked around the room, smiled and rose to her feet."Tomorrow, Judge?" When he nodded, she took her exit.

As my English-born cousin would have said, "What a woe-man!" Alwyn remained seated with eyes closed for a few minutes after she left. He seemed to be concentrating, almost as if he was unable to move. As the seconds ticked away, he finally stood up, stretched, rubbed his eyes and said, "That was something else. Eerie but amazing. A lot of memories scratched."

"What did she mean?" curious Mike asked, "about not marrying? Not obeying Daddy?"

"She was close to the mark. Only it was my mother's admonition, not my dad's. I am sure I told you the time I called or visited this friend from Central at her home one Friday evening, and who would show up? My dad, of course. The girl and I were sitting in the front room and in he walks, suit and tie. I suppose he was visiting the mother, since there was no father, but I didn't stay around to find out. My mother probably knew about it or there may have been others and maybe she was trying to tell me something with this advice. No, my dad and I never discussed it and I never talked to that girl again."

"George, tell us in plain Guyanese what the phrase 'na brace em, na tase em' means."

The Judge began to titter." 'Na brace em' is one piece of advice you are not going to relish. It means you have to keep your zippers up, no fooping for six weeks. Only thing I don't understand is when does the time count begin? Six weeks from now or six weeks from the time you meet your soul mate?"

Just then someone cleared her throat and we turned our attention to the door to greet one beautiful woman by any standard.

"Ah, there you are. Come, dear, and meet some old comrades." The Judge introduced his wife Evelyn who then joined us for a few minutes. She had a soft dulcet tone to her voice and was very attractive with short curly hair and smooth brown skin. She was of medium height and was wearing a pink blouse, short white skirt, and white sandals with heels. Just looking at her, we knew she was a dugla; we learned her mother was East Indian and her father was of African descent. After she left, the Judge said, "Isn't she a doll?"

We concurred. He was thankful that he was associated with bright, sensible women. Granny Holder, a recent entry into his life, who pretended to be a simple country girl, had graduated from Bishops High School, one of the leading high schools for girls. She had been outstanding in both academia and athletics. After high school she worked as an administrative assistant at the Ministry of the Interior and spent some years in the hinterland close to the border with Brazil where she developed an interest in folk medicine and psychology. All her spare time was devoted to enhancing her knowledge in those disciplines, and because she was in an isolated area, she was able to maintain her focus. When she thought she was ready, she resigned her day job and devoted her time to her calling, as she referred to her work. Evelyn had a double degree in anthropology and sociology from a university in the U.K. and was doing research toward a book on the Arawaks and the Wai-Wais, two indigenous tribes in the country. And of course, there was Charlotte, who was more than a servant, as I have already explained.

Boogie arrived and we were invited for some more gustatory delights—large curried shrimp, which were called prawns. Since we had left for the United States, offshore fishing had become a giant industry. Local entrepreneurs were in on the business along with Japanese and American interests. These very prawns—or I should say, their relatives—had found their way into the supermarkets of North America. The Judge suggested we sample his medicinal soup and it was surprisingly appetizing. No wonder he was on the fast track to recovery. It was a very relaxing and enjoyable reunion but we knew we were intruding on his schedule, so we reluctantly bid adieu. George kept some parting words for us: "Want to have a happy married life?" Without waiting for confirmation, he continued, "Have low expectations of your mate. Have a safe trip and stay in touch."

We teased Alwyn telling him later that the Judge was giving him a parting message since only he was the marrying kind. The Judge did recover and he and his family were able to spend some time with us in Toronto. My Uncle Pat had a different slant on the same subject: "Tek her to the Sea Wall for a walk. If you got to keep up wid she, dat's no good. If she walk side by side wid you, dat's not too bad, but if she always a little behind and you got to slow down, dat's the one. Keep her."

Before leaving Guyana we promised to visit Kaieteur Falls, located in the interior on the Potaro River. While we were making arrangements for our trip, the receptionist at the hotel told us to be sure and look for the rainbow over the falls. We were indeed rewarded with a view of a circular rainbow that radiated below and above the falls. Kaieteur Falls drop over seven hundred and forty feet and most visitors claim it is more spectacular than Niagara. Years later on another visit to Kaieteur my wife-to-be was with me and it was there, marveling at the cascading waters and colours of the rainbow at the foot of the falls that she agreed to change her name.

Despite our wonderful reunions, we were in one way not sad to leave, though for me to leave my mother, grandmother, and Uncle Pat, the emotion was quite mixed. During our conversation on the plane ride to Toronto the subject of returning to Guyana on a permanent basis did come up several times. Once we had landed and were driving through the regulated traffic, observing with admiration the well-maintained parapets on the sides of the highway and the clean streets, each of us realized it was not so easy to go home again.

Being inseparable friends for such a long time, we were surprised to discover on our trip back to Toronto that Alwyn had kept a part of his life in D.C. a secret from Mike and me. Apparently Granny Holder had had a profound influence in his motivation to confess. In the middle of his revelation, I became introspective, wondering what lies I had told them, lies of omission or commission.

While we were in D.C. I was able to find work for Alwyn at the Cairo after one of the bellhops had completed his job of robbing a bank and was about to leave undetected when an off-duty policeman tried to prevent his escape. Instead he was rendered helpless by an uppercut he was too slow to see coming. From this very bellhop who had taken me under his wing when I started working at the Cairo, I leaned how the term bellhop had originated. In olden days if the clerk at the desk wanted to page a guest a young man handling the baggage was given a slate with the person's name on it. He traversed the lobby ringing the bell until the person answered. The name then was bellboy and later changed to bellhop when men took over the job. I suppose they had to do some hopping as well. Of course the modern bellhop has to greet guests as they arrive, get their luggage, and lead them to the registration desk. Sad to say that the genus of the bellhop has virtually disappeared.

I secured the job for Alwyn when the bellhop-bankrobber became persona non grata in and out of the Cairo Hotel. He was still new at the job working the three-to-eleven PM shift when a guest without luggage visited the hotel. This suggested to the cognoscenti that even though the gentleman was obliged to pay the full price, he did not plan to stay the usual length of time (in the inner city I was told a room could be rented for two or three dollars for a couple of hours or more), especially since he was accompanied by a beguiling young model type. The gentleman hooked up with Alwyn on his first visit requesting whiskey, ice, chasers, and special cigars. When Alwyn told me he had him running all over the block to procure these items, I had to sit him down and indoctrinate him in the ways of a successful bellhop. Every job had its own style and to be frank, its own hustle. Even though Alwyn's service was not up to par that first time, he received a folded bill in his palm instead of the quarter he expected. We had decided to call his client Diamond Jim. Jim was his first name and he had diamonds everywhere—rings, cufflinks, tie pin. The appellation was on the mark.

On his next visit, although Alwyn was occupied with another guest somewhere in the hotel, Diamond Jim waited until he was available to take him up. Alwyn wasted no time, hurrying down again immediately to fulfill the request. Since the order was the same as before he had the Jim Beam, ice, chasers, and special cigars ready to take back up in a jiffy. Here is Alwyn's story in his words.

"The tip was more than considerate. I would have taken a quarter just to see that seductive witch on the bed. As I was taking my leave, Jim said, 'Care to join us for a drink?' 'Us' meant Jim and the delectable young thing, sprawled on the bed with the shortest of negligees, showing off long beautiful legs and thighs and full boobs with nipples like very large raisins, maybe the colour of raisins but more the size of grapes waiting to be suckled.

'No, sir, wish I could,' I replied without a trace of enthusiasm, 'but I am on duty, you know.'

'Oh, please, Al, for my sake.' This from the lady in the most syrupy voice I have ever heard.

'Okay, a short quick one then.'

Jim poured me a stiff drink and while I was sipping it and wondering what was really going on, he whispered, 'I have a proposition.'

'Yeah? What kind of proposition?'

'Ethel here wants you to bang her while I watch.'

He must have seen the expression on my face because he immediately retorted: 'Okay, I'll go in the closet, close the door, and peep.'

I protested vehemently but Ethel begged so much I had to acquiesce. I could not stand there and see that beautiful woman ruin her makeup. And that was the start of a liaison that went on for the duration of my stay at the Cairo. Each week Jim came in with a different model and the tip went up every time."

"Models, my eye," Mike laughed mockingly. "Hope you don't go blind in your old age."

"Don't be a skunt," Alwyn replied.

Alwyn's excuse for not telling us about his injudicious conduct at the Cairo was quite understandable. He believed his relationship with Peeping Diamond Jim was a behavioural solecism, a grave indiscretion which was not something to shout about. Alwyn's revelation started me thinking that Granny H possibly had an effect on all of us, even though her attention was focused on him. Maybe her thoughts were like a leaking umbrella drenching all of us standing under it. Before realizing what I was about to relate, I started telling them something in my past that I thought only two people knew at the time, and one was no longer living.

"Remember that Old Year's party I took you to? It was given by a Guyanese entrepreneur who owned beauty salons around Washington and was making his own beauty products."

"Of course we remember," Mike replied. "That's when you met that pre-med student from Guyana and had your nose wide open."

"Right. I went home with her and the next day I left for the Cairo from there."

"Yes, and you came home and said how you had fooped all night and day and you were as tired as a stray dog," said Alwyn.

Mike added, "How you had a hard time because she was a virgin."

"I remember saying all that and most of it is a lie."

"Say what?"

"That's right. I made up the fooping part. We never did. She said she had never been with a man in that way and that's the way she was going to remain until I was ready for the ceremony. 'So I would have something to look forward to,' she had giggled."

"Is that the truth?" Alwyn queried.

"That's the truth, I swear to it. You remember she went to medical school in France shortly before I left for Nashville? I still have some of her letters from Paris."

"Yes, and I remember she died there while she was in school."

"Sorry again, my man," Alwyn muttered.

"That's a first for you lying about women."

"That time I did and now I'm sorry."

"Her name was Minnie, wasn't it?" Mike asked.

"Never knew you had such a good memory."

"I remember important things, my friend. Maybe it's the rarefied air we're breathing. But I too have to correct something I told you both." Mike became quiet, thoughtful, and very fidgety.

"What's the matter? Cat got your tongue?" Alwyn asked.

"Remember I told you the reason Joy and I broke up?"

"Sure, because of your bent attitude." I said.

"Because you caught her in bed with a bald-headed midget?" Alwyn laughed.

"Get serious."

"We give up."

"I caught her in bed all right, but it was with a woman."

"Get outta hey!"

"I caught her in bed with that bitch April. I did not want to tell you because I was sure I would never hear the end of it. A woman taking my woman away. That I was not man enough."

"We would never be that cruel, man." said Alwyn.

"No more secrets from now on, okay?" I said.

"Right."

"Right."

So we had visited Guyana, had seen old friends and family and had arranged to pay back some dues by setting up the scholarship fund. Back in Toronto it didn't take us long to get into the groove. Two weeks after our return we honoured our first invitation. It was at Sharon's and when we arrived about ten, the party was in full swing. Sharon and Betty greeted us like lost relatives and introduced us to some people we had not met. It was truly a diverse ethnic mixture. The hosts looked radiant in floor length dresses and could have been models for the Wonder Bra outfit. Betty brought us drinks and snacks and made sure we mingled with all the guests. Later in the evening I noticed Betty and Alwyn in animated conversation, only to be foiled by Sharon dragging him to the dance floor. Did I tell you he was a very good dancer? I always have this picture of him doing the splits at one of the dances we crashed when we were teenagers, long before we ever thought of the United States. Why do some images make such indelible impressions on my memory? I guess the splits have disappeared like the jitterbug—he was master of that too. He seemed to be really enjoying himself, dancing with both Betty and Sharon and some of the other beauties.

The day after the party Alwyn came over. There was nothing unusual about his visit, except this Sunday he seemed restless, pacing up and down, as if he was carrying on his broad shoulders the problems of the entire world.

"What's the matter with you today?" Mike blurted out. "You seem so fidgety."

"You notice."

"Did either of you see anything out of place last night at the party?" Alwyn asked after clearing his throat several times.

"Nope"

"Nothing unusual?"

"No."

"Didn't Betty seem more carefree than in previous times?"

"Maybe she was free at last," Mike said, trying to be humourous. "No?"

"And where was her partner?" Alwyn continued.

"Man, if you have something to say, say it. Don't beat about the bush."

"All right, here it is. Betty made a confession to me."

"Another?"

"That's right. She is not a lesbian. Never was."

"Then why the heck did she—?"

"Say she was?" Alwyn interrupted. "She thought that was the only ruse she could use to end our relationship. That Betty Bad episode had nothing to do with it either. I believe there is no memory of that afternoon."

"That's it?"

"Yes, that's all there is to it. Now she wants us to remain friends."

"Well, that's wonderful, Shortman."

Another season for golf had arrived and I would see Sharon on and off the golf course. At one particular course where she and her parents held a membership and where I golfed occasionally I would sometimes arrange a game with her. She had a respectable handicap as befitted a talented golfer. She had started golfing in British Guiana and when she arrived in Canada, was smart enough to seek out a coach. As a matter of fact, it was a family affair, as her parents had a passion for the game and took lessons from the same coach. When they hosted their annual tournament, guests came from as far away as Buffalo, New York.

Sharon was a frequent visitor to our house on weekends, as were many unattached male and female friends. And Alwyn, of course, was over every weekend; he did not need an invitation, as he still had his key to the place. Those warm days of summer were our days of glory. Alwyn with his karmic reasoning always wondered whether our abhorrence of the cold winter days was one way of teaching us about suffering, which he said is inevitable. Mike laughed at the idea and I pleaded for time to think about his theory.

One Friday Alwyn called to invite us to a late lunch the next day. Bring one of your kangalangs. We may go out to eat at a restaurant later.

"I beg your pardon?" I said sarcastically.

"Bring a broad and don't be late, giving me the time he expected us to arrive."

The invitation was for Mike and me to bring dates. Mike had his Bibi and I was undecided on my choice of date. Although Uncle Pat had advised me about variety being the nub of youthful pleasure, I am sure I was not consciously listening to his counsel.

I thought of Mrs. K

Do you remember Mrs. K? She had befriended us early when we arrived in Toronto. I had met her through my first professional employment and she had actually encouraged us to purchase our first property. She would invite me to her home where we would listen to the music of Miles Davis and munch on cheese and crackers while we quenched our thirst with homemade wine. Although I was a also a fan of M. Davis, I nevertheless took a couple of records of Nina Simone and a recording of Mark Holder who was making a name for himself in the Caribbean world. He is also my mother's nephew.

Mrs. K always dressed casually, wearing those muu-muu dresses of the period that concealed all shapes and sizes. She had a very attractive face, was about five seven and in her thirties. I never did ask the lady her age. She never asked mine, though I'm sure she would never have guessed. Throughout my life I have always been thought to be younger than I really was. She was what women these days euphemistically refer to as full-bodied. Romance never entered the picture.

Two months before Alwyn's party Mrs. K had telephoned and invited me over. She had a favour to ask. She had to be away for about six weeks and wanted me to keep an eye on her property. "Make it look like I am still here," she explained, meaning that I was to turn on some lights and keep an eye on her plants. I took my assignment seriously, checking in every day and doing what I had promised to do. After a little over six weeks Mrs. K returned and when she greeted me at her door, she was wearing a smaller version of her muu-muu. An opening from the waist up revealed cleavage that I always suspected was there. Confirming it in the flesh, I almost felt giddy.

"Have I come to the wrong address?"

"You certainly have not. Come on in and make yourself a home," she said, grabbing my hand.

I had just finished playing nine holes of golf and was glad I had the prescience to shower and change clothing for what seemed to be an invitation to lunch. I remember just about everything from that day, including the menu. Chicken in champagne sauce followed appropriately by several glasses of champagne. We listened to *I Loves You Porgy* several times, among other songs by Nina Simone. People keep saying money can't buy happiness, well, perhaps not, but what about beauty? That fat farm had sold Mrs. K something. Now she had a body to match her face.

The night before Alwyn's brunch I called Mrs. K and invited her.

"Oh, let me check my calendar. I don't just sit and wait for your call, you know."

"I am sure you don't."

"Okay, I am free tomorrow."

I told her what time I would call for her and she sounded very happy to be included. The next day I picked her up with Mike and Bibi and drove to Alwyn's home. We arrived a few minutes before our scheduled time and Mike said, "Let's be very English today and surprise him." The English for the most part are always on time. West Indians, and I am including Guyanese, are always late.

"It's the heat that slows you down, Pappy," one of my daughters once told me. "The sun saps your energy." When I arrived on campus at Howard I could almost always spot the Americans because they walked briskly around the campus. They had to, growing up in the cold.

We did not upset our host by our early arrival. He greeted us in a relaxed, effusive and gracious manner in his expensive smoking jacket. He seemed more carefree and elegant than I had observed him to be for some time, and thinking it was the jacket that created his mood I considered purchasing a smoking jacket also.

Of course, we were never slouches in our custom-made suits. A new one every three or four months from an Italian tailor on Dundas Street in the latest style. Imported fabric was standard fare for all of us.

Being the first ones there, we sampled the spread, especially the warm black pudding that Phyllis our cook prepared for him on a weekly basis. In our teens our trip to Camp Street in Georgetown on a Saturday evening was never complete without copious portions of black pudding from yes, the Black Pudding Lady. Ending up on Camp Street and the intersecting Regent Street was the equivalent of my daughters and their friends going to Whyte Avenue in Edmonton or the way it used to be on Yonge Street in Toronto in the sixties. Alwyn left us munching and reappeared with the beautiful Sharon dressed in an almost floor-length black dress with a low-cut top that showed a gold golf pendant on a gold chain. They were holding hands and smiling from bicuspid to bicuspid. Mike whispered so everyone could hear: "Dis could be the start of something large," then hummed, "You're nobody till somebody loves you."

I introduced Mrs. K to Sharon. Almost immediately the other guests arrived. There were four in the group—a married couple and a couple living together. The married ones were Heinz, a German immigrant, and his Jamaican-born wife Marjorie. He was a trained mechanical engineer with qualifications from Germany but because of the protocol and energy he would have had to expend to be certified in Canada, he opted to open a motor car repair business, catering mostly to import cars. With his skill and hard work he was able to turn it into a successful business. His wife was a registered nurse and their only child was a young son who was proving to be a musical prodigy.

The relationship of the other couple I found intriguing. Malcolm came to Canada with his parents from Trinidad when he was ten and was product of the public school system. He himself graduated as a public school teacher, and started playing in a band on weekends and holidays. He enjoyed his second job so much and was in such demand that he quit his day job and became a full-fledged musician, fronting his own combo. His instrument was the piano and he was well regarded by the public as well as other musicians. His girlfriend Jessica was of a different stripe. During the day she worked as an efficient assistant for one of the larger legal firms on Bay Street and at night became a high-priced call girl. Malcolm was quick to point out that Jessica was not really *une fille de joie*. He could never allow himself to call her a harlot. She was not involved in any sexual activity but was only titillating the imagination of her clientele—men who were all rich and strange. Her identity was never compromised, since she was always in costume, her features covered with a variety of masks. He claimed that this was his most satisfying relationship. Previously he had women whom he let stay at home and when he was at work, they found time to play and give it away freely. He summed them all up by paraphrasing Ray Charles—"I took them to the night club and the whole band knew their names."

Later we did go out to dinner at the Royal York Hotel opposite Union Station and had a wonderful meal including wine. Alwyn grabbed the check, actually snatching it from the fingers of Mike. We ended up on Yonge Street listening to some jazz by a group from the United States.

Malcolm and Jessica were our hosts for this sector of the evening. Almost immediately upon arriving at the club, Malcolm was coerced into joining the band. His virtuosity on the piano had us mesmerized once more. When he played *Time After Time*, Mike shouted: "Move over, Oscar P" and when he followed with *Misty*, Mrs. K stood up and screamed, "So long, Errol." My aural senses reminded me of my mother explaining what a busman's holiday is and Malcolm's performance reinforced that memory. It was truly a night to remember; love was finally in the air.

Alwyn had found communion with Sharon and now they spent most of their free time together. No longer did they have to meet surreptitiously, arriving at our place and pretending it was accidental meeting. Now they arrived and left together. One day after work he came alone and I was in a small room next to the kitchen. It used to be a pantry but Mike had it converted into a workshop where I could tinker with my clubs. I was replacing a shaft and concentrating on the task, when I heard him say, "See my grip?"

Naturally I thought he was referring to a suitcase, which he kept at our home with shaving supplies and underclothes, if he had to sleep over. You have to understand that growing up in British Guiana, anything that held clothing for traveling was known as a grip. My reply was, "It's in the place where you always keep it."

"What you talking 'bout? Look here." I looked and he had one of my clubs in his hand. "Don't be daft I want you to show me how to grip this club."

"What for?" I replied. "You don't golf. Or are you taking up such a pedestrian game?"

That was when the cat was let out of the bag. Sharon had introduced him to the game and her coach. Mike was yet to be converted.

I did not have the heart to tell Alwyn what pleasure and disappointment were to be experienced by him if he continued to play the game. Hard work too since golf is not an easy game and knowing him, I was sure he would want to excel or at least see some improvement.

Early in the fall, Ulric called and suggested a trip to Barbados. His technician, who was in charge of his laboratory where they did some o f their work, was Barbadian-born and was offering the use of a cottage. He had a brother in Barbados and we would have a car at our disposal. Ulric drove to Toronto and parked his car at the terminal and we flew from there to Barbados. He had brought a friend Dale, who was a lieutenant in the Detroit Police Force. He was no stranger to me as we had golfed in the Detroit area a few times and we had met socially on other occasions. This was Dale's first visit to the West Indies and he was truly impressed that the country was governed by leaders who were of the same ethnic origin as he was.

"You sure about that?" Dale queried as I tried to explain that the British had long departed.

"Sure, I am sure. Just as I am sure that Miltiades, the thirty-second pope was of African ethnicity and a Catholic."

On our arrival we were met by our Barbadian friend and driven to the cottage, given the keys to both it and the car, along with his phone number to call any time we needed anything. There was a well-furnished bar and a kitchen cupboard with breakfast supplies and a well-stocked refrigerator.

We did not waste much time getting to the golf course the next morning. The sun was in its glory and although it had been some time, I still enjoyed the tropical flavour—that is, the heat and warm breeze. Even with carts we may have expended too much energy playing twenty-seven holes, so we decided to take respite from the fun and games. Both Ulric and Dale planned to enjoy a midday siesta while I had other thoughts reverberating in my soul.

I availed myself of the opportunity to put into action a plan that had occupied my mind for some time. My maternal grandfather was Barbados-born and as a young man he worked in the sugar industry in a skilled position. Many Barbadian as well as Guyanese men would take advantage of their talent and work in both Barbados and British Guiana during the harvest seasons: cane to molasses to rum. My grandfather visited British Guiana as a young man and loved it so much that he stayed and never returned to Barbados. My project was to trace his roots, as I had no knowledge of his background except his name. There is an area in Barbados called Holder's Village, and since that was his surname, that's where I intended to start.

I hired a driver and we proceeded toward that destination, stopping in some of the shops or stores to ask anyone whom I thought might be old enough to know. I spent the better part of three hours without getting a snippet of information. Not wanting to give up too easily, we continued until I spotted a little house on a quiet street that caught my attention. It was well-kept, painted white with green shutters that opened outward, and a green fence surrounded the property, which was large for such a small house. There were bougainvillea in the front and what looked like a vegetable garden at the back. We had driven around the block a few times without seeing any activity. A sign read: Property of J.A. Holder. No Trespassing.

I dismissed any apprehension I was feeling and knocked on the front door. An older man opened the door—a tall, brown skin man with hair slightly grey on the sides, darker on top, and cut to about half an inch in height. He was over six feet and must have weighed about one hundred and seventy-five pounds, but it was hard to guess his age; his height and weight I fathomed from comparison to me. He had a grayish, thin moustache, and a beard, also grayish, extending to the angle of his chin. He was holding a pipe in his right hand and looked so familiar that right away I thought of my Uncle Pat. I could hear my grandmother's voice whispering to me, "Family can't hide."

I suppose she was telling me that it is easy to see the resemblance in families. I can recall going downtown with each of my daughters and have her mistaken for one of her sisters. And they had all lived in that small town until they left for college.

"Mr. Holder?" I ventured.

"Yes. Do I know you?"

"No, sir."

"Then how can I help you?"

"If I can have a few moments of your time, perhaps I may be able to judge."

"All right. Come in."

Almost immediately I knew he was living alone. It was a large room that served as a living and dining area. Bookshelves took over the expanse of one wall and a couple of guitars and a banjo lay on a shelf on another wall. Two couches, coffee table, three chairs, and two rocking chairs were the extent of the furniture. A well-fed brown cat with light stripes was enjoying his siesta on one of the couches. He was stretched out, fully relaxed. After a quick look in our direction, he indulged in a hearty stretch and wide open yawn, then covered his eyes with paws and completely ignored us. Mr. Holder pointed to one of the rocking chairs at the coffee table for me to sit and he took the other.

I told him of my quest to find the genealogical tree of my grandfather, giving him his three given names, his surname, and his job description. Nothing rang a bell. I could see he felt ineffectual at not being able to help. If he was circumspect when I knocked on his door, he was now more relaxed and hospitable. When he apologized for not being able to offer any insight, I remarked that the two initials on the No Trespassing sign were the same as mine: I then asked him his full name. "One out of two ain't bad," I said to him when he told me.

"What do you mean?"

"We have the same first name, you know."

"How could that be?" he asked, looking overwhelmed.

"I can't tell you, sir."

Nothing was said for a minute or two, as he stood up and walked to the kitchen, then returned almost immediately. "You had lunch yet?"

When I said no, he offered to prepare lunch for me and my driver, who by now was sound asleep in the car. Mr. Holder was an efficient cook, having already begun marinating before we arrived. *Le déjeuner du jour* was boned Barbados flying fish in a sauce, with homegrown carrots, greens, and rice, washed down with a bottle of *Beaujolais Moulin-à-Vent* no less. Mr. Holder explained to us that there are Beaujolais and there are Beaujolais. Some are deemed young wines, which meant consumption had to be within two to three years. The one we were enjoying can age in the bottle and get better with time. Uncle Pat, to my knowledge, was never a wine connoisseur, but was fond of saying: 'The older the wine, the sweeter the taste.' I have a feeling he was thinking of something else.

No matter what the reference was, I told Mr. Holder it was indeed a privilege to share such a precious commodity with him. Although there was no proving it, he said he felt a deep sense of kinship between us and invited me to visit whenever I was on the island. In his younger days he was a musician and was employed on one of those tourist ships that frequent the Caribbean. He had formed a relationship with one of the passengers and every year she would bring him bottles of French wine. She was well-connected and when she stopped traveling she made sure a supply of precious French wine was delivered to him.

Let me explain the mystery of the flying fish. When I was still a boy in short pants in British Guiana and had heard of Bajan flying fish, I always conjured images of fish flying above the water like birds. Mr. Holder explained that during a particular time of year the water reached a certain temperature which facilitated the fish in leaping out more like high jumpers. This gave the impression that they were flying. Perhaps it was a similar phenomenon that accounted for the crabs walking ashore in that part of the Atlantic that touched Fredericksburg.

Bajan is a contraction of Barbadian, by the way.

Later he lit his pipe and brought out fresh glasses and poured us each a drink from a keg sitting on a shelf. We drank it the way he did, straight, no chaser, and it was as smooth as syrup. We talked for awhile, killing time, sipping our drink, and when we thought an appropriate interval had elapsed before saying thank you and farewell, Mr. Holder objected with "Oh no, no. A bird doesn't fly on one wing." He proceeded to pour us another drink and I noticed that it was noticeably less than the previous one this time.

Back home December brought weather not to our liking. Continuous snowfall ushered in cold temperatures. My cousin Patrick was to pay us a visit from the United Kingdom and we hoped the weather would show a kinder face by the time of his arrival. We kept up the Guyanese Christmas tradition of preparing black cake and ginger beer weeks in advance. Patrick was known as Brap when we were young, and some names, false ones in the case of Brap, remain throughout the person's life. So Patrick was still known as Brap in the U.K. by friends and acquaintances. Brap was the cousin who accompanied me to the punt trench for our afternoon of swimming when we were confronted by my mother on our return home. He had been living in England for years where he was the leader of a steel band, then became a bodyguard for a well-known actor from British Guiana and parlayed this relationship into bit parts in the movies. This was his first visit to North America and we were determined to make his visit a memorable one.

Christmas day started early with a bang, playing the appropriate music, even some recorded steel band music which Brap was kind enough to bring. Our annual custom of garlic pork, pepper pot, and ginger beer transported us to a different time and place for the rest of the day. We were back in the British Guiana of our youth. Boxing Day we paid a visit to the Casa Loma ballroom where Byron Lee and the Dragonnaires, originally from Jamaica but more of an international group at that time, and with their peripatetic lifestyle they probably returned to Jamaica only to catch their breath. Needless to say, Brap knew the members of the band and they knew him.

Casa Loma is really a castle in Toronto, built around 1914 by a financier to fulfill his childhood dream of owning such a palace. Hard times befell him and the city of Toronto became the owner. For many years the castle was unoccupied and the city fathers were contemplating tearing it down until in 1937 the Kiwanis Club of West Toronto suggested turning it into a tourist attraction. Casa Loma is now still owned by the City of Toronto and operated by the Kiwanis Club. We used to be entertained there quite frequently. After all, we lived just a few minutes away on Walmer Road.

We tried to entertain Patrick as best we could with the weather being the determining factor. Patrick was not enamoured of the cold or snow. He often mentioned the only ice he cared for was in the glass that held his Glenlivet. We did visit Hamilton where we had a friend who played for the Toronto Argonauts football team, and we also took him to Niagara Falls.

Around the middle of February Ulric called to suggest we register for a course which was to be given in Orlando, Florida. This was not an unusual request, since he and I had both been participating in these continuing education courses for a long time. In Florida we could avail ourselves of the warmth and sunshine and play a round or two of golf. And why not, indeed, I replied. During our conversation he casually recalled his New Year's Eve celebration. He was having a ball on the dance floor and his next recollection was waking up in a bed at one of the hospitals in Detroit. He had suffered his first heart attack and when I asked him where he was going from there, in other words, what his doctors recommended, he replied in an almost inaudible tone, "Surgery."

"And when is this to take place?"

"Oh no, not so fast, bro. I am seeking other opinions and after that is done, we can hightail it to Florida."

I couldn't help remembering the course I took at the University of Michigan, once a week for over a year. If weather allowed, I would leave early from Toronto and drive straight to Ann Arbor, but if not, I would catch the bus to Windsor after work, get there about six in the morning, rent a car and drive to the university. At the end of the course I always drove to Detroit to visit Ulric before driving through the tunnel to Windsor. No matter how late I arrived at his office Ulric would be charging full steam ahead as if his day was just starting. He would greet me exhausted after his last patient, as was natural after such a daily marathon. Because he was so occupied with business he never did take enough time to eat quietly or as my mother would have said, properly. Whenever he stopped for lunch, he would patronize the greasy spoon a few steps away and would find a similar place after work.

When he called me back two weeks later and we co-ordinated our itinerary, I asked him: "What did your new doctors have to say?" He did not broach the subject of his health himself.

"I was told I could wait for at least two years. In the meantime, I am to take an aspirin daily and follow an exercise regimen."

"Does that mean no surgery? What about the first recommendations?" I asked.

"What do you expect surgeons to say? They do surgery, so that's what they are going to prescribe, right?"

So there we were in Orlando, I with my golf clubs, and he without. Without golf clubs or medication of any kind. I went out and purchased a bottle of low-dosage aspirin. I was determined to get some practice in, so we went to the golf course and he watched me hit balls. I was concerned that he was showing no interest in golf and what bothered me even more happened when we discovered a restaurant that served what he referred to as soul food. It was delicious to the taste but sour in digestion—ham hocks and black-eyed peas, okra, pork chops and string beans, marinated spareribs, barbecued pig feet, and as desserts: pecan pie, sweet potato pie and more rich selections. It was a smorgasbord to beat all smorgasbords. We could eat as much as we wanted for as long as we wished.

Ulric turned to me. "Pinch me," he said.

"What for?" I queried.

"I feel like I've died and gone to heaven. What a feast." So I pinched him.

In the afternoons we went for long walks and Ulric could never resist the ice cream stores. No simple cones, but ice cream topped with nuts and bolts and every other trimming available. I have often wondered how such a smart individual did not seem to care. Perhaps he believed in the goddesses of Fate—Clotho, Lachesis and Atropos—who determine the birth, life and death of men. He shared this belief with many. Only the other day when there was thunder and lightning on the golf course and I was racing our golf cart to seek shelter, my partner said, "Why rush? If it's our time, it's our time." I almost pushed him off the cart. Many people in Guyana also share this view. They say 'wa' fo happen, go happen.' *Que sera*, according to the Spanish. I suppose avoiding heart surgery was a reinforcement of Ulric's belief.

Before I left for Orlando my cousin Patrick had called and had given me the name and telephone number of a friend there. A few days into our stay, I made the call and he invited us to dinner the day before we were to depart. He picked us up and took us to his home, met his beautiful wife and had scrumptious meal of chicken curry washed down with luscious drink. Later our host who was born in British Guiana drove us back to our hotel. We were staying in separate rooms and were due to leave the next day. Ulric had an early reservation and mine was for later in the day. I waited for him to call to say good-bye and when he did not, I called his room. There was no answer. I went down to the registration desk and discovered he had checked out without saying boo. I thought it very strange indeed.

On my return home I tried calling Ulric and for three days I could not get in touch with him at home or at work. When I finally got through to his office, I was relieved to find out he was well. He had been away at a business meeting and had omitted telling me. He called when he returned. I was glad to learn that his silence and abrupt departure were not due to health reasons, only a lapse in manners.

Five of us from our dominoes group in Toronto attended Expo 67 in Montreal. Dennis and Greville invited Mike, Alwyn and me to join them on the trip as they had procured lodgings in a flat belonging to some Jamaican students. We boarded the train at Union Station and enjoyed a very pleasant ride to Montreal, a maiden voyage for us three. It was a sparsely furnished apartment, a large barracks of a place and as clean as a whistle. Each of us had a cot of his own. Some of the cots had to be folded and put away in a closet in the mornings to make room for navigation. It was centrally located and it was quite easy to negotiate our way to the Metro and to the grounds of the Expo.

Our first visit was to the French pavilion as it was the first one we encountered. We only paid a courtesy call, meaning that we did not spend a lot of time there, but did return later after visiting pavilions that held more interest for us, like the Jamaican and Guyanese. In our homeland pavilion you could count the number of visitors there on your two hands. We could not believe our eyes when we ran into Chumel. He was the one who had telephoned me many moons ago when we were in Washington, D.C., telling me of Coraye's apartment. He was now a practising psychiatrist and had recently returned to Guyana to live and work and dabble in some business ventures. He told us about the Guyanese reception scheduled for that night at one of the hotels and exhorted us to attend. He would introduce us to the Prime Minister again and maybe he would remember us this time. We did go and a wonderful time was had by all, including our Jamaican friends.

On our return to Toronto we talked more and more of the prospect of returning home. In truth I don't believe we had ever stopped. I had flown to Guyana filled with grief at the passing of my grandmother. Baba and I had spent many hours together and the memories of our trips and the battles she fought on my behalf would always brighten my day.

As much as we would like to think that 'we are monarchs of all we survey,' circumstances can play a great role in the decisions we make, decisions that change lives profoundly.

Bibi was getting a promotion and a transfer to the embassy in London, England, and Mike was in the throes of making the big decision—to break up his business partnership and leave his friends and follow his heart and travel to England. We entreated him to consider this move carefully. When he started speaking in a phony English accent and talking of English pubs, we knew he had made his decision. When asked why was he leaving North America or Guyana to go to yet another country, of which he knew hardly anything, his reply was, "Boat gone a falls, he can't turn back, and this is Kaieteur Falls."

By his statement we assumed the wedding ceremony was imminent.

"Well, when is the wedding?" Alwyn asked.

"You hear me mention marriage?" Mike quickly replied. "Never put all two feet in river if you want to test how deep the water is."

The writing, however, was making its way onto the wall. If Mike was on the verge of leaving then we would have to start planning for the dissolution of the business. The accountants began their task.

Alwyn was trying to decide how many guests were to be invited to his wedding and I was seeking advice on the sale of my practice. Alwyn and I were definitely returning to Guyana. The only piece missing in the puzzle was the timetable. Of course, the decision-making was not easy. It was not handed to us on a platter. After years of long hours and hard work, I had built my practice to a financial success. In conversation Alwyn and I wondered if we would be able to adapt to a country which had changed since we left. We certainly had changed. Could we accept the change in a society from the one in which our attitudes were inculcated? In Toronto we still could leave our doors unlocked for extended periods of time and park our imported cars, also unlocked, on the street when we did not feel like putting them in the garage. And we were never concerned for our personal safety. Since we had left British Guiana, most homes had protected barriers on doors and windows and private security guards were employed by those who could afford to bear the cost. We considered all the negatives and rationalized that home was home and that was where we belonged. With each passing week we crept closer and closer to our decision.

Mike and Bibi left for England six months after the matrimonial union of Alwyn and Sharon. Three months later plans were set in motion for our repatriation—a high-faluting way of saying our minds were made up to return to Guyana. It would seem that we rushed things but it took us over two years after our visit to Guyana to bring the wish to fruition.

Once we returned, it was not that easy to set up shop. In his profession Alwyn would have no problem finding office space; he could start small and move to larger quarters later, when he saw fit. For me, setting up a private practice became a drudge, finding a place to live became a challenge and getting used to the tropical heat again became a lesson in adaptation. Fortunately, I was staying with Boogie during my reorientation and that helped to dilute the frustration. Finally, after looking all over central Georgetown I found a building that could be converted into both residence and surgery and I was able to engage some relatives to do the job. The building was centrally located a few minutes away from Bookers, the expatriate store and was close to Water Street, one of the main business areas. The library was just around the corner and so was the Tower Hotel, where we had stayed when we set up our scholarship fund, which by the way, had borne fruits beyond our expectations. St. George's Cathedral, said to be the largest wooden structure in the world, was just a few steps away. Although I was not a member of the Anglican denomination, I did attend a few services there now and then. I could not see any harm in getting a different point of view, if there was one. I had met the priest at Boogie's home and continued to meet him at different functions and we became friends.

While the office was being constructed, I was appointed dental officer for the Guyana Defence Force and dental surgeon for a large school district covering schools in the East Bank, clinics for adults and a few schools in the Demerara River district. These could only be reached by small boats. Most of the clinical work comprised teaching dental hygiene and extractions. I was able to persuade the representative of a toothpaste company to let us have toothpaste and toothbrushes at a reduced price which we distributed free to the schools.

Of course, it was not all work and no play. I was able to get in a few rounds of golf, mostly on weekends. In retrospect I did put in a number of hours doing pro bono work without any acknowledgement. Traveling up the Demerara River to treat school children, flying into the Berbice interior to treat members of the National Service and spending two days at the camp, flying into the interior to treat soldiers a number of times. If my pay was assessed by the hour, the wage would be negative. I am not complaining, just stating a fact. I have often wondered why I had to make such a sacrifice for so many years. On a more pleasant note, just about every week there was some social event to attend. A few times, without co-ordinating our agenda, I would meet Boogie and Alwyn and their wives at a function. Since I was still flying solo, I was free to escort whomever was willing to accompany me. That was the way it was until I met Manet who later became my wife.

There was an American dental surgeon who was doing volunteer work for the Seventh Day Adventist Church and we became friends. Whenever I had some time to spare, I would volunteer at his clinic. When I visited their home for a sit down dinner, Karl and Joan introduced me to Manet, who was in the country volunteering with CUSO, the Canadian University Student Organization, and was teaching French at three high schools. She had met Karl and Joan at one of the gatherings of expatriates and they became friends. Joan and Manet managed to find time to visit some of the public schools in Georgetown to teach the students the proper way to brush their teeth, using puppets and models to illustrate the maintenance of dental hygiene.

When Karl and Joan moved to another residence on Almond Street, they held a house christening and invited us, giving us directions. We left North Road, where we lived, made a circle right around St. George's Cathedral and turned right onto Church Street which took us to Vlissengen Road. As soon as we reached Almond Street we saw a party in progress in the lower flat of a two-storey house and we found a place to park. As we approached we could see some of the guests sitting staidly or sedately on straight-backed chairs—the windows were wide open to let in the fresh air, of course. We knew right away they were expatriates or non-Guyanese, because Guyanese speak with their hands and would have been more demonstrative. We walked right in and with a quick glance, I recognized some patients and exchanged a wave. Just then a man emerged from the other side of the room, walked up to us with two glasses and beckoned us to follow him to the bar, asking us the choice of our beverage. That was when I discovered our grave error: we were at the wrong house, the wrong party. I apologized, explaining our dilemma to our host. "Not to worry, old chap. Come back anytime," he replied, still intent in offering us that drink. We shook hands and with sheepish grins left there as fast as a bullet.

Many of our high school buddies had remained at home and joined the work force seeking employment in the civil service, which at that time fulfilled our dream. Others opted for the military and the police force and worked diligently to achieve promotion to the higher ranks. On our return one of our friends was the Superintendent of the Police Force. One New Year's Eve he had invited me and Manet to join him and some friends in celebrations. I started to decline, explaining that I had promised a friend arriving from Toronto that I would pick him up at the airport.

"Leave that to me," he said. "What's your friend's name and when is the time of arrival of the plane?"

I supplied the information and my friend from Toronto never felt so important to be greeted by the local gendarme, assisted at Customs and Immigration and deposited at our home.

Westey, a friend from our days at Central and an original member of Les Amis had climbed the civil service ladder of success and was the ranking officer in the Ministry of Home Affairs, which dealt with law and order, the police, and diplomatic affairs. He and his beautiful wife Sybil were frequent visitors to our home and were always present when we had most of our rollicking parties. When the Chinese Ambassador invited him to dinner and asked him to bring a friend he asked Manet and me to join him and Sybil. The four of us were the dinner guests of the Ambassador, the Deputy Ambassador and their wives. That was quite an experience and that's no hyperbole—an eight-course dinner of Chinese cuisine, accompanied by a different wine selection for each course, but who was counting? After dinner and dessert we were shown a Chinese movie with subtitles in their private theatre.

When Mr. Trudeau, the Prime Minister of Canada, visited Guyana in 1975, Manet and I were among the privileged few to attend an informal reception at the residence of the Canadian High Commissioner. I was introduced to the Commissioner by a member of the Lusignan Golf Club when the Commissioner joined us for a round of golf. This member was a minister of the Guyana government and we used to have a game from time to time. Later I would encounter the Commissioner at the swimming pool of the Pegasus Hotel and we would exchange pleasantries.

Manet and I were in conversation with some other guests when word filtered our way that Mr. Trudeau had arrived and was in another part of the building. Manet and one of her friends, Sarah, a Canadian by birth and also married to a Guyanese who was an engineer, scurried to the area where the Prime Minister was. I decided to stay put and maybe take my time and visit later. I continued my conversation with a guest whom I had met a day previously at the outdoor bar at the edge of the Pegasus swimming pool. He was a visitor from Saskatchewan and was an advisor to the government on matters pertaining to agriculture. Shortly thereafter, another guest joined our small group and said to me, extending his hand (I had a feeling he had already met my man from Saskatchewan), "I am Bruce and I am a Scorpio." I believe the astrological introduction was one of those fads, a seven-day wonder, as the saying was in Guyana at the time.

He was in his mid-forties, I would say. I am always in trouble when I try to guess the age of North Americans.

After some more mundane chat, he continued, "I am a writer, you know."

Some admonitions I never forget, like the one from Trini: Don't ask anyone what he does for a living. So I said, "You don't say! What kind of writing?"

"Fiction mostly. Short stories. I have been working on a novel for two years and I have a long way to go."

"Is that right? Where do you live?"

"Ontario, Toronto to be specific. Have you ever been to Toronto?"

"Sure. I did have the pleasure of living there for a number of years," and anticipating his next question, added, "in the Walmer Street/Bloor area. Do you know Austin Clarke, the writer, by the way?"

His reply was in the negative. I was disappointed. Not that Toronto is a village like Fredericksburg where everyone knows everyone else but I always thought there would be a fraternity for writers where the wannabes would try to know the successful ones, like Austin who had published several books and appeared on national television from time to time. This was not the same as a patient asking me upon my return from Toronto, "My cousin Johnny Higgins lives in Canada. You ever see him over deh?"

Just as I was becoming too introspective in this flashback to my Toronto days and my curiosity about why a fiction writer from Toronto was traveling with Mr. Trudeau who lives in Ottawa, Manet appeared. She was more excited than I had seen her for quite awhile as she announced that Mr. Trudeau wanted to meet me. When I did not move fast enough, Manet actually dragged me to meet the Prime Minister. He was still where she had left him and she did not want to miss too much. The same group surrounded him: her friend Sarah, a business man who managed a shirt factory, and a Canadian woman who owned a large grocery store with her Guyanese husband. As soon as I arrived, he had the prescience to put me at ease.

"Your wife tells me we have at least one thing in common," he said, after we shook hands.

"What is that, sir?" I asked, trying to control my voice.

"We both married women from the west."

Everyone laughed loudly. Mr. Trudeau did make us feel important that evening, spending so much time with our group. There was a photographer snapping pictures and some of those pictures ended up in albums, then to commemorate his death on the walls of our home. These days a picture should be worth at least five thousand words.

The Guyana Defence Force had its social affairs as well. For example, there were special dinners for officers and perhaps a special guest would be invited. At other times wives and sweethearts and friends were included. When the president of Nigeria paid an official visit to Guyana, the officers of the Defence Force had a special dinner for him and he was introduced to each of us.

Ulric visited and I became a tourist guide. We visited Kaieteur Falls as well as the falls at Orinduik, the same falls where Mr. Trudeau did some swimming on his visit. Mike and Bibi also returned from England twice during our stay in Guyana. The first time they came they seemed to be still enraptured with each other.

"When are you going to stop living in sin?" Alwyn asked Mike when we were all together—Alwyn, Mike, Boogie, and me.

"Never trouble trouble till trouble troubles you," was Mike's reply. Apparently he was not yet ready for the big event.

On their next visit about two years later we had decided not to tease him about his matrimonial plans. Mike brought it up himself.

"Say what?" Alwyn asked.

"I said we decided to jump in the river together."

"You don't say," said Alwyn. "What river and when?"

"Sooner than you think. I have to return to the Registrar's Office tomorrow and then we'll be all set."

A few days later Mike and Bibi quietly took their vows in our back yard, attended by Bibi's parents and sisters, relatives and friends. Also present were Mike's two sisters Caroline and Eunice, Boogie and Joyce, Alwyn and Sharon, Manet, Cousin Boyo, the Judge and his wife Evelyn, and Westey and his wife Sybil.

Mike insisted on short toasts from a select number of guests. Bibi's father, in the tradition of Guyanese weddings, was eloquent with what we referred to as big words. Mike's sister Caroline could not hold back the tears. Bibi replied for the couple thanking her parents for their participation in all aspects of her life, including the welcome and love they gave to Mike. She closed her speech with "I used to tell Mike after we had known each other quite well that among the reasons I love him so much were his wisdom and compassion. I used to call him Buddha. Recently, and by recent I mean the past seven weeks or so, I have revised my opinion of him and now call him Jesu. You see, after all this time he has been transformed into a carpenter building a crib, swings and playpens." She then pointed to her father, exclaiming, "I cannot keep the secret any longer Papa. You are to become a grandfather." There was utter silence followed by cheers and hand clapping.

Bibi's father gave orders to the waiters, who were listening to the speeches, to start serving the champagne. The celebration lasted until late in the evening or early in the morning. The bride and groom were driven to the Pegasus Hotel where we had arranged to meet them for lunch later.

Alwyn, Sharon, Boogie and Joyce were among the last to leave. On arriving home in the early morning, still ebullient from the nuptials of the preceding evening Alwyn and Sharon were not prepared for what was to follow. Seated in one of their chairs was a short, rough-looking stranger in short pants and dirty tennis shoes with a knife in one hand a gun on his knees. He seemed so sure of himself, Sharon said later.

At the side of his chair were two stuffed pillow cases, which served as a cache for his booty. He ordered them into the nearby study where the light was still on. Sharon took off her broad-rimmed straw hat, bought specially for that day, and placed it next to some bound books on the table. Under the hat she placed her small evening bag. When the bandit demanded money, Alwyn explained he did not keep cash at home, then emptied his pocket, placing a few hundred dollars on the table.

"Dat's not enough!"

"Well, that's all I have."

He then focused his attention on Sharon. "Okay, gie me all you jewls."

Sharon complied, taking off her gold necklace with its locket, her wedding rings, and her gold bangles.

"Na worry. Ah got you other jewelry a'ready from yu bedroom." He smiled for the first time, displaying a mouthful of gold.

"Well then, you have done well for yourself. Please leave."

"Ah leave when ah ready. You two stay right deh."

Throughout all this Sharon remained close to her hat and purse. He started to backpedal, the knife still in his hand, the gun now in his pocket. As he picked up the pillowcases on his way to the door, Sharon retrieved her evening bag from under the hat. When he reached the door, she said to him in a cold, steely voice: "Mister, you forgot something."

"Ya, wha?" Still sure of himself.

"This." She slipped her hand in her purse where she kept her .22 calibre revolver and shot him first in the groin, then as he buckled, in the left knee, then followed by the right knee.

Alwyn made a single telephone call and within minutes a uniformed police patrol was on the premises, followed by two plainclothes detectives. Soon after an ambulance arrived. The detectives identified the perpetrator as a wanted felon who was accused of committing a spate of armed robberies and was also wanted for allegedly killing a policeman. They accompanied the ambulance to the Georgetown Public Hospital, but by the time the patient reached the emergency station, he was pronounced dead on arrival. Rumour had it that he was helped to an early demise by the detectives who disappeared once the ambulance reached the hospital.

Sharon had been taking target practice at Police headquarters since her return to the country and her proficiency was due to the instructions of a Sergeant Peters. Three months after her display of marksmanship Sergeant Peters was promoted to Inspector. In Guyana everyone knew the meaning of 'Na who you know, but who know you.'

Alwyn and Sharon closed their home and moved in with us for a couple of days. Later in the day after the botched robbery we gathered pool side at the Pegasus to continue the celebration of the nuptials with the newlyweds, Boogie and Joyce, Alwyn and Sharon, Westey and Sybil, and a few others. Sharon showed a lot of patience and composure in repeating the details of the robbery; she had already answered questions from the police and later the press. Alwyn decided when to put an end to her interviews but he allowed her to repeat the story to her friends who did not want an iota of detail to be omitted. Mike and Bibi stayed in Guyana for another week and soon we returned to as much of a normal routine as was possible.

Life was such a breeze. During our stint in Guyana Manet and I, on different occasions, had visited Barbados and Trinidad, Grenada and Antigua, Jamaica and the Bahamas. We also visited Tortola in the British Virgin Islands where my father's nephew was a judge. From Tortola we traveled by hovercraft to the U.S. Virgin Islands where we went sightseeing after lunching with a banker of Guyanese origin who had visited us in Guyana on holiday there. To this day I still think of a wonderful long weekend trip we took to Suriname, previously known as Dutch Guiana. From Georgetown we drove to Rossignol, crossed the Berbice River by ferry and drove from New Amsterdam to Springlands located in the county of Berbice. At the Customs and Immigration in Springlands one of my patients was in charge. Through his influence the captain of the motorboat which was to transport us to Nickerie where we were to clear Customs and Immigration again, allowed us the privilege of sitting on the bridge with him. From there we flew to Paramaribo, the capital city, and took a taxi to our destination.

We were given a self-contained bungalow where, if we desired, we could prepare meals. A private swimming pool was just outside our unit, and I say private, because during our stay, we were the only users of it. At night we swam in the buff and no one was the wiser. There was a small restaurant in the compound where we had our breakfast. An efficient bus service took us to the city and we enjoyed the short ride trying to engage in conversation with passengers who looked every bit like residents of Georgetown. The difference was that most of them spoke only Dutch, their native language and that fact kept reminding us that we were in a foreign country. Some friends in Georgetown had persuaded us to call their friends when we arrived and we were so glad we did. One person turned out to be the assistant Police Chief and he became a friend. We toured his department and had lunch with his aunt who was a member of their legislature. She lived in a beautiful older home and her front yard was a delight to see with its most intricate network of vines and beautiful flowers that were reminiscent of some parts of our famous Botanical Gardens in Georgetown. The other person was a self-employed accountant who with his wife took us out to dine at one of their best restaurants and later to an international hotel where Manet tried her luck at slot machines and did win a few coins. The next day they took us on a tour of the city and showed us some beautiful homes along the Suriname River.

When in my younger years I would take off from Toronto to visit my mother and relatives in Guyana, I always used to wonder why many of the older passengers had waited until their grandchildren were of a certain age to take their first overseas holiday. I picked up that information from them because they were so excited to be winging their way south. I am glad we did our traveling early, as the exorbitant cost these days would not permit us to enjoy a fraction of what we did back then.

As much as I had returned to a lifestyle to which I was born—servants at my beck and call, a chauffeur to fight the traffic, a masseur who visited the home once a week—certain aspects of my life had changed. I am referring to the pitter patter of little feet that reminded me of my responsibility. After seven years of a nirvanic experience with no savings we started our preparations to return to Canada, this time as a family. We settled in rural Saskatchewan and what a contrast it was for our little girls whose dress code was 'less is more.' We arrived to find streets piled with five-foot snowdrifts in March, when winter is supposed to be over, but their adaptation was instinctive. Now they have all matured and become beautiful women with families of their own.

978-0-595-44864-7
0-595-44864-X

Printed in the United States
84698LV00003B/69/A